THE
DOMINO
EFFECT

Center Point
Large Print

Also by Davis Bunn and available from
Center Point Large Print:

The Patmos Deception
Strait of Hormuz
Unlimited
The Sign Painter

**This Large Print Book carries the
Seal of Approval of N.A.V.H.**

THE DOMINO EFFECT

Davis Bunn

CENTER POINT LARGE PRINT
THORNDIKE, MAINE

This book is dedicated
To three remarkable gentlemen
Who introduced me
To the art and discipline
Of honorable politics.

James B. Hunt

E. Lawrence Davis

James R. Hinkle*

*Esse Quam Vedere***

*In Memoriam
**To Be Rather Than To Seem
(North Carolina State Motto)

"Recent market swings are a sign that something is awry with the capital markets. . . . A fast market is not necessarily a fair market, and . . . will cause the public to lose confidence in the markets."

Richard Grasso
Former CEO, New York Stock Exchange
September 11, 2015

"In recent years the world's top twenty banks have paid fines totaling 235 billion dollars for bad behavior."

Donald MacDonald
Chairman, Institutional Investors Group
October 2015

"Major banks operate in a privileged heads-I-win-tails-you-lose bubble. There is widespread rigging of benchmarks for personal gain."

Mark Carney, Governor, Bank of England
Chairman, UK Monetary Policy Committee
October 2015

THE
DOMINO
EFFECT

1

Thursday

Esther Larsen hurried along the corridor, racing the clock.

She arrived at the boardroom five minutes late. Jason Bremmer paced the corridor outside the conference room. Esther's boss hated to be kept waiting. But she had only learned about this meeting when the bank's CEO had personally phoned her. Esther's boss hated that most of all.

Jason stood with his back to the conference room and put serious heat into saying, "Not one word. Not one *breath* out of line."

Esther did not respond.

She followed her boss into the room. The bank's chairman, Reynolds Thane, stood facing the plate-glass wall and the Charlotte skyline. Esther knew he had been studying the room's reflection, waiting for her to show up. "Everyone here now? Excellent. We've called this meeting because the investment banking group has requested an additional temporary allocation of two billion dollars."

"So the bank can earn another hundred million," Jason replied. "In two days. Possibly more money in less time."

Reynolds took many of his meetings like this,

dressed in a striped shirt with a white collar and the pants to a Savile Row suit, suspenders from the St. Andrews golf course gift shop, gold cuff links and tiepin. Standing with his back to the room, fascinated with the city he dominated. "You claim to have identified a sure-fire investment."

"Not claim, Reynolds. We've done it. This is solid gold."

"Your floor already controls eight percent of the bank's total assets. And now you want more."

"We've made money year on year," Jason replied. "We will again this year. If you give us the green light here."

"Your division is down for the past two quarters."

"Just on paper, and only because we hedged on longer-term gains. Which means we can't pull out of these positions without posting unnecessary losses. But this new investment will put us in the black for the quarter and the year."

Esther stared at the polished surface between her hands. She did not need to look up. She had sat through enough of these meetings to know exactly how things stood. Jason had come with four of his traders. They were all eager, smart, polished, and vicious. Just like their boss. They would say whatever Jason told them to say. This blind willingness to do whatever it took was how they had arrived at this point. Making the big bucks. Sitting with the power players. Looking at how much higher they might climb. If they made the cut. If they bet right with the bank's money. There was no reason to dwell on the downside, no profit.

That was the job of Esther and her analysts.

Reynolds asked, "What if I told you the bank could only allocate half a billion?"

"The deal won't work. I can give you the figures if you want. But the trade requires the full two billion outlay."

Jason did not actually lie. But in the nineteen months she had worked for him, Esther had learned that Jason took pride in manipulating the truth to his own ends. She felt her muscles lock with the effort it required not to speak.

Reynolds asked, "What if the bank requires time to draw together these funds?"

"The memo I sent you this morning was marked urgent for a reason," Jason said. "The door opens, the door closes. If we're going to act, it has to be now."

Esther had a distinct impression of observing the conference room from a vast distance. Jason was in control here. Forget the titles on the doors. Everyone else was frozen into position. Including Esther. They played the game according to his rules.

"Walk me through it one more time," Reynolds said.

Jason was one of the best at pitching deals Esther had ever heard, and she had heard some of the finest. It would be so easy to believe in what he was selling.

When Jason was done, the room held to a singular tension. Jason's crew tensed with genuine fear, knowing just how dangerous their boss could be, how their careers were all on the line. Each and every day.

Reynolds asked, "Is there any reason why I shouldn't approve this deal?"

Esther knew without looking up that Jason's attention was trained on her now. Taking aim.

Reynolds asked, "Is there any potential down-side lurking in the shadows?"

Two hours ago, Esther had been called into Jason's office. Her report on this deal had been there on his desk. Jason had planted one fist on the pages and told her that she was never to mention this to anyone. Ever. He did not threaten because he did not need to. Esther knew Jason had only one way of dealing with staff who did not fall into line. He chopped them off at the knees.

Reynolds, of course, did not care about Jason's hostility. Esther suspected the bank's CEO actually approved of his senior trader being a vengeful tyrant. Reynolds Thane was interested in one thing, and one thing only: making more money this quarter than last.

The bank president rocked up on his toes once, twice, and said, "Do it."

Jason could not have risen faster if his seat had been spring-loaded. "You'll have the documents ready for your signature in an hour."

Esther rose with the others. As she filed from the room, she risked one glance back, hoping the CEO might ask her to remain. But Reynolds stayed as he was, smiling at the skyline and his own reflection.

Jason did not speak until the elevator doors slid shut. Then he looked at Esther with all the menace she knew he carried. "Good work, Larsen."

Esther nodded in response. She felt dwarfed by the five men in the elevator, despite her five-foot-eight height and gymnast's physique. She wore her dark hair swept back and held in a plain gold clasp. Today's dress matched the mood, somber and gray. She shifted slightly from one foot to the other, observing her reflection. In the bronze elevator doors, her mask shattered and reknit, over and over.

She walked down the carpeted corridor, across the skyway, and halted by the entrance to her department. Esther leaned her forehead on the door and wished she could find enough air to take one easy breath.

2

Esther met that evening with a group she'd known for several years. Once every month the friends came together for dinner and a relaxed gathering in various homes. There was no agenda. The individual or family who hosted also offered some theme or thought or whatever. The discussion flowed from there. It lasted an hour, two, occasionally until after midnight. These informal gatherings were as close to intimacy as Esther came.

Tonight they met in the home of a neurologist, Donald Saunders. Esther loved their sprawling home, its walls of exposed brick and the free-standing chimney forming a natural barrier between the kitchen and dining areas. The open spaces suggested a home without boundaries. A life completely alien to the way Esther lived.

Most were gathered in the living room, talking in the easy manner of old friends. Esther helped Patricia, Donald's wife, unpack the bowls and platters brought by the guests. Each time someone offered to help, Patricia shooed them away. Esther carried a tray of sliced beef tenderloin out to the dining table, and when she returned, Patricia said, "I keep hoping one of these evenings you would open up."

"I'm really not comfortable talking about myself," Esther replied.

"Don't I know it." Patricia Saunders was a heavyset woman with an easygoing manner. "You are about the most tightly wound woman I've ever met. Do you ever allow yourself to just relax?"

Esther did not know what to say.

"And another thing. I've noticed the way you watch all of us. Like you're taking mental notes. Analyzing. I bet you know more about me than anyone else here, outside my own family."

"Patricia Saunders, born Richards, October 1972. Dartmouth BA with honors in art history. You met your husband your senior year and opted not to continue for a master's, though you'd already been accepted to Duke's graduate school. You wanted nothing more than to marry Donald and raise a family." Esther concentrated on spooning hummus from a plastic deli container into a ceramic bowl. She knew Patricia was frozen in place, watching her. Esther had no idea why she was talking like this. Probably because she had to release the growing pressure somehow. "For years you and your husband took in foster children, often special-needs. But the last one turned out to be a very difficult experience, especially for your youngest daughter who had just turned fifteen. Lacy is now a junior at UNC, in premed. You miss her terribly."

"You *researched* us?"

"No, Patricia, I *listen*. That's what analysis is all about. A good investigator often pulls together things that are hidden in plain sight."

"So . . . you're a private investigator?"

"I suppose, in a way."

"But I thought you worked for a bank."

Esther turned around. "I do. I'm the senior risk analyst in the investment banking division."

Patricia Saunders was not so much large as solid. She coached children's soccer, which helped to keep her weight down. But the years and the birthing of four children had added an unyielding thickness to her frame. Patricia picked up the salad without taking her eyes off Esther. "This is the most I've ever heard you speak in . . . how long have you been part of our group?"

"Two years and three months."

Her husband called from the living room, "Patricia, the natives are getting restless."

"Coming." Patricia asked Esther, "When dinner is over, will you tell us something about yourself?"

Esther felt a decisive shudder run through her. "If you want."

But Esther's courage vanished long before dinner was over. Esther ate very little and managed to slip away while the others shifted from the table to the living room. She was out the door and down the curved front walk before anyone noticed.

As she drove away, Esther glanced back and saw Patricia's silhouette in the doorway. The home looked inviting, and Patricia somehow emanated a genuine disappointment. Yet Esther knew it was for the best. There was nothing to be gained from sharing her burdens. They couldn't help her. After it was over, she would be right where she was now, driving back to her silent home. Only they would have been burdened now as well. No, it was far better to keep her fears down deep. Where they belonged.

3

Friday

As with most senior analysts and traders, Esther's home office was linked to the bank's system. She left the four monitors on twenty-four-seven. She was in the habit of crossing in and out of the office as she prepared for bed. Whenever she could not sleep, like now, she climbed out of bed and went over to stand in front of the monitors. The images told a story, changing with every day, every hour, sometimes every few heartbeats.

Toward dawn, Esther watched the European exchanges race through another turbulent trading day. The Middle East crisis continued to trouble the global markets. She gave up on trying to sleep and made herself a pot of coffee.

She slipped into workout clothes and packed her business outfit in a large tote her assistant referred to as the mother ship. Back when times were easy and her life seemed on track, Esther had bought a house in the Dilworth section of Charlotte. The neighborhood formed a green boundary to the high-rise downtown area, its stately homes set on oversized lots. She had spent happy weekends with her brother and a pair of semi-retired carpenters, turning the old house into a haven for the family she hoped one day to have. Eight years on, Esther's plans had come no closer to reality. As she backed her car down the tree-lined drive, she reflected on the fact that she had never been more successful . . . or felt more alone.

The predawn hour was Esther's favorite time to work out. The bustling city was calm, and many of her problems were asleep. She loved entering the gym and being surrounded by others who were equally determined to get a head start on the world. She knew many of them by name but felt no need for small talk. No one was here to socialize, unlike the after-work crowd. Esther had developed a routine all her own, starting with a long stretch and then light free-weights to keep her upper body toned. This was followed by the stationary bike or an elliptical machine, always with reading material positioned in the handy tray by the controls. Today Esther scanned a series of *WSJ* articles on her tablet, then finished with another stretch.

She ignored her reflection in the surrounding floor-to-ceiling mirrors. She had never been defined by how she looked. She had a fairly extensive wardrobe and bought a new business outfit once every quarter. She tended to go for designers she trusted, since how she looked was part of her persona.

She had known two important relationships, one in college and the other during her first year with the bank. Both had turned out to be disasters. The men had wanted to *confine* her. Nowadays she stayed busy enough to ignore the yearning for a husband and family and a life beyond the bank. The only time she really noticed the absence was when she woke in the night, her pillow wet with tears from dreams she could not remember.

As she drove along East Boulevard, Esther used the hands-free to call her office. Esther managed a team of seven analysts and nine admins, all of whom she considered the best in the world. Jasmine, her number two, answered with, "Everything is too calm."

"What time did you show up?"

"Early. Might as well. I sure wasn't sleeping." Jasmine was half African American, half

Bahamian and spiced her speech with a hint of the conchy's accent. She had been raised dirt poor, her father a seine fisherman on the Alabama Gulf. Her brilliant mind had taken her to the University of Miami and then to UNC-CH and finally here. She said, "I kept waiting for the world to explode. It didn't. Lucky me."

It was an old joke and normally good for a smile. But today the words only sparked the same fears that had kept Esther up most of the night. "I think I'll stop by and see my brother."

"Good idea."

"If anything comes up, my phone is always on."

"Why should I bother you? I mean, other than the bank going bust or markets entering total meltdown, right? Jason won't be asking for any new investment analysis, that's for certain. Our division is so overextended, if I went hunting the aisles, I couldn't find a loose nickel."

"You're not making me feel better."

"Oh, I'm sorry. I thought my job was to analyze risk. Silly me."

Esther cut the connection. Many of the bank's traders found Jasmine hard to take. She was smarter than all of them, and her comments turned biting when she confronted a trader's blind optimism. Jason's team referred to Esther and Jasmine, the slender white analyst and the dark-skinned former athlete, as the Downside Twins.

Esther drove past the Carolina Medical Center,

Charlotte's largest hospital, and a block later pulled into the rehab center's parking lot. As she stepped from her car, she was halted by the sight of three dogwoods whose blooms were just emerging. It had been a warm March, and now the trees were defying the crisp April dawn. They hinted at a season Esther almost could not recognize. She felt captivated by the trees' delicate beauty. Their limbs were bare as pale bones, which heightened their sense of defiant hope.

As she entered the medical center, an all-too-familiar voice said, "Esther, excellent. You've just saved me a phone call."

Carter Cleveland was an osteopath who a decade earlier had left active practice to build and run Charlotte's finest rehabilitation center. He was an angular man in his sixties with no bedside manner whatsoever. Esther considered him something of a bully. "I need to see Nathan."

"And you will, right after we've talked." Carter reached out a hand, and the nurse was alert enough to know which file he silently indicated. He cut off any further protest with, "We can do this here or in my office. But we're doing it."

The foyer was empty save for the receptionist and duty nurse. "Here."

"Your brother needs to be moved. Sooner rather than later."

"Nathan is comfortable. I really want him to stay here."

"Your desire was enough to keep him here this long. But the time has come—"

"I pay on time."

"Money is not the issue. Well, that's true and not true. Money is always an issue. But the simple fact is that your brother is not getting better."

"Give him time."

"Esther, we've given him seven months, which is a new record for our center." Carter opened the file. "For nine weeks now your brother has refused to participate in his daily treatments. His vitals are declining. There is nothing to indicate he—"

"I'll talk with him."

"Esther, if talking to Nathan could make any difference at all, you would have had your brother up and jogging long ago."

Seven months and eight days ago, Esther's brother had been involved in an accident on the interstate that had killed his pregnant wife. The police were fairly certain that Nathan had been speeding. Esther suspected Nathan's unresponsiveness derived at least in part from guilt. "I don't understand. Where am I supposed to take him?"

"I see your court-appointed guardianship is in order." Carter shut the file. "I suggest you consider moving him to the Davidson Mental Health Hospital. They have a long-term wing that may be ideally suited to your brother's requirements."

"Out of the question."

"Esther, from time to time I am faced with a patient who simply does not want to get well. The mind is a powerful instrument. If the patient has given up on life, there is only so much modern medicine can accomplish."

"But Nathan . . ."

Carter gave her a moment to complete the sentence. But Esther found no strength to shape the words, *Nathan is all the family I have left.* He said, "There's a social worker on duty at the hospital next door who has considerable experience with this. I urge you to give her a call. She can help you prepare for the transition."

4

Nathan's rehab center was the finest in the state. It was also outrageously expensive. Esther's brother had previously been a freelance graphic designer, which had paid quite well. But he had never bothered with private top-up health insurance. Why should he, since neither Nathan nor his late wife had been sick in years?

The upshot was as devastating as it was simple. Nathan's seven months in the center had racked up a debt almost as large as Esther's mortgage. She had not hesitated to pay, not for an instant. They had lost both their parents when Esther was still in grade school. They went to live with their mother's parents, a silent couple who treated their presence as an imposition. Nathan was nine years older and had fitted himself into the role of Esther's surrogate parent. The following year, he left for university. But Esther had never felt abandoned. Nathan had joined her for every vacation and many weekends. For her sixteenth birthday, Nathan paid for them to have a month together in Europe. Of course she was there for him now. The cost was manageable.

So long as Esther kept working for the bank.

The clinic's front lobby and halls had oak wainscoting and wallpaper with a soothing beige pattern. The patients' rooms were decorated like an elegant inn, and the food was excellent. There was even a wine cellar. The center delivered its guests the best of everything.

Esther knew Dr. Cleveland and the clinic nurses all assumed Nathan was simply a loser at life, content to play patient while he sapped all the finances he could from his pliant sister. The doctor probably thought he was doing Esther a favor, inflicting on them both the tough love Nathan deserved.

Nothing could have been further from the truth. Esther knew her brother did not care whether they kept him or shipped him off. The exquisite décor and fine lifestyle was lost on him.

Nathan was simply looking for a place to die.

• • •

As she rounded the corner and arrived at her brother's room, Esther was halted by the sight of a stranger seated in her chair.

For months she had been Nathan's only visitor. Esther was sure she had never seen this man before. He leaned in close, a smile creasing his handsome features. He gently prodded Nathan's arm with two fingers in time to his words, an intimate gesture like a friend might make while telling a joke.

Esther felt oddly excluded. Her brother's body language was the only part of the scene she recognized. Nathan's face was turned toward the window on the bed's opposite side. He had started doing this about nine weeks ago. He was sleeping more and more these days, or at least pretending to. Shutting out the world as best he could, using drugs and slumber with equal ease. His determined dismissal of any interaction had punctuated her every visit for over two months. But if the stranger even noticed Nathan's lack of response, he gave no sign.

Esther returned to the front lobby and approached the nurse-receptionist. She held to an air of polished elegance that fit the station. Esther detected a faint glint in her eyes, suggesting the woman agreed it was time that Nathan became someone else's problem.

Esther asked, "Who is that in my brother's room?"

The receptionist's frosty expression softened. "Oh, that's Craig."

"I'm sorry, who?"

"Craig Wessex, a divinity student at the local university. He's a friend of Dr. Cleveland. They've known each other forever."

Esther wanted to tell the woman her comments explained nothing, but she felt jarred by the warmth and approval in the receptionist's words.

The woman took Esther's silence as an invitation, and continued, "Craig started coming in here, oh, it must be a couple of weeks ago. It's part of some class assignment. Craig is wonderful. Would you like me to introduce you?"

"No, I . . . Another time." Esther pretended to check her watch. "Right now I need to get to work."

When Esther arrived at the bank, she followed her normal routine, first crossing the main trading floor, smelling the air, taking its pulse.

The chamber was dominated by young, fiercely aggressive males. The few women scattered among them tended toward rather severe suits and assertive manners. They had to compete with the men. Success in this business was based on maintaining solid alliances and being the first with new intel. Either the women developed an aggressive attitude and a tough shell or they were erased.

Esther had never been interested in going for a place on the floor, though a good trader could earn ten times her salary. And she was certain she could have been very good indeed.

The trading floor was fairly quiet today because the investment banking division was over-extended. The tension was a palpable force. The traders sat focused on their trading screens, flexing rubber balls or flicking pens. Esther knew they hated the forced idleness. They loved the risk. They wanted *action*.

Esther also thought they looked scared. Which, given the circumstances, was probably a good thing.

She crossed the skyway and pushed through the main doors. Her assistant met Esther as she entered the analyst division. Jasmine Dubrot had played basketball for the University of Miami and moved with an angular grace. "There I was," Jasmine said to Esther, "driving to work and listening to some talk-show host ask her listeners what they were going to do with their weekend."

Esther made a face. "Why were you wasting time on that?"

"Boredom and tension in the same blender. Couldn't listen to the news. I kept scripting that the bank collapsed and my future was gone." Jasmine waved that aside. "So this woman calls in, and she spends five minutes complaining about how her awful mother-in-law was coming over for an outdoor barbecue and bringing the worst potato salad anybody ever fed to some poor dog."

"She didn't need five minutes to say that," Esther replied. With Jasmine, there was no telling where these exchanges would take them. Which was why Esther enjoyed them so much.

"Okay, maybe it only seemed like five minutes. Probably lasted ninety seconds. Do you have any idea how long ninety seconds can be?"

"The woman caller," Esther reminded her as they entered the office.

"Right. So I start talking back to the radio. Asking the woman what she knew about anything. Did she have any idea how lucky she was, having a mother-in-law in the first place?"

Esther set her briefcase on the desk, crossed her arms, and waited.

"The woman goes, 'You got no idea what you're talking about. You want this woman, you got her. Matter of fact, you can have the potato salad *and* her son. Take the whole package.' Can you imagine?"

"Wait," Esther said. "You actually phoned the radio station?"

"From the car. Don't worry, I used my hands-free."

"I don't care if you . . . They put you on the air?"

"That was strange, let me tell you. Talking to my steering wheel and hearing my voice come out of the radio. With that woman. The way she talked about her mother-in-law, I hope the old lady lives in Borneo."

"Excuse me?"

"Somewhere without electricity. On account of how otherwise some busybody neighbor is gonna run in and say, Turn on your radio and listen to the trash coming out of your daughter-in-law's mouth."

Esther sat down behind the desk. "For an extremely intelligent and highly gifted analyst, you are making no sense whatsoever."

"I know it. Don't I just know it? Who am I to be worrying about what some old woman thinks about her son's wife?"

This was one of Jasmine's many gifts, her ability to temporarily ease Esther's worries, all in the space of one absurd comment. But today was crunch day, and there was no putting it off any longer. Esther looked up at Jasmine. "Anything new?"

"Not a thing. Not a whisper. Seems like the markets are holding their breath. Along with the rest of us."

Esther's computer system had cost the bank one hundred and seventeen thousand dollars. She scanned the screens. They all told her the same thing. "The markets are holding stable."

Jasmine paced like a caged tiger. "How long do we have?"

"Sit down and I'll tell you. You're making me nervous."

She sat, but twitched like a schoolgirl in the principal's office.

Esther said, "The portal closes in thirty-two minutes."

"So we're half an hour from the wire."

"Unless the bank opts for another trade."

Jasmine's response was halted by a knock on Esther's door. Jason's secretary entered and said, "Jason wants to see you. Now."

Esther grabbed her tablet and cell and followed Jason's secretary back across the skyway to the trading floor. She knew most investment banks separated their various trading divisions, arguing that this fostered a greater sense of competition and also limited the risk of a bad decision or faulty information striking at multiple levels. But Esther's company had been the first in Charlotte to develop a full-scale investment banking group. Originally called Carolina First Mercantile, the bank had been through so many acquisitions that almost none of the younger executives had any notion of the group's origins or the role it had played in developing the city. Nor did they care. What they saw was a mildly out-of-date trading floor housed in a massive cube.

The open space was almost exactly the same size as the nightclub many of these young employees frequented. There were 146 trading stations, each powering a minimum of three monitors. The front wall held six of the largest flat screens ever made, each nearly seven feet wide. The incoming data being fed into this chamber might have been somewhat quieter than the nightclub's din, yet the energy was just as frenetic. Many of the traders went straight from the trading floor to the club.

Jason's secretary led Esther into the executive conference room and asked if she wanted coffee. When Esther declined, the secretary said, "I'm instructed to say that he will be with you shortly and you are to wait for him here."

Esther felt tendrils of uneasiness creep through her gut. "I thought you said this was urgent."

The secretary was a battle-hardened veteran with less than two years to retirement. "I have learned it is best not to question the boss when he is in one of his moods. Know what I mean?"

Esther did not reply.

The secretary smiled, as though Esther's silence was the correct response. "Let me know if you change your mind about that coffee."

Esther swiftly realized the conference room was scrubbed. The word was old-tech, from pre-internet days. Originally a room was scrubbed when all listening and observation devices had been eliminated. Nowadays it signified a room where electronic access was denied.

Esther's tablet would not link to the bank's system. The flat screens at either end of the room were blank, the controls nowhere to be found. Walking to the outer windows made no difference. When she picked up the conference room phone, it buzzed straight to Jason's secretary, who asked, "Can I help you?"

"I need an outside line."

"And I will need to get back to you on that."

Esther set down the receiver and said to the dead air, "You do that." She returned to her chair feeling exposed, vulnerable. She knew what Jason intended by this confinement. He wanted Esther to understand that he held the authority to deny her total access. All real power was held by him.

She also understood *why* he was doing this. The mock imprisonment had nothing to do with the bank's current exposures. Jason wanted Esther to understand that he fully intended to take the same risks again.

Jason had no plans to return the two billion the bank had granted him for this trade. He would fight tooth and nail to keep the money on his division's books. Jason did not care about her reservations. He was after power.

And to a certain extent, his silent tactic worked. Esther was indeed frightened.

But mostly it made her angry.

Esther could hear nothing within the sound-proof room. Through the interior glass wall she could see the electronic ticker tape flowing around three sides of the administrative bullpen.

The clocks below the data stream counted down the minutes. Esther felt increasingly constricted, less by the room's walls than her solitary tension.

She took a deep breath to calm herself and focus. Wall Street's latest derivatives craze was called capital-relief trades. In this particular instance, Esther suspected "craze" was absolutely the way to describe them.

Capital-relief trades were means by which banks could hide their high-risk assets, at least temporarily. When a bank identified a potential shift in the market that might draw their derivatives portfolio into dangerous territory, they had only two choices. Either they dumped the hazardous asset, which meant taking a loss. Or they slipped beyond the boundary for risk-weighted assets set by the US Securities and Exchange Commission, which meant fines and snooping regulators and bad publicity.

Traders had invented capital-relief derivatives as a short-term fix. These credit derivatives allowed them to transfer some of this risk to another bank.

There were two kickers, as far as the Jasons of this world were concerned. First was that the acquiring bank received a very high rate of return. Second, the legal framework was iffy. And intentionally so.

The purchasing bank was not actually buying the tainted asset. Instead, the asset remained on the books of the original bank and a *derivative* of the asset was sold.

The question was, if things went south, who would have to pay up? And the answer was, unless things went south, the question did not matter. At least as far as the acquiring bank was concerned, the cloudy nature of the acquisition lowered the risk while creating a higher rate of return.

Esther had heard traders laughing over the hazards, proud of their new way of slipping things under the rug.

If deals went bad, the lawyers would spend years fighting over who held the downside. But this was precisely the sort of high-risk venture that had brought down Enron. Hiding risk did not mean it went away. Sooner or later the markets would turn against the trade.

But none of this mattered, so long as the markets held steady. As far as Jason and his team were concerned, this was as close to a win-win situation as they could find in today's market.

Esther watched the summary of currency and interest-rate swap positions sweep around the walls. Finally the target moment arrived. The portal shut. Only a slight uptick to the currency markets signified the completion of that trade, meaning the bank had survived. She did a swift calculation. Jason's gamble had netted the bank one hundred and eighteen million dollars. In seventeen hours and forty-three minutes. She knew that was all the board of directors would care about. The potential downside would be overlooked.

Doing business was all about taking measured risks. Jason and his team had been proven right. So the money would stay on his books, and he would go hunting for the next gamble.

Three minutes later, Jason's secretary opened the door and smiled her apology. "It looks like he won't be able to see you today after all."

Esther slipped past her and reentered the trading floor. The atmosphere was jubilant now. The traders cavorted like a high school team that had just won the state championship. Esther slipped down the back aisle, completely unnoticed. She glanced up to the narrow balcony that ran along the western floor. Occasionally the board or other senior executives would slip in to observe the animals in their feeding frenzy. Today the balcony was empty.

The truth was there on full display. What they all refused to see was how close Jason had brought the bank to utter ruin.

And now they had a green light to do it all over again. The only thing they could see was the future commissions this represented.

But only if they stayed lucky.

As Esther left the trading floor, she felt as though she were being trailed by cinders and smoke from a fire not yet lit.

It was only a matter of time.

5

The trading floor's southern exit led to a hallway and the glass bridge passing over Seventh Street. The bank's satellite building was an older structure that had once contained a textile warehouse. Esther's division had been relocated here in the early days of Jason's reign. She minded, but only a little. Jason's attitude toward his analyst team was guarded and mostly hostile. He did not want them telling him what the risks were. He liked to think he already knew everything he needed about such threats. What Jason wanted from his analysts were two things, and two only. Where the next opportunity for profits lay. And how to increase his division's gain while remaining legal. And if not legal, how to keep his actions under the SEC's radar.

The majority of Esther's team were typical geeks—too fat or too thin, sallow-faced, and scraggly-haired. They were also astonishingly brilliant, excellent at their jobs, and intensely loyal to both her and the bank.

They did their best to fit into some version of banker attire. But Esther doubted if her four males had ever spent more than ten dollars on a tie. Or if any of the women besides Jasmine fully understood the art of applying cosmetics.

When Esther returned to her division, she was greeted by sixteen very tense and worried faces. They all knew what the day's trading success really meant. And there was nothing she could say to reassure them that was not a lie.

Jasmine reported, "Some hack from the executive floor was in here looking for you. Apparently Reynolds Thane wants to have a word."

"When was this?"

"About five minutes after you left. What was Jason after?"

"I have no idea. He . . ." Esther stopped in midflow.

"What is it?"

"Nothing. I'd better go see what our chief wants."

Esther returned to the main bank building and took the elevator the traders referred to as the Boss Rocket. Previously it had halted only at the lobby and penthouse levels, but then Jason insisted a new stop be inserted for his floor. Esther considered this a very strategic move. Every board member was suddenly made aware of the tectonic shift of power. For the nine quarters since Jason's promotion to division chief, investment banking had generated more profit than the rest of the bank's activities combined.

As the elevator shot her up to the thirty-fifth floor, Esther tried to formulate a response to what the CEO was bound to ask: What was her take on the risks embedded in Jason's trade? Esther still felt caught by Jason's silent warning and had no idea what to say. Which was hardly the mind-set to carry into a meeting with the bank's president. But when the doors opened on the board level, Esther realized it no longer mattered.

Reynolds Thane stood in the elevator's lobby with another gentleman in his late sixties. Both men possessed the ruddy sheen of out-of-season tans. Reynolds gripped an imaginary putter while the other man smiled indulgently. Sir Trevor Stanstead was CEO of a British conglomerate that owned the third largest bank in Europe. The group had recently acquired four percent of CFM's shares. The following month, Sir Trevor had been named to CFM's board.

Sir Trevor had snow-white hair and a genteel manner that most people found charming. He dressed in tailored clothes even when headed for the golf course, like now. Sir Trevor wielded ultimate power with refined grace. She was certain Trevor Stanstead eviscerated his enemies with polished charm.

Reynolds smiled benignly. "Ah, Ms. Larsen, they found you. Excellent. Sir Trevor, this is Jason's top analyst."

Trevor Stanstead had a piercing gray gaze the color of a polished blade. "I say, well done, Ms. Larsen."

Reynolds held the private elevator doors open for his guest. He clearly had no interest in Esther joining them. "We'll need to reschedule our chat, Ms. Larsen. Perhaps early next week. Speak with Grace and set it up."

Esther waited for the doors to shut, then moved over to hit the button for the slower-moving elevator. When she stepped inside, she felt as if the bronze walls were closing in on her.

As the floors pinged past, Esther said to her fractured image, "They are already celebrating."

When she exited on the seventeenth floor, her phone chimed. Esther had downloaded a special ringtone for Jason's calls and messages, the opening bars of Wagner's "Flight of the Valkyries."

The message from Jason was five words long. *Find me the next one.*

6

Ten minutes into her homeward journey, Esther's phone rang. Patricia Saunders said, "Tell me I'm not interrupting something important."

"I just left the office."

"Good. Do you have plans for tonight? I'm asking because my sister is coming over for dinner, and we thought . . . well, would you like to join us? I know it's spur of the moment, but I've found the tactic works better with busy people. My husband included."

Esther did not need to think it over. "I would like that. A lot, actually."

Forty-seven minutes later, Esther pulled into Patricia's driveway. She was twelve minutes early, but it appeared that others had already arrived. She turned off the motor and sat there, listening to the night through her open window. The urge to join them in the house was as strong as hunger. Even so, she remained where she was, captured by the memory of losing her parents. She rarely permitted herself these recollections. But tonight, surrounded by a soft Carolina spring, she remembered. She remembered everything.

When she was eight, her mother had departed this earth. That was how their father had described the event that had ended her mother's battle with cancer. Like the woman had stepped away for an evening or a weekend. Nine months later, her father died from a heart attack. Esther had been small and quiet even then, able to tuck herself into the shadows of their home's central staircase and hear how one person after another described her father as having spent nine months trying to live with a broken heart.

Sitting in the parked car, Esther recalled how angry she had felt at the time. Her mother had suffered and died. But her father? He had *chosen* to abandon them. How was that even possible?

Esther had not cared about all the reasons, how wonderful her mother had been, or how much her parents had loved each other. None of that had mattered *at all*.

What Esther remembered most about the entire episode was how she never cried. The anger did not let her. This rage carried her through the terrible transition to her grandparents' home. They were very quiet, very set in their ways. Her mother had been so full of joy. She had spent hours humming snatches of tunes as she worked. Esther knew even then that her mother's music represented a lifetime of filling the empty spaces created by her taciturn parents.

Nowadays Esther rarely listened to music. There was always the risk of having a song come on the radio that her mother had hummed, and being wrenched back to those awful days.

Two things had saved her back then, both from her own rage and the home's constant silence. One had been her love of numbers. The power of math had formed a compass heading during those difficult early years and on through university, graduate school, and into a profession she loved. Until recently.

The other remedy had been Nathan. Her brother had fit himself into the role of guardian and caregiver. Esther knew there was bitter irony in where Nathan was now, repeating his father's pattern. And once again she was helpless to do anything about it, except give to him without reservation.

Esther knew it must have been challenging for Nathan to love the child she had once been, withdrawn and perpetually hidden behind her walls of abandonment and rage. So she did not criticize him now. She had not raised her voice even once in the face of his silent defeat.

Esther closed the window and exited the car. As she started up the front walk, she silently repeated the familiar refrain. She would lovingly grant Nathan the freedom to make his own choices.

So long as she kept her job.

Esther always enjoyed spending time in Patricia's home. Tonight's visit carried a special poignancy. As soon as she entered, Esther felt struck by everything the home contained that her own did not. Laughter rang from the living room. Aromas drifted down the front hall. Patricia greeted her with a warm hug. All the components of a life that many people took for granted.

Patricia said, "Lacy is back from school. We didn't know she was coming until about two hours ago."

Their daughter was a junior at Chapel Hill. "Anything wrong?"

"She won't say."

Esther asked, "Issues with her boyfriend?"

"That's my guess." Patricia lowered her voice

further. "Speaking of which, my sister's brought a friend."

"A man friend? A *single* man friend?"

"Well, yes."

Esther saw the unease Patricia was trying to hide and guessed, "You knew about this when you invited me."

"Oh . . ." She waved her hands like her fingers burned. "Donnie says I've never been able to keep a secret or tell a fib in my entire life."

"You can *tell* one," Esther corrected. "You just can't get anyone to believe it."

"Yes, I knew Rachel was bringing him. Yes, I told her it was okay. Yes, I am being manipulative. Are you mad?"

To Esther's surprise, she could honestly reply, "No." Then she added, "Not if I don't have to like him."

"You don't even have to speak to him." Patricia showed dimples. "But he is kind of nice."

"Kind of?"

"Okay, he's hot. There. I've said it. Even Lacy thinks so."

"How old is he?"

"I have no idea. Late thirties, I suppose. But that didn't stop my daughter from describing him as a 'major drool.' "

They both were laughing as they entered the living room. Which made Esther's shock impossible to hide.

"Esther Larsen, I'd like you to meet—"

"Craig Wessex," she said.

He was taller than she would have imagined, but of course she had only seen him seated. And he was even better looking than he had appeared in silhouette, leaning in close to Nathan, poking her brother's arm.

He frowned at Esther. "I'm sorry, have we met?"

7

Esther replied, "I saw you at the clinic today. You were with my brother Nathan."

Craig nodded slowly. "Of course. I can see the resemblance. And the nurse said you had stopped by, but then needed to leave."

Patricia looked at Esther. "I didn't know you had a brother."

Esther's heart sank under the weight of everything that would now come out. The whole mess with her brother, her past, everything. But Craig must have seen something in her expression because he said, "Nathan is a topic for another night."

"Of course," Patricia said. "Duly noted. Filed under tomorrow or the next day."

And just like that, they moved on. It was remarkable how smooth the transition went.

The evening proceeded at a comfortable pace.

As usual, Esther did not join in much of the conversation. She was grateful no one saw any need to press her. Patricia's sister Rachel was an art historian working for the regional museum, her husband a professor of American history at UNC-Charlotte. Which was how they knew Craig, a divinity student who showed a quiet passion for almost every topic. His cheekbones punched hard against the skin beneath his eyes, and his brows were shaggy as an old dog's pelt. But his most remarkable feature was his eyes. They were gray like a mist at dawn and almost translucent.

Patricia's daughter Lacy looked like the walking wounded. Esther was rather certain now from the few comments the young woman made that she had been emotionally crushed by a man. The family's response was far more interesting to Esther than the reason for Lacy's severely bruised state. They showed the silent care of people who intimated with their every gesture that they were there for her, that she could turn to them whenever she chose, for whatever she needed.

Over a dessert of pecan pie and fresh-brewed coffee, Patricia asked Craig about his return to school. "How does it feel, going back?"

He smiled. "Don't you mean, why did I do it at my age?"

"Oh, all right, yes. That's exactly what I meant."

Craig replied, "The direct answer is, my wife left me and took our two daughters with her."

An intense silence was followed by Patricia asking, "What happened?"

"She fell in love with another man. That was, let's see, four years ago." Craig hesitated, then added, "My daughters . . ."

Rachel said quietly, "They don't like him."

"Probably better to say they're having difficulty adjusting," Craig said.

"They wouldn't need four years to adjust," Rachel replied. "His two girls are convinced their stepfather doesn't want them around."

Craig sighed, but did not speak.

Patricia asked Rachel, "You know his daughters?"

"The older girl, Samantha, is friends with my daughter," Rachel explained. "They miss their dad, and they don't like their current situation."

Patricia asked Craig, "Why can't they live with you?"

"The courts say they should stay with their mom." Craig's voice was very low.

Patricia asked again, "So why did you return to school?"

"After the divorce, I spent eighteen months going through the motions. Finally I accepted that my former life no longer held any meaning. I was working seventy-hour weeks for nothing. So I moved on."

"What did you do back then?" Donald asked.

"I was an accountant."

Esther spoke for the first time. "What was your field?"

"I was a corporate auditor with KPMG." He was watching her openly now, for the first time that evening. "I heard you work for a bank."

"CFM," she replied, the shorthand for Carolina First Mercantile, so widely used it was now on the bank's letterhead. The bank actually preferred it. The board thought *Carolina* to be too provincial a heading for a global brand.

Craig asked, "What do you do?"

"I am head of risk analysis."

He leaned back in his seat. "What department?"

"Investment banking. Primarily the currency markets, but these days we deal with all forms of derivatives."

"The old lines of demarcation are being erased," Craig said.

Esther noticed the intensity of his focus. "You worked on bank audits?"

"Never had the pleasure. But I was a partner, and KPMG handled external audits for a number of financial groups."

"Not us," Esther said.

He smiled. A new quality entered his voice, the spark of former days. "Not for a lack of trying. My former partners would have traded their firstborn for that account."

Patricia said, "I'm hearing words but not understanding a thing."

"The lady across the table is passionate about numbers," Craig said. "She can pierce the veil and see things that others assume are well-concealed."

"Like you?"

"Oh, no. Accountants are a dime a dozen." Craig's gaze held Esther's. "We gather on street corners and stare up in awe at the offices of risk analysts like Esther."

Patricia demanded, "But what does that *mean?*"

Esther liked how she could talk directly with Craig even while the others listened in. "My favorite part of the Carolina spring is when the nights get warm enough for me to go outside and sit on my deck and watch the sky. I love studying clouds blown by the wind."

"Turned silver by moonlight," Rachel put in. "I know, it's so beautiful."

"I was going to say," Esther continued, "this is the closest approximation in the physical universe to risk analysis. Clean numbers stretched across the universe, then clouds of risk come and go. My job is to predict the clouds' pattern and their course."

Craig added, "And identify which stars will remain clearly defined, uninterrupted by the clouds."

This time a little shiver touched her reply, "Exactly."

• • •

Esther gathered dishes and helped carry them to the kitchen. On her third pass through the dining room, she was halted by the sight of Lacy seated on the floor by the living room sofa. Her family all listened with grave expressions. Esther doubted the young woman was even aware of the tears dripping off her cheeks.

Esther turned and slipped silently across the kitchen and let herself out the back door. She was trying to decide which patio chair had the best sky view when the door opened behind her and Craig asked, "Mind some company?"

She stepped over to the brick wall housing the grill, feeling its heat rise against the back of her legs. "It seemed like a good time to become invisible."

"No one objected when I excused myself," Craig agreed.

Esther could see through the rear windows that Patricia had left her husband's side and moved around to hold her daughter. She said, "For what it's worth, I'm sorry for everything you've been through, Craig."

"Thank you." He settled onto the brick wall. "I think there were kernels of transcendent truth in my tragedy. I missed years of signals because it was easier to focus on the pressures of work. I had to be really smacked down hard to pay attention."

49

"Kernels of transcendent truth," Esther repeated. "That's a lovely turn of phrase."

"It's not original with me. A Supreme Court justice said it first."

"Do you know which one?"

"Roberts. Heard him on the radio. I was driving to work, oh, it must have been about a year after my wife left me. I was still trying to climb out of the black hole, but I kept coming up against the same awful question—what was the point of it all?"

"Hearing the words helped you."

"They did. I realized that so long as I returned to what had cost me so much, there *wasn't* any point. The question was, what could I possibly do differently that would give meaning to my days?"

"So you decided to become a pastor."

He was silent so long that Esther feared her rather offhand comment had offended him. Then, "Not exactly. At least, it doesn't feel that way to me."

"But . . ."

"What happened in the car that morning was, I started looking for something *more*." He turned toward her. "Why do you think they invited us here tonight?"

Esther was glad he could not see the crimson flush rise to her cheeks. "What kind of question is that?"

Craig did not appear the least affected by her

sharp-edged response. "I mean, beyond the obvious. They are concerned about you."

"They told you this?"

"Not in so many words. But Patricia is not the only one in that family who can't keep secrets. They care for you, Esther."

"They hardly even know me."

"And why is that?" Craig's tone was gentle, but he was also insistent. "Rachel described you as beautiful, intelligent, and troubled by something you either can't or won't discuss."

"So they're using you to pry free my secrets?" Esther knew her charge sounded awful. Even before the words were fully out, she wished she could take them back. "Sorry, I just, I don't—"

"You are perfectly correct. I am out of line. And I won't say anything else about this unless you speak first. I mean it. Even if we meet again at your brother's or anywhere else. Just let me ask you one question. Do you have anyone you can confide in about the burdens you're carrying? Because I sense there's more at work here than . . ."

Craig stopped talking, because Esther had spun around. She watched as cinders rose from the grill and joined with the night. The backyard was bordered by a stand of Carolina pine that cut a jagged silhouette from the city's glow. Esther felt a sad lump rise from the empty place where her heart should reside.

Behind her, Craig said softly, "Everybody needs a friend. Even a hyperintelligent analyst." His footsteps carried him back across the patio. She heard the door to the kitchen open and close.

8

The dinner party was well into wind-down mode when Esther reentered the house. She stood on the periphery where she could observe and remain unnoticed. Esther saw how they comforted Lacy, shared her pain. She followed them across the foyer and out the front door. All Esther's familiar reasons for staying silent clamored for her attention. But the arguments no longer worked.

They gathered on the home's curved front portico, its five steps descending to a path of the same fired brick. The faint whiff of new magnolia blossoms hinted at an awakening season.

Esther gripped her arms around her middle, terribly conflicted.

Patricia laid a hand on her shoulder and asked, "Esther, honey, what is it?"

She looked from one face to the next, seeing exactly what she expected to find, what she *needed*.

Esther whispered, "I'm so scared."

Patricia declared that whatever it was Esther wanted to share, it wasn't meant for the front porch. The family and their guests reformed in the living room, this time with Esther at its heart.

Rachel went into the kitchen and put on a fresh pot of coffee. Craig drew a hardwood rocking chair over and invited Esther to make herself comfortable. Lacy seated herself on the bottom step of the stairs leading up to the bedrooms, pulled the sleeves of her sweater down so they covered all but the tips of her fingers, and wrapped her arms around her legs. Patricia and Donald sat on the couch. Craig carried in a chair from the dining table and seated himself across from Esther.

After a moment's silence, Esther confessed, "I have no idea what to say."

Patricia suggested, "Why don't you tell us a little something about yourself."

"Most of the time I feel like a total alien around other people. I suppose I have all my life. My parents passed away when I was very young. But I remember my mother calling me her changeling. She was a specialist in medieval literature. A changeling originally meant a child of forest sprites who had been snuck into a home." Esther found it easier to address her words to the empty fireplace. "I like Italian operas and Victorian architecture. I am a student of Talleyrand and Churchill and Machiavelli, whom I consider the three greatest strategists when it comes to risk management."

She knew the words were disjointed and random. A new thought welled up so strong it nearly choked off her air. She whispered, "I need to tell someone."

Craig asked, "Is this about your work?"

"Not the bank. But yes. In a way."

"The economy?" When she nodded, Craig said, "What frightens you, Esther?"

"In the days following the Wall Street crash of 2008, I started what I call my Doomsday List." Esther could hear the tension in her voice, a jagged quality she had never noticed before. Then again, she had never spoken of this. Not once. Not to anyone. "It began as two books. Book One contained all the certifiable factors that led to the collapse. I took no single source for what went in this first book. Every issue was confirmed by a minimum of three respected experts."

The others had gone rock still. The only motion was when Rachel handed around coffees and then joined her husband on the loveseat. Craig asked quietly, "How many factors do you have listed in the book?"

"Five. I call them dynamics. Each holds a confirmed level of destructive force. None of them alone could cause another financial institution as large as Lehman Brothers to default. But put several of them together and that would cause a major meltdown."

Craig now served as the group's moderator. "You know this because you've calculated their potency, correct?"

"Yes. Book One now has six volumes, almost seven hundred pages of notes and calculations along with corroborating support."

He nodded slowly. "And Book Two?"

"This contains other activities employed by financial institutions that I am fairly certain played a major role in the worldwide economy's near collapse. This list holds another eleven dynamics."

"But you can't confirm their role."

"Correct. Most of those dynamics are based on rumor and innuendo." Esther hesitated, then added, "I also used sealed documents from Senate investigations."

Craig asked, "And do you have allies who share your concerns?"

"A few."

"These allies are professionals who trust your abilities as an analyst."

Esther did not know what to say, so she remained silent.

"These dynamics," Craig continued, "many of them are illegal, aren't they?"

Again Esther did not reply.

"Which means you cannot confirm in any concrete way that they played a role in the economic mess." Craig gave her a chance to respond, then asked, "Do you have a list of the banks you suspect use these methods?"

Her heart hammered in her chest. "They are on the front page of Book One."

"How many banks are engaging in these dynamics?"

"In the US, sixteen. Globally, another forty-seven."

"You notice I didn't ask how many employed these dynamics prior to the 2008 crash."

It was Esther's turn to nod.

"Which means you are not simply doing an analysis of past events," Craig said.

"Correct."

"You are looking at the situation today."

"Yes."

"And that is what alarms you."

"Yes." Esther waited for someone to object. How the SEC held new regulatory powers. Or how the banks certainly must have learned the lessons of 2008 and pulled back from the wild maneuvers that had pushed the global economy to the brink. But no one breathed, no one moved.

That was when Esther hit the wall.

Her geeks used that phrase a lot. The wall could be anything—fatigue, stress, or simply an analysis that did not come together. Whatever the reason, the outcome was the same. One minute the data was pouring in, the analyst was cooking, the intel read like a good novel. The next minute . . . total confusion and panic.

Esther sprang to her feet, startling them all. Her mind scrambled for a way to take it all back, make the confession simply vanish. But all she could think to say was, "I have to go."

They followed her to the door, but the gathering's collective nature was gone. Craig seemed deeply concerned by her abrupt departure. Esther offered lame thanks for a lovely evening and hurried out to her car. As she drove away, one refrain echoed continually through her mind: They probably thought she was crazy. And maybe they were right.

9

Saturday

Esther awoke expecting blowback. The term came from the military, but it had spread via electronic games and was now adopted by geeks everywhere. Blowback meant any repercussion from a forward movement, especially one that risked exposure to incoming fire. As she prepared her morning coffee, Esther saw any number of potential sources of worry and threat, starting with her own internal alarms. She was surprised not to have been repeatedly awakened by their clamor.

She took her coffee out to the rear deck and

watched the pale wash of dawn grow in the east. The birds were especially strident this morning, cardinals and mockingbirds and jays and robins, all shrilling their amazement at a new season. The air was crisp and the city weekend quiet, so Esther decided to go for a long run.

Esther left for the bank at nine. The downstairs guards were in laid-back mode. The trading floor was closed, the executive level vacant. In her group's converted factory space, her team hummed along at the typical weekend pitch. Esther surveyed her crew with a sense of deep affection. Even the admins tended toward geeky and awkward, yet they were *her* geeks.

Jasmine greeted Esther with, "So where do we go from here?"

"Assemble the team," Esther replied. "Conference room. But give me fifteen minutes. First I want to check the traffic."

Esther rarely used the conference room assigned to her team. They shared it with the accounting division responsible for all mortgages the bank kept on its books. The bank's home-loan portfolio was growing by leaps and bounds. The market for bundled mortgages and all their derivatives had dried up after 2008 and never fully recovered. The SEC kept too close a watch. This meant the bank was keeping a larger portion of the loans they wrote on their own books. The accounting division treated the conference room as their exclusive turf. They considered Esther's team usurpers. She used it today because she wanted the solemnity of a structured environment. As usual, she included her admin staff as well as the analysts. It was her way of showing that they were all in this together.

She began the meeting without preamble. Lengthy sessions tended to send her geeks into severe withdrawal mode, as it disconnected them from their computers and data streams. "You know how much the bank made from the trade they concluded yesterday. I have orders from Jason to find another target."

Jasmine frowned, but did not speak. Their newest member, a recent graduate with a voice as high as a squeaky toy, did so. His name was Bradley, but his first week he had repeatedly bragged about his alma mater. Now everybody simply called him MIT. "Is that wise?"

"It is inevitable," their lone Pakistani spoke up. "If they want to make another hundred mil in a week."

Jasmine said, "So Jason isn't giving back the two billion."

Esther replied, "The note from our boss said nothing except 'find me the next one.' His exact words."

"Does the top floor realize what that does to the bank's exposure?"

"When I went upstairs yesterday, Reynolds and

Sir Trevor both complimented us on the role we played. I assume the answer is that they know what they want to know." Esther held up her hand, halting further comment. "Our task has been set. Let's focus on the objective."

Once the discussion started, Esther allowed Jasmine to take over and did not speak again. Nor did she pay close attention to the swirl of talk and calculations. Instead, she concentrated on her own internal debate.

When the meeting broke up, Esther returned to her office and lowered the translucent screens over her internal windows. That was her signal for the team to leave her alone unless there was an impending tsunami. She faced her monitors, both because the team would see her familiar silhouette and because she found the data stream reassuring.

Esther left the office at midafternoon, pausing only to review the half-completed ideas her team was putting together. She ordered them to leave by six, a command she knew most would ignore. She drove home with her windows open to the cool spring air, then sat in the driveway, staring at her front door and facing her internal realization.

The status quo no longer worked.

Remaining silent, not speaking, that was what had weighed her down the most. More than the plight of her beloved brother. More than the risks the bank currently exposed itself to. Her time of remaining on the sidelines and simply observing was over.

But what possible good could come from the actions of just one person?

Esther prepared a packaged dinner of rice and stir-fried vegetables with Thai sauce while watching the business channels' weekend roundups. The Dow had ended the week down by over four percent, which left the stock market's key indicators in negative territory for the entire year. The talking heads were gloomy in their forecasts for the next week. All their discussions carried a sense of grim foreboding. Esther agreed with their predictions, but not the reasoning. They focused almost exclusively on the American economy. And the problem was that their answers did not fit with the questions.

As she switched between channels, the voices became a unified anxious chorus. Junk bonds were down to their lowest level in seven years. Stocks were sinking across the board. The economy seemed to be stagnating. In the raw-material sectors, four years of rising values had been wiped out. Investors were acting like herd animals, fleeing the first rumble of thunder beyond the horizon.

But what Esther did not hear anyone discussing were *next steps*. What were people supposed to do? How were they to protect themselves, their families, even the country? Esther pulled out a pad and pen and began sketching out her thoughts. She felt many of the answers were right there, waiting for someone to lift their gaze beyond the horizon of this single economy and look at the bigger problems. As she ate, she watched half-formed concepts take shape.

The longer she sat there, the more certain she was that the time had come to act.

Midway through her meal, the phone rang. When she answered, Patricia asked, "What are you doing tomorrow after church?"

"Same old," Esther replied. "Go to the gym, then swing by the office. Prepare for the coming week."

"Could you take time for lunch at our place?"

"Twice in one weekend? I don't—"

"Please." Patricia's voice carried an unusual level of stress. "It's important. Really."

"What is this about?"

"Have you been watching the news?"

Esther huffed a humorless laugh. "Pretty much all the time. That's part of my job description."

"We've all been talking about what you said. Craig feels . . ."

She brightened at the sound of his name. Which was silly of course. "What?"

"Craig insists that you are someone we can trust to get it right."

Esther did not know how to respond.

Patricia said, "There are some people we want you to meet."

"Well, I suppose—"

"Great." The words came at a rush now, as though Patricia feared Esther might change her mind. "It's a potluck. Bring whatever. Veggies or salad would be nice. And we tend toward informal on Sunday afternoons."

That night Esther watched a movie starring Cary Grant, her all-time favorite actor. He played a jewel thief on the Riviera and drove a convertible roadster and never got caught by anyone except the beautiful blonde.

Esther thought Craig Wessex resembled the star to a certain degree. She was surprised at her disappointment that he had not called. Esther felt like a teenager as she carried the phone with her into the bedroom. She was a grown woman. An executive with a regional powerhouse. She could get his number from Patricia and make the call herself. But the last thing she needed right now was another failed romance.

As she drifted off, Esther realized she had not checked the monitors in her office since returning home. She decided it could wait until she arose in the middle of the night. But she fell asleep almost instantly and slept until morning, as well as she had in years.

10

Sunday

Esther drove along wet and windswept streets. The Carolina spring was astonishingly beautiful, even in the midst of a storm. This time of year, the rainfall carried a softly apologetic note, as though regretting the need to disturb the day. Esther felt no closer to finding an answer to her quandary. Even so, there was an odd sense of comfort in knowing she had at least identified a new compass heading.

Providence Presbyterian Church was one of Charlotte's oldest. The first log structure had been erected in 1767. Entering the compound gave Esther the feeling of being anchored to the city's early days. The structures resembled the church of her childhood. Esther smiled a greeting to Patricia and her husband, accepted their quick embraces, and allowed herself to be guided to the row where Rachel and her husband sat.

Today's service was lost to the sweep of memories. Esther stood and sat along with the congregation, but the intensity of her recollections dominated everything. She had loved her early Midwest upbringing. Their family had lived twenty miles west of Minneapolis, near Lake Minnetonka. Many of her fondest memories were about numbers. At age three she had made a secret pet of the number nine. At six, she had tested out at high-school-level mathematics. The instructor responsible for supervising those tests had never seen anything like her. He designed a pair of logic questions to determine if she could derive the fundamental concepts of calculus. Esther offered him the correct answers before he had finished writing out the problems.

Esther's parents had been both proud and supportive of her gift. That was how they described it. Her gift. The children at her school were kind and nasty in turn, but most of the time Esther was content with her own company. Church had been a weekly delight back then.

Two years later, her parents died within nine months of each other. Her life, quite simply, fell apart.

Her grandparents saw her passion for numbers as a childhood oddity. They wanted her to behave. They wanted her to disturb their silent calm as little as possible. Her presence was already an unwelcome fracas. She was a perpetual stone thrown into the still waters of their existence.

As a result, Esther's attitude toward numbers underwent a drastic shift. Gone was her passion for the purity of math. She knew she was gifted. That at least had not been lost along with her parents and her home and her church. By age eleven, Esther had already taken aim. She decided to use this gift and fashion a way out for herself.

She took the state exams at twelve, four years earlier than normal. This was followed by SATs at thirteen, for which she received a near-perfect score. With Nathan's help and support, she applied for early admission to four universities. She was accepted by all of them. At fourteen she entered the University of Chicago because they offered her a full ride and because it was the farthest removed from a house that had never been a home.

Esther's grandparents had belonged to a church as stifling as they were. At university, she stopped attending. She did not forget how to pray. But the tyranny of the urgent, the sense that God had abandoned her, all reshaped her perspective.

Nowadays the pressures of her upwardly mobile job left her content to spend a few hours on Sunday communing with her past, then leaving. She often wondered if she ever really had a faith of her own.

Esther was mildly surprised when the church service ended. She rose and followed the others to the Sunday school classroom she usually attended. The majority found seats in a wide circle that held twenty. Esther took her customary position in the second row. People had long since grown accustomed to her silent presence.

Craig's words echoed through her mind *The*

transcendent truth. Esther wondered what that might possibly mean to her own life.

Esther stopped by her home to change clothes and pull a bowl of endive salad from the fridge. When she arrived at the Saunders home, the driveway was already full with more cars lining both sides of the street. So Esther left her car farther down the block. Three couples by the front door turned to stare at her. She could see others watching through the home's front windows as Patricia rushed down the brick walk. Esther shifted her bowl so that the larger woman could embrace her. "What's going on?"

"A lot of folks are worried, is what." She settled an arm on Esther's shoulders and pressed her forward.

"I don't understand." But she did understand, in fact. The stares and Patricia's obvious tension added up to only one thing.

These people were gathered here because of her.

"The economic news has been so awful this past week, all Donald had to do was mention you and your ideas, and people begged for the chance to meet up. Then Craig had the idea for us to invite some people over for a lunch. But let him explain."

Eyes followed the two of them as they maneuvered through the crowded rooms and entered the kitchen. Craig was deep in conversation with two couples, but when he spotted Esther he broke off and approached with a small smile. "It's good to see you. I'm glad you agreed to come."

When Esther deposited her bowl, he led her outside. Esther waited until they were in the back garden to say, "Who are all these people?"

"A few are friends of mine. Donald and Patricia and Rachel called around. Their contacts phoned others. Did you see the news last night?"

"Yes."

"Everybody is worried what the markets are going to do this week. I simply made a suggestion. Donald and Patricia offered to set this up."

The same dual sense of internal pressure and deep-seated need were still with her. And growing stronger. Esther found herself confessing, "I've pretty much decided I have to do something. The question is *what?*"

Craig was clearly pleased by her words. "When did this happen?"

"It's been growing for some time. But really the actual decision for me came during church today."

He revealed a warm smile, there and gone in an unsteady heartbeat. "May I make a suggestion?"

"Of course."

"Don't talk to them. Talk to me. I'll ask you some questions."

"Like the other evening?"

"Just like that. You say what is on your mind and heart. When you're done, just sit there. And see what happens."

"I don't understand . . . what are you expecting from this?"

"Two things," he replied. "First, you'll realize you are not alone. Second, well . . ."

"What?"

He shared another smile as he said, "You'll realize what you need to do next."

11

The size of the gathering actually made it easier for Esther to ignore them. Normally her presentations were restricted to senior traders or bank executives, a dozen at the most. Esther had learned to adapt to the spotlight by researching each listener in depth. She knew them, she understood their backgrounds, she anticipated their aims. This was impossible today. Patricia's home held over forty people. They filtered in and out of sight. They ate seated in all the downstairs rooms and lined the central staircase and filled the back patio with plates balanced on their laps. Most were in their thirties and forties, but several were quite a bit older. Rachel bustled around one gentleman in his late sixties, who walked with a distinct limp and used a cane. Esther thought she recognized him, but she was swept away before she could fit the face to the memory.

Esther was offered a place at the dining table but opted for a spot in the kitchen, where she could stand by the rear window and focus on the trees and the sunlight. She had no appetite, which was normal for her during such times. And yet she felt no jitters. Craig stood beside her, a silent assurance that he would stay with her and help guide her. Through what exactly, she had no idea. Even so, despite her natural avoidance of public attention, Esther had the distinct impression she was where she should be. She hoped it was not merely because she was glad to see Craig again. She didn't think so, but she could not be certain.

After lunch there was a gradual shift into the living room. Several couples had brought young children, and they were let loose to play in the backyard. A few kids, however, caught their parents' somber mood and remained close at hand.

Craig brought in two high-back chairs from the dining room and set them by the fireplace. He placed them at an angle, so that she could look out over the gathering if she wanted or focus solely on him. "What do you think?"

Esther nodded, her throat tight. "Could I have a glass of water?"

"You can have anything you like," Patricia replied.

"Water is fine."

The living room became jammed with bodies. They filled the sofas and all the dining chairs. Couples who had changed into casual clothing sprawled on the floor. Others took their places on the window seats, dragging in extra cushions from the television area. When the living room could hold no more people, they crammed into the doorways.

Donald excused himself to switch on the air conditioning. When he returned, Patricia said, "Craig, somebody needs to run this show. You're it."

"All right." He swiftly recapped their dinner conversation, hitting all the salient points. Esther found herself calmed by his professional manner. Craig listened well, and what was more, he remembered. When he completed his summary, Craig turned to her and asked, "Ready?"

"Yes."

"Okay. You have listed sixteen US banks who have resumed practices that carried us into recession in 2008, which you call dynamics. But these sixteen banks aren't the only ones who are running such extreme risks, are they?"

"Probably not."

"These are the ones you've been able to confirm. The ones you have hard evidence against, yes?" He nodded in time to her response. "But there's something more about these sixteen that troubles you, isn't there?"

"Yes."

"It's their size, am I right?" He rewarded her nod with a smile of encouragement. "Where do they stand in the national ranking, Esther?"

"All of them are in the top forty. Three are in the top ten."

"So if they were to fail, they could have the same seismic impact as the collapse of Lehman Brothers, correct?"

"Not any one of them. A number of safety measures have been put in place since the recession, most importantly the financial stress test overseen by the SEC. These new rulings mean the economy is somewhat better protected than it was in 2008."

"But if, say, three of them were to be hit by a calamity at the same time . . ."

"Then the markets would probably crash."

"And by markets, plural, you mean the global economy?"

"Correct. This is no longer about a US recession. The world financial markets are too intertwined."

Craig gave that a beat, as if preparing for a new line of questioning. In the pause, a voice from the room said, "I'm not clear on what we're doing here. I mean, I was already worried. I don't need—"

Donald broke in, "For this to work, we need to let the two here finish their analysis. We'll have time for discussion afterwards. But until they're done, it's important that everybody stay quiet." He nodded to Craig. "Back to you."

Esther was pleased to discover that the interruption did not faze her. Craig kept his eyes glued to her, and she to him. Craig used the disruption as an opportunity to change directions. "Let's take just a minute and talk about your background. Where did you study?"

"I did two undergraduate degrees in accounting and econometrics at the University of Chicago."

"How old were you when you graduated?"

She had the distinct impression he already knew the answer, which was very interesting. Both because it meant he had researched her, and because the knowledge did not trouble him in the least. "Seventeen."

"Maybe you should explain what econometrics actually means."

"It's the mathematical and statistical analysis of factors impacting the economy."

"But you didn't stop there, did you?"

"No, I did a master's and a doctorate at Caltech. My focus was the development of algorithms that could be used to track future economic trends."

"Which brought you to the attention of CFM. How long have you been with them?"

"Going on nine years."

"And when did you first begin to grow concerned about trends in the nation's financial system?"

"My final year at grad school. Then following the 2008 crash I began focusing on what I hoped would never be repeated. I thought . . . it's naïve, but at the time I thought the banks had learned their lesson."

"But that hasn't happened."

"No. In fact, the trends are now moving in the exact opposite direction."

"Why is that?"

"Because the decision-makers at these banks are all focused on one factor above everything else, short-term profits. Their goal is to make more money this quarter than last." The thoughts came more easily now. The lid was off her internal cauldron. She was revealing her fears. At long last. "The biggest impact the 2008 recession had on the financial industry was to raise the size of their bets."

"Same question, Esther. Why is that?"

"First of all, you need to understand that the investment banking divisions of major banks is a lie. They don't invest, and they're not banks. They're gamblers. They were the cause of the 2008 recession and they are the ones . . ."

"Pushing us to the brink again."

"I think so. Yes."

"So these gamblers are betting larger sums. Why do you think that is happening?"

"The margins are smaller. The SEC and similar groups in other countries are restricting their movements. So when a potential source of income is determined, they go at it full bore."

"They bet the house."

"Exactly."

Craig leaned back and smiled. "Do you need a break?"

"No, I'm fine."

"Okay. For us to understand what these risks really mean, and why they are so dangerous, we need to come to grips with one thing above all else, correct?"

Esther nodded, totally in sync with him now. "Derivatives."

12

The original usage of the word *derivative* was in the higher maths. A derivative measured the sensitivity to change of one factor when impacted by another. This measurement forms one of the central pillars of calculus.

A financial derivative was actually based on this concept, though most traders had no idea the connection existed. For a trader, derivatives were contracts that *derived* their value from the performance of an underlying entity. Traders usually referred to these assets as *underlies*.

The element on which the financial derivative was based could be a paper asset the bank owned like a home mortgage. It could also be a fixed asset such as currency, gold, or bonds. But the most powerful of the derivatives were not based on anything so concrete. Instead, these were based on *positions*. The structure of interest rates, the measure of economic growth, the future value of an asset that was not actually in the bank's possession—any and all of these formed the basis for new derivatives. All the bank needed was for someone to measure their value and someone else to buy them. The financial system had a word to describe all such derivatives. That term was *exotic*.

Esther had another word for them. She called them toxic.

By this point, Esther had become so involved in her explanation that she no longer had room to be nervous. She rose from her chair and took the four smallest photos off the mantel behind her. She then knelt on the carpet and put the photos facedown on the coffee table, four gilt-edged frames around blank felt squares. "Okay, we need an example to show what's happening in the market. Let's say these four are derivatives either held or being acquired by a major bank. They are all interconnected. That's a key element of exotic pairings like this. There must be a logical correlation, something that can be measured."

She touched each of the felt squares in turn. "So let's say here we have commercial mortgages. These are normally cross-border, which means they represent buildings in half a dozen different countries. And here we have one block of currencies that are used to value these mortgages, say, US dollars and Mexican pesos. This third group includes three other currencies—the euro, Swiss franc, and yen. And this final block are euro bonds issued by banks and real estate holding groups. Clear so far?"

Craig pulled his chair in closer and leaned over. "Very," he said.

Esther lined up the four frames like little square soldiers. "This is how they're bought. One and then another and then another. Before they're purchased, we run two sets of numbers. The first is standard risk analysis. What is the likelihood the value will swing in our favor and the bank will make money? In this case, we are betting against the market."

"Betting," Craig repeated. "How much?"

"Each of these represents many hundreds of millions. Billions in the case of interest-rate swaps and some currency trades."

"So, a lot."

"Yes, but for many derivatives the bank does

not pay the full value of the underlie. The bank pays a percentage, and this percentage is hotly negotiated."

"Just like a private trader working on an account."

"True, but that's not the important thing here. Well, it is, but it's not . . ."

"You're doing great," Craig said gently. "Tell me what's important."

"The real risk, the *important* risk, comes from this." Slowly Esther reached out and drew the four into a single tight square. "The bank bundles them."

"They take the four assets and make one," Craig said.

"Right. And this joining creates a completely different risk structure. We can measure this too. The bank has a series of algorithms specifically designed to measure how risk changes according to such groupings."

"So you buy them separately and then bundle them, and the risk changes, and so does the price," Craig said. "That's brilliant."

Esther rose from her crouched position and returned to her chair. "It's also highly dangerous."

"Why is that?"

"Two reasons. First, these bundlings don't happen overnight. A legal structure has to be formed. That can take weeks, sometimes even months. Then the bank's traders have to go out and sell the new product. This means analysts at other banks make their own calculations and determine whether the claims of our traders are real."

"Which means you're holding the assets on the bank's books," Craig said.

"They don't just hold the assets, they hold the risk. And so long as the market moves as we anticipate, as we have measured, the total risk goes down, which means the assets we hold go up in value. But what if the *economy* goes down? I don't mean, enters into recession. I mean, what if there is even a *fractional* shift in the factors that govern this particular area of the global market?"

Craig's voice had become as tense as her own. "What happens, Esther?"

"The risk is magnified beyond all the bank's carefully constructed boundaries."

"And the downside becomes a threat to the bank, possibly to the economy."

Esther nodded. "Now we apply the second factor, the reason this has become such a menace. The *size* of these bets."

"Billions," Craig repeated.

"These four components of this one bet represent a sizable portion of the bank's total assets. If the market swings in the wrong direction, the response within the derivatives market would be like a catapult. A small adjustment downward becomes a huge change in the asset value."

Craig's eyes had gone dark. It was remarkable how they seemed to change color according to his mood. "And it's not just one bet, is it?"

"No, there are many. Every day. And the risk they represent overlap. Banks tend to follow the trends that make them profit. That means they become overweighted in one sector."

Craig watched her with unblinking intensity. Then he leaned back. Not disconnecting. The energy between them was strong as a steel cable. He said, "So you think there is going to be another financial crash."

"I do."

"Have you developed a timeline?"

"I have, yes."

"How long do we have?"

"Perhaps six months."

"Perhaps?"

"Yes."

"But it might be less, correct?"

She paused, then let out a sigh. "It could be a matter of days."

Craig turned to the group. He showed them open palms. Inviting them in. And not even that gesture changed the feeling Esther had of being connected. The simple motion invited her to join with the entire gathering. She looked up and met their gazes. She was pleased to find it did not frighten her.

In fact, it felt exquisite.

The same man who had spoken earlier asked, "I have the same question as before. Is there anything we can do?"

She nodded slowly. "I've been thinking about that."

"And?"

"I have an idea. Actually, it's just part of one. But I think it might make a difference. If I'm right."

When she stopped, the others let the silence linger until Patricia asked, "Will you tell us?"

13

Half an hour later, Esther and Craig emerged from the Saunders home. The mid-April afternoon had warmed, transforming the earlier rainfall into a humid blanket. In a few weeks, such days would be oppressive. Now the air was crystal clear and fragrant. Esther said, "All I can see are the holes in my ideas."

"At this stage I'd say that's pretty normal," Craig replied. "Where is your car?"

She pointed down the block. "Do you think my structure has potential?"

Their footsteps were punctuated by shrieks of children playing in the street. He was silent long enough for Esther to fear he thought her idea lacked merit. Instead, Craig said, "Do you really want my opinion?"

"Of course."

"You're asking the wrong question."

She stopped where the sunlight pierced the branches overhead. "Explain."

"The real issue is, why are you doing this? I know, I know, the economy is under threat. But you could easily build yourself a financial bunker and wait it out."

A fitful breeze shivered the high branches, sprinkling the sidewalk with a few raindrops. Where the sunlight touched them, the rain shone like gemstones. "I don't follow."

"Why are you so concerned, Esther? What is the purpose behind your feeling this need to speak out? Is it some vague notion of punishing the wrongdoers?"

"There's nothing vague about this."

"No, you're absolutely right. That was not the right word. I apologize."

She had not expected such a quick retreat. Esther could see he was ready to drop the subject entirely. It troubled her in a way she could not explain, as though his words had worked beneath her skin. Still, she felt a faint resonance, a need to understand. She said, "Tell me what the answer is."

That pleased him. "You're the analyst. And this is your issue, not mine. You need to reach the conclusion yourself."

Once again she felt as if she were not staring at a handsome man but rather an internal mirror. She had no idea how to respond.

"Here's what I think. You've been so worried for so long, you've not permitted yourself to think beyond the problem. But you're no longer alone. You have allies now. You have the workings of a plan. But this is only the first step."

"I know I need to work out the details."

"Not the plan, Esther. The plan is fine." Craig pointed back toward the house. "You have a lot of people in there right now who are claiming the plan as their own. They'll flesh things out. That's why I suggested we leave, so they can build the wings your plan needs to fly."

She turned away from him and squinted into the brilliant light. She knew he was right. But she still did not see . . .

"The people inside that house came because they are worried. They're *afraid*. They've spent months and years feeling totally *helpless*. And until you showed up, they could not name what scared them. Only that something about their financial world was *wrong*."

Esther could see the tiny shards of an answer flickering in and out of focus in the sunlight. But try as she might, she could not bring them together into a cohesive whole. Finally she said, "I need to think about this."

Craig waited for her to beep her locks, then

opened her door. "Will you see your brother tomorrow morning?"

"Seven-thirty."

"May I join you?"

"I'd like that."

"So would I." He looked down at her for a long moment, then said, "You did really, really well in there."

14

Monday

The next morning, Esther woke up feeling weightless. The sensation was so unfamiliar, she had finished at the gym and was on her way to the clinic before she could actually identify what was happening. The previous day had marked a major transition, far deeper than divulging secrets or spending time with a very nice man. Esther had chosen a different course. She did not regret the move, not even when the normal boundaries of her life were being erased. She was scared, but she had been living with fear for months.

She pulled into the rehab center's parking lot and wondered which car belonged to Craig. More than her growing interest, stronger than her hope that this guy might actually be different, was a relief that she was not entering this transition alone.

But when she entered the building, she was met by a very different man. Craig Wessex looked ravaged by his own set of midnight ghosts. Esther walked with him down the corridor and entered Nathan's room. She shut the door and kissed her brother's cheek. Then she asked, "Will you tell me what's the matter?"

Craig tried to shrug it away. "We have more important things to focus on."

"Craig, please. Something clearly is wrong. Tell me what's happened."

He took a long look at the man lying in the bed. "There are times," he said, "when I envy your brother."

Nathan had adopted the same position for the past nine weeks, rolling over so all she saw of him was his back. He would remain inert and silent until she kissed his cheek a second time and departed.

Craig said, "Yesterday, after our session, I visited with my daughters. They don't like their stepfather. And they blame me for their having to live with him."

When he went silent, she prodded, "How old are they?"

"Abigail is eleven. Samantha will be fourteen next month."

"Those are difficult ages to be facing this kind of issue."

He gave no indication that he had heard.

"They're angry with me. They think if I had been a better father and husband, none of this would have happened. The fact that my wife was the one who left doesn't change a thing in their minds."

"And you feel helpless," Esther said.

"Of course I do. Everything I say to them, every attempt I make to improve things only makes it worse in their eyes." He kept his gaze on Nathan. "I let it slip yesterday that I had stayed in Charlotte because of them. Theology training at UNCC is fairly weak, and I feel frustrated by how much more I could be doing at a better seminary. I could have studied anywhere. I was accepted . . ."

When she was certain he had run out of steam, she said, "How did they respond?"

"Abigail has adopted her mother's attitude. She says she's embarrassed that I want to enter the ministry. She says I should go back to being an accountant—that's the only thing that makes any sense."

"And the older girl?"

"Samantha says I'm just making things worse by being here." Craig sighed.

"You know they don't mean what they said. They are deeply hurt and angry. And Samantha is a teen. She's lashing out at you because she can."

Craig ran a hand through his hair. "Maybe they're right."

Esther waited. When he finally looked up, she said, "It's easy for me to sit here and give you advice. But I think you should wait."

"Wait for what?"

"For them to come to you."

"But that could take years."

"Possibly." She pointed to the figure in the bed. "When our parents died, we went to live with our grandparents. I never got along with them, even when my parents were alive. Nathan left the following year for university. He chose a school in Minneapolis so he could visit me as often as possible. And most of our weekends together I spent ranting. I was angry all the time. Nathan didn't argue with me. Instead, he helped me reshape my anger into something that . . ."

"Brought you here," Craig finished for her.

The sense of being understood, of sharing the helpless moments with another individual left Esther fighting back tears. "He was such a good brother."

"What *happened* to him?"

"A traffic accident on the interstate. A truck blew a tire and crushed the passenger side of their car. His wife was killed. She was three months pregnant. The police say he was probably driving well over the limit. I suppose Nathan blames himself." So much power compacted into a few short sentences. "His wife meant everything to Nathan."

They walked out together. Though they did not touch, it seemed to Esther that the moment carried a new intimacy, as though some juncture had been reached through the act of sharing the impossibles of life.

When they reached the sunlight, Craig's phone buzzed. He pulled it out, sighed, and told her, "I invited a couple of friends from school to join us yesterday. They phoned last night to ask if you'd be willing to speak on campus."

"When?"

He lifted the hand holding the phone. "They just texted me. This afternoon at three?" When she hesitated, he said, "I can put them off."

"No, no, it's okay. I just . . ." She inspected him. In full daylight his features looked physically bruised. "Did you sleep any last night?"

"A little."

Which meant she would have to carry the entire session on her own. But Esther replied, "Tell them yes."

Esther drove straight from the clinic to the bank. The difficult time with Craig and Nathan had not entirely erased her earlier sense of weightlessness. This shielded Esther during a pair of tense meetings. The first was with Jasmine, who laid out the team's own sleepless weekend's worth of calculations. They had identified three projects with genuine potential to repeat the previous week's gains. Esther could see that Jasmine had failed to evaluate fully the underlying global conditions. Jasmine was very sharp, and she had a firm grasp of the bank's risk measurements. But she had not spent years analyzing the core elements that supported the world's economies. Esther knew she owed Jasmine an explanation, but it would have to wait until her own course was clear.

The second meeting was chaired by Jason, who drew Esther's analysts into his normal Monday meeting with the senior traders. She told Jasmine to handle the pitch. Esther had done this several times in the past, giving the pedestal to a team member who had actually done the work. Esther knew Jason considered this a sign of weakness, but Esther did not care. Especially today. She listened as Jasmine and three of her team ran through the potential investments. The senior traders responded with the hungry excitement of pack dogs.

Jason rewarded them with a grudging nod, the only approval she or her team ever received from their boss. For the first time, though, Esther remained isolated from the tension and attrition that dominated Jason's division.

As usual, Esther ate lunch by herself. She opted for a smoothie and a bagel at a local health-food store. She returned to the office only long enough to check the markets, then told Jasmine she was lecturing at UNCC. They both occasionally were asked to speak at business schools or industry groups. The only difference today was that Esther did not ask her number two to make the presentation. Jasmine relished being the intelli-gent and attractive black woman addressing a sea of mostly white male faces. Usually Esther was only too happy to let her go out and rock their boats.

Esther drove over to the UNCC Center City Building. The university's main campus was located ten miles from downtown on a thousand-acre neo-Georgian campus. However, the university had recently completed construction on a unique academic tower located in Charlotte's First Ward.

First Ward ran east of the intersection of Trade and Tryon Streets. Until just before Esther arrived, First Ward had been the most dangerous place in Charlotte. Which was saying quite a lot, for as recently as the eighties Charlotte had one of the highest per-capita murder rates in the United States. But the Charlotte city fathers had turned their trouble spots completely around. First Ward was now the hottest nightlife and arts quarter in the Carolinas. The university's Center City Building was the new jewel in the First Ward crown. The tower was, quite simply, a show-stopper. The building was designed as a series of semitransparent cubes that rose as three rotating masses.

Esther parked across the street and spotted Craig pacing in front of the entrance. When she approached, he said, "Maybe this isn't a good idea."

"I said I would do it, and I will."

"No, listen, I invited the academic dean yesterday. He's brought some people from the business school."

Esther placed her hand on his arm. "It's okay."

"What if word gets back to the bank?"

"That's my job, worrying about how the bank might respond."

He seemed to see her for the first time. "You're so calm."

"I've been thinking a lot about what you said yesterday. I haven't reached any conclusions, but I know you were right."

Craig looked genuinely confused. "About what?"

"About my need to start asking the right questions." Only then did she realize it was the first time they had touched. She left her hand there a moment longer, then dropped it and said, "Let's go inside."

15

But when Esther pushed through the glass doors and entered the crowded atrium, her sense of calm confidence evaporated. A man she recognized from the previous day rushed over to them and said, "This thing has gotten totally out of hand."

Craig cast a worried glance her way. "Dean Molier, Esther Larsen."

"Dr. Larsen, I wish I could say this was a pleasure." He turned to Craig and continued, "Apparently several people who attended yesterday made calls of their own. Almost a third of our trustees are here."

"You want to call it off?"

"What I want . . ." The dean stopped at a chime from Esther's phone.

She had coded in a ringtone shared by everyone on her team, a refrain from *Tubular Bells*. Esther said, "Excuse me a moment. I have to take this." She took two steps away and answered with, "This better be urgent."

"That doesn't go far enough," Jasmine replied. "Can you get access to the markets?"

"Hold a sec." Esther turned and asked the dean, "Does your building have Wi-Fi?"

"Of course. The code is UNCC Guest. ID and password both."

"Thanks." She settled onto a side bench and drew her laptop from her case. "Okay, Jasmine. I'm good to go."

"I'm shooting you a link."

"Got it." Since Esther was outside the bank's system, there could be no access to any of the confidential data links. Instead, Jasmine had given her the address for a public Bloomberg site.

"The Shanghai index opened and just tanked," Jasmine told her. "Hong Kong followed. The Chinese government closed both markets. Jason went with the second option this morning, which means all the underlies are based in Japan, Singapore, and Australia. They had already laid out the full two billion when this happened. We're freaking out over here."

"How are the other Far East markets?"

"Stable so far. Wish I could say the same for our boss. He's climbing the walls. And blaming us for the fiasco."

Esther checked a couple of the news sites hosted by business analysts whose perspectives she trusted. They all noted the same stability while acknowledging the crisis. A lot of adrenaline-drenched opinions were being bandied about, but the data held firm. "I'm going with the data."

"Excuse me?"

"Go tell Jason I think the investment remains solid."

"Are you looking at the same intel I am? Because this looks anything *but* solid."

"Jasmine, take a deep breath."

"This could be just the tip—"

"Stop!" Above the laptop screen, Esther saw attention turn her way. But there was nothing she could do about that. "I don't have time to deal with Jason. Which means you have got to *get a grip*."

Esther hardly ever lost her cool, one of her defining traits. Speaking sharply now had the desired effect. When Jasmine eventually responded, she said, "Okay. I'm good."

"Are you sure?"

"Yes."

"All right. Here is what you tell Jason. Last year's tumult resulted in almost all foreign capital being withdrawn from the Chinese stock markets. Tell me you understand what I'm saying."

Jasmine dragged out the words against her own panic. "The downturn is contained."

"So long as the Chinese currency remains stable, there is limited international fallout. That's why the other markets are not responding like they did last year. International banks currently hold almost no exposure in either Shanghai or Hong Kong. Close to zero. And that is *exactly* what you will go tell Jason. Clear?"

"Ah, yes. Yes. Okay."

"Have the team keep a minute-by-minute watch

of all the eastern exchanges. Ditto for the currency markets. The *instant* you see a shift, you phone me. Got it?"

"Yes, boss."

"Now go pull Jason down off the wall." Esther cut the connection, shut her laptop, and rose to her feet. Only then did she realize how silent the atrium had become. All eyes were on her as she walked over to the dean and said, "Perhaps we should begin."

The morning's alarm only solidified Esther's certainty that she was making the right move. She did not have clear answers yet to Craig's questions. But Esther was certain the issues he had raised were crucial. She was not doing this for herself. The issue was far too large for her objectives to be either personal or selfish. So why was she up here, in the uncomfortable position of addressing a completely packed assembly hall? What was her desired outcome? She did not know. Not yet.

She watched Donald Saunders slip into the hall late, accompanied by three men and two women, all in the regional hospital's whites. An older gentleman she vaguely recognized from the Sunday gathering waved his cane and gestured to empty seats beside him. Once again Esther felt she should know him, but this was not the time to hunt through mental data.

Craig fumbled her introduction, but Esther found she did not mind. She stepped up beside him and covered the microphone with one hand. "Why don't you sit this one out?"

"Are you sure you don't need me?"

The question was made tender by how Craig did not realize what he had said. Esther replied, "Just sit in the front row so I can focus on you."

As Craig left the podium, Esther's first words to the crowd were, "Some of you may have heard my side of the phone conversation in the atrium. A few hours ago, the Chinese stock markets went into serious decline. This is the second such massive downward spiral in less than twelve months. Beijing has already responded the same way they did last time, by freezing the exchanges and injecting billions through their central bank.

"During the previous crisis, most of the global markets teetered on the brink. Berlin, Paris, London, and the Dow Composite all dropped by more than seven percent in two days. This time, the markets are holding stable. As I just told my assistant, over the past ten months almost all foreign asset managers have reduced their exposure in the Chinese markets to near zero. This means the crisis will mostly affect local investors. But because so many small share-holders have financed their investments through personal loans, the impact inside China could be severe. In order to maintain political stability, the government will probably order state-owned institutions to prop up markets by buying more shares of endangered companies. This tactic works, but carries consider-able long-term risk. And that's all I will say on the matter for now."

She opened her laptop and positioned it on the podium beside the microphone. "I've been asked to speak to the issue of a potential global crisis. As you've no doubt already heard, I do believe this is going to happen. I'll begin by addressing directly the financial analysts in the audience. This will mean entering into the mathematical realm of risk structure. I know some of you will not understand, and I apologize. But this is a rare opportunity for me to present my evidence and have it checked out by people who can challenge any errors I might have made. If I am correct, I think you will all agree this action is justified."

A bearded young man in socks and sandals slipped up to the podium, offered her an apolo-getic smile, and plugged in her computer to the podium's system. He touched a pair of switches, then offered a thumbs-up to someone at the back of the room. The overhead lights dimmed, and the image on her laptop's screen appeared on the giant screen behind her.

Esther's laptop had an internally illuminated keypad. As she typed she gave a brief overview of Sunday's discussion. She had always been able to talk and type at the same time. What was different today was how a third part of her brain remained distanced from the entire process. She observed herself, saw the calm demeanor, and listened to her steady voice.

On the screen behind her flashed a series of calculations. Like most mathematicians, Esther used software that allowed her to press several keys at once, forming the notations and symbols of formulas. She told the gathering, "What you see here is a single grouping of algorithms, a mathematical procedure used to solve a problem that involves a high number of variables. It is named after its creator, Mohammed al-Khwarizmi, an Iraqi mathematician and a member of Baghdad's royal court in the eighth century. Algorithmic calculations involve a carefully defined series of steps that take the investigator from an initial state, through a series of clear and concise stages called the execution, to a measurable outcome." She looked up from her keyboard, glanced at the larger screen, and added, "Though some of you might question my use of terms 'clear and concise.' "

The sound of laughter stopped her. She looked around the darkened room, pleasantly surprised by the crowd's response. Occasionally she had wondered if she even possessed a sense of humor.

She went on, "The sort of algorithms taught in introductory calculus are known as 'deterministic,' which means that each transition from one portion of the calculation to the next is set out in advance. Such computations terminate in a final state, a clearly defined outcome.

"What you see here is different. This is known as a *randomized* algorithm. This means that along the way, between the initial input and the final outcome, there are vacuums. These random variables, or auxiliary inputs, aren't known until the moment when they are inserted into the calculations. And whatever these random variables might be, they all can have a major impact on the final outcome."

At this point, Esther cut off the computer. There was a rustling sound in the darkened auditorium, then a single spot of light focused on her face. "There are two things you need to understand before we go any further. First, these are not the algorithms employed by my bank. Those are proprietary, and my revealing them to any outsider is prohibited by law. These are a new series of algorithms I have designed specifically for the purpose of looking at the global markets.

"I do not consider the global economy to be a unified whole. But I do think the economies, the trading markets, and the current banking system are all interlinked. Joined by satellite, fiber-optic cable, hedge funds, and global investment banks.

The fate of one market now determines the futures of all the others."

She turned on the computer, started typing again, and added, "I hope you are paying careful attention, because there will be a test."

16

Reynolds Thane was big on turf. As in, he wanted to control the situation before the first word was uttered. He was seated now in his favorite chair, positioned so that his guest faced the bronze Rodin. He poured Sir Trevor tea from an antique silver service that had once been used by Russian nobility in St. Petersburg's Winter Palace. Reynolds enjoyed relating the remarkable tale of how the service came into his possession. He treated each of his precious belongings as a component of his own story.

But Reynolds did not speak of such things now. He knew Sir Trevor viewed him and his possessions as typically American. Sir Trevor's family had been rich for centuries. Four hundred years ago, Sir Trevor's ancestors had owned some minor fief in the middle of nowhere. But they had wisely recognized the Plantagenet's time as rulers of England was over. They backed the usurper. And when the House of Orange took control, Sir Trevor's family was amply rewarded.

Reynolds had visited Sir Trevor's country estate on several occasions. The Jacobean manor was nestled among three thousand acres surrounded by an ancient stone wall. Sir Trevor treated any treasures that had actually been purchased as merely symbols of new money. Sir Trevor thought those who possessed new money had not yet learned the subtleties of wielding power.

Reynolds asked, "Milk?"

"Just a thimble." The Limoges cup was so thin, Trevor's fingers were visible through the china. "Tell me about this lady. What is her name again?"

"Esther Larsen." They had been through this before, but Reynolds did not mind. He was coming to understand Sir Trevor a little. Beneath his mild-mannered exterior beat the soul of a cautious assassin. "A genius. She entered the University of Chicago at fourteen, then earned her doctorate from Caltech, now here."

"You know what they say about geniuses." Trevor sipped, nodded approval of the tea. "They're useful only so long as you keep their wings clipped."

"She has a brother. A tragic tale by all accounts. Lost his wife in an accident. A basket case ever since. Apparently loves playing the parasite."

"Is that enough to keep her in line?"

"She spent a small fortune acquiring a home in Dilworth and renovating it to the nines. Quite simply, if we threaten her employment, she loses the house and her brother dies."

"I suppose that should be enough of a hammer. Just the same, we'll need to keep a close watch on her, given these latest developments."

Reynolds tasted his own tea. "You would have made an excellent wartime strategist."

"Or a spy. I actually considered that in my youth. But my father threatened to sever the family purse strings. And spies these days are paid such a pittance." Sir Trevor smiled. "Tell me about her professional abilities."

"Esther tends to focus on the negative."

"Hardly a surprise. She is, after all, paid to assess risk." Sir Trevor poured himself a fresh cup. "Thank you again for sharing those three new proposals her team developed. I had a trusted young man take a look. He said they all held unique potential."

"If the markets hold for another two hours, we will net ninety-three million from this latest trade, despite the Chinese markets tanking."

Sir Trevor leaned back in his seat. "Can she be bought?"

"We'll need to ask Jason," Reynolds replied. "He's waiting for us in the conference room."

But as they stood, Sir Trevor halted him with an outstretched hand. "You can of course confirm that none of Jason's chosen candidates have any close family ties."

"All good traders tend to be lone wolves," Reynolds said. "Jason assures me these five take that trait to the extreme."

"This is very important, you see. Vital. We can't have anyone asking questions if things . . ."

"Go south." Reynolds nodded.

"Quaint, but correct." Sir Trevor indicated the door. "Shall we?"

The first moment Reynolds Thane knew he could happily forge this partnership had occurred while watching Sir Trevor handle Jason Bremmer fourteen months ago. At the time, Sir Trevor had been nothing more than a competitor, one who could well have planned to steal Jason away. And to his credit, Trevor did not try to fob off Reynolds's concerns. Sir Trevor's silence was message enough. Either Reynolds trusted the Brit or he didn't.

Sir Trevor had revealed a killer's charm, taut and subtle and pleasant to observe. Jason's one dominant mood was latent rage. But within half an hour, the man had relaxed enough to actually enjoy himself.

At the end of that lunch, Reynolds confessed, "I have just watched a master at work."

Sir Trevor accepted the compliment with a regal nod. "May I share a little secret with you?"

"Please."

"The English private school system is loathed

by most, and rightly so. I was taught young and well by masters in the craft of ruling others. My headmaster at Eaton was a terrible snob, but he also possessed a remarkable ability to pierce the veil."

Reynolds had reserved CFM's executive dining room for this meal. Theirs was the only table occupied. The waiters knew not to enter unless summoned, and the room was swept twice daily for bugs. It was a place made for sharing secrets. "I envy you that early start."

"You've managed quite well on your own, I daresay."

"Clawing and scrambling and taking years to learn what you were taught in your youth."

"Fed it with a silver spoon," Sir Trevor cheerfully agreed. "But I missed a good deal in the process. I seriously doubt you would grow faint at the sight of blood."

"Not if it belongs to an enemy," Reynolds said. "And neither would you."

"But reaching that point cost me a very great deal. Now then. Where were we?"

Reynolds knew he was being handled, but he did not mind in the least. "Early lessons and silver spoons."

"My headmaster. Yes, thank you. The old gentleman must have seen something in me, for I had the great good fortune to be taken under his wing. He had served in the cabinets of two prime ministers and spoke with the quiet authority of a man who knew what it meant to send men off to die. He told me something I have never forgotten. Something that has served me well in any number of confrontations with people like your Bremmer."

"I'm listening," Reynolds said.

"Most people live broken and fractured lives," Sir Trevor said. "And remain willfully blind to any chance they might have of healing and moving on."

Reynolds had the odd sensation of their being in sync. "They pretend their internal situation is someone else's fault. They blame their plight on destiny. Or past burdens. Or present circumstances."

For a brief moment the man's ice-hard gaze melted a fraction. "I see it would be a great misfortune to underestimate you."

"The headmaster," Reynolds reminded him.

"Quite. The old gentleman tested me rather harshly. Forcing me to identify the cracks in other people's personality or character or past. Which meant learning their innermost secrets. Which led to developing the talent of disguise and discreet manipulation."

"The best of Britain," Reynolds said. "The lessons that made you rulers of the world."

"At least for a time. Of course, you know what formed my headmaster's next instruction."

"Never threaten outright. Never reveal all you

know." Reynolds used these tactics every day. "Be certain they know you hold the ax, and that you are willing to use it. But only if absolutely necessary."

Sir Trevor exposed what Reynolds thought was his first glimpse of a smile. "I'm so glad to know my hopes in you were not misplaced."

The selection process took all of ten minutes. Long enough to assure the three men and two women whom Jason had brought together that what they had heard was indeed true.

Most top traders were big-city mutts who possessed enough drive to stay clean and get out. They had learned to compress their wounds and old pain into a single nuclear fury that seared away all barriers. Their loyalty was strictly on a pay-as-you-go basis. They were ruled by an insatiable hunger, a vacuum at the core of their being. They surrounded themselves by a world that reflected this internal void. Whatever they earned, however rich they became, their lifestyle always required more. They were never satisfied.

And these five traders were poised to become extremely rich.

If they succeeded.

There was really no decision at all. The five personnel files had already been carefully vetted. Reynolds and Sir Trevor knew Jason had chosen well. They were here because the new team needed to understand they had the board's unofficial backing. Secretly. Silently.

Nothing was spoken about their new task. After all, there existed the slim chance that one government agency or another might eventually ask some very disconcerting questions. So there was nothing these five could say except that they had attended another meeting in the board-level conference room.

The second reason for this meeting was to calm Jason down. The man was livid. Justifiably so.

The five traders sensed Jason's rage and immediately fled the boardroom. They were only too happy to leave the battleground before bullets started flying.

When the three of them were alone, Jason growled, "Tell me this is not what I think it is."

Reynolds replied easily, "It's not what you think."

"You're siphoning five of my top performers off to the competition?"

"Sir Trevor is partner in this new project."

"Holding four percent of the bank's stock doesn't make him a partner of anything," Jason shot back.

Reynolds tapped the table once, twice. "We are not handing part of your team over to Sir Trevor. Now that's all the rope you're going to get. Your job is to shut up and listen. Either pay attention or go back downstairs and bid your team a fond farewell. Because if you refuse to accept the new reality, you no longer have a place in this bank."

Jason blinked. Reynolds did not threaten. It simply was not part of his genetic pattern. The streets of Charlotte were littered with the corpses of opponents who never saw it coming. "I don't understand."

"There is no way you possibly could. As far as the rest of your team is concerned, your initial assessment is correct. These five are gone, never to return. They have been stolen away to work for Sir Trevor's group. It is essential that our remaining traders have no reason to suspect anything else."

Jason's gaze shifted back and forth between the two men. He was an expert at reading markets and discovering the unseen road to profit. Not being in the know left him extremely unsettled. "Then what—?"

"In nine days, Sir Trevor's group is making a public offer to acquire CFM outright. The board has secretly given its approval."

Jason's mouth opened, but he made no sound.

Reynolds glanced at his new partner. This was the crux, the moment they had been working toward for five long months.

Sir Trevor explained, "A new trading arm has been established in Bermuda. Officially it is merely an expansion of an existing Bermuda-based bank. Secretly, my group owns this bank outright. As far as anyone outside this room is concerned, you are going to take a brief holiday. During this time, you will serve as a consultant to the Bermuda bank. If anyone asks, Reynolds owes the president of the Bermuda group a favor and has reluctantly agreed to loan you for a time. You will then establish a new investment banking division. Your five subordinates will oversee it, along with five carefully selected traders from my own bank."

"They'll have the resources to bring in support staff," Reynolds added, "but we want them to run this operation as lean and mean as possible."

"Secrecy is a primary element," Sir Trevor emphasized.

Reynolds said, "If they succeed, if their operation remains below the official radar, if they refrain from letting any of their associates know where they are or what they are doing, they will receive a sizable bonus."

Jason was tracking the two men, his attention focused as only a trader knew how to do. "What size operation are we talking about?"

"Seven billion," Reynolds said.

"How are you going to keep a seven-billion-dollar transfer off the radar . . . ?" Jason was then punched back in his seat by the realization. "The merger."

"There is a temporary window," Reynolds confirmed. "Confusion created by two conflicting systems. Accounts and clients in forty countries. A maze of regulations. Different auditing requirements."

"We will let the outside auditors in both countries think they are competing for the one unified account," Sir Trevor said. "They will tread very lightly, and they will take all the time we ask them to take before officially notifying us of the missing funds. When that happens, we fold up the Bermuda tent and it's back to business as usual."

"After we have lined everyone's pockets," Reynolds added, "including yours."

Jason's swallow was audible. "How long do we have?"

"Thirty days," Reynolds replied. "Six weeks at the outside."

Jason said, "You want me to play the cutout."

"As of today," said Reynolds, "you are temporarily appointed chief of the new Bermuda division. This will be in addition to your current responsibilities."

"What's my take?"

"Double your standard commission."

"And the traders?"

"Standard commission for the duration. If they succeed, and if they manage to keep this quiet, then a final payout of five million dollars. Each."

Sir Trevor added, "Needless to say, the bonus

will be paid in Bermuda. Outside American tax records."

"For five million free and clear," Jason said, "my team will hold their breath if required."

"That is our expectation," Reynolds said.

"So . . . what's the target trade?"

"We want you to return to pre-2008 tactics."

Jason nodded slowly. "Makes sense."

"The two latest trades you've made, they risk alerting the SEC. Move all such future tactics offshore."

"The rest of my group will scream bloody murder," Jason said. "Those trades are the only reason we're in the black this quarter."

"They must be kept quiet," Reynolds insisted.

Sir Trevor said, "Once the merger goes public, they'll understand."

"The whole team will need to receive a bonus," Jason said. "Otherwise we'll see attrition along with the kind of questions we don't want."

"Promise them whatever you feel is appropriate," Reynolds replied. "I'll sign off on any such request."

Jason walked to the door, then turned back and said, "I want a completion bonus of my own. Ten million."

"Jason—"

"Take it or leave it."

Reynolds gave what he hoped was not too theatrical a sigh. "Done."

When the door closed behind the bank's senior trader, Reynolds let the silence linger. The question they both faced almost glowed in the window's warm sunlight. Finally Trevor asked, "Do you think he bought it?"

"Hook, line, and sinker." Reynolds replied. "We spoke the only language Jason understands."

"I must say, you showed a master's touch," Sir Trevor said.

"Jason sees an opportunity to make a huge amount of money," Reynolds continued. "The fact that it's a scam means he has to keep it quiet. He won't want to dig further because it will risk his take."

Which was very important. Vital, in fact.

Because everything they had told Jason was a lie.

17

Tuesday

The next day rocked Esther's world before she had even opened her eyes.

She woke from a dream about her father. Since childhood, Esther had not been able to think about him without a burning rage. This morning was different in every possible way. The dream was very brief, scarcely the length of a dozen breaths. Any longer and the years of regret and anger would have jerked her awake. In the dream, she was nestled in her father's lap. He read to her from his favorite book of the Bible, the one after which she was named. Esther watched him turn the page and begin relating elements that brought the story to life. She knew the story already by heart, but she loved to hear him repeat the tale.

When she awoke, she was sobbing.

Esther put on a robe, made a pot of coffee, and sat on her back porch watching the day strengthen. She was drawn back inside by the ringing of her phone. When she answered, Craig said, "I hope I didn't wake you."

"I've been up for hours. Did you sleep?"

"Some. A little." He sighed. "Not well. Never mind. I wanted to tell you the dean called. The faculty agrees with your assessment."

"I suppose I should be glad."

"One of the university trustees has told the dean he wants to contact you."

"Did they say why?"

"I asked. Either the dean wasn't told or he's been instructed not to say." When Esther did not respond, Craig said, "I can ask to put them off."

"No. No, it's fine. Well, not fine, but . . ." Esther did not want to talk about her analysis or the trustees. "When are you seeing your two girls?"

"I'm picking them up from school. Their mother . . ." Another sigh. "I'll take them somewhere for dinner."

"Bring them over here. I'll make us something. I would like to meet them."

"Esther . . . they can be extremely difficult."

She looked out over her back garden. But what she actually saw was herself as a young teen, raging against a destiny she refused to accept as her own. "It will be fine."

Esther dressed and gave the markets a quick scan. Everything was holding steady, so she decided to visit Nathan. She phoned her office from her car. Jasmine answered, and she asked, "What's new?"

"Oh, like you're not calling to give me a big I-told-you-so."

"I'm sorry I was sharp with you."

"Girl, I needed that more than I need a steady man. And I need that man bad."

"Even so, I shouldn't have snapped at you. You handled Jason?"

"I walked over and I repeated what you told me. Minus the instructions for him to come down off the wall he was climbing. He didn't fire me. If that means he was handled, then yes."

"When does the portal close?"

"Two hours and counting. Listen, Esther . . ."

"What?"

"You remember how during the last countdown the whole trading floor just got . . ."

"Frozen," Esther recalled. "Tense. Extremely nervous."

"Yeah, well, this time it's different."

"Different how?"

"Girl, if I knew how to describe it, would I be stumbling here?"

"I was going to stop by and see my brother, but maybe I should come in."

"And do what? Nobody's trading. We haven't heard a peep from anybody all morning. They're all just in there sulking."

"You're not making sense."

"Check on your brother, then come see for yourself."

"I won't be long," Esther said, then clicked off.

But thirty minutes later, Esther had only just finished another difficult meeting with the clinic's director. As she finally walked down the hall to her brother's room, a newly acquired document weighed down her purse. Across the top of the first page was written *Legal Notification of Patient Transferal*. It felt like an order for her to cease and desist.

She entered the room but did not sit down. She stared at Nathan's back, sensing as usual that he was awake yet intent on willing the world away. She said softly, "This week you're going to be moved." She sought for something else to say, to warn him of what was about to take place. But in the end, all she could manage was, "Nathan, don't leave me. Please."

18

On the drive to the office, Esther was struck by a sudden thought. She called Rachel, Patricia's sister, and asked, "Don't you have a teenage daughter?"

"Sure thing. Why, are you in the market for one?"

"No thanks."

"We'll let her go cheap. Today only, special price."

"Actually, I'm calling for some advice."

"Sugar, the only thing I can help you with is how to lose your temper."

"I have an angry almost-fourteen-year-old and her eleven-year-old sister coming to dinner tonight."

There was a longish pause, then Rachel asked, "Are these Craig's girls?"

"Well . . . yes."

"Oh, wow, give me a minute to finish my dance around the kitchen."

"You know they're going through a tough time."

"And putting Craig through it with them. Yes."

"I want them to feel, well . . ."

"At home. How totally cool is this."

"I'm just trying to help out a friend."

"Yeah. Right. Whatever." Rachel laughed. "Listen to me. I sound like my daughter."

Esther stopped in the bus zone before the entrance to the bank's parking garage. She didn't want to lose the connection, no matter how much Rachel's laughter embarrassed her. "What should I do?"

Esther started by walking across the back of the trading floor, reading the invisible signs. The atmosphere was highly charged as usual. What was different was the sullen rage she saw on every face, as though Jason's latent fury had infected the entire floor.

Jasmine was up and moving as soon as Esther entered her department. "See what I meant about the mood on the floor?"

"What's going on?"

"Soon as the bell rang yesterday afternoon, Jason was called to a meeting with Reynolds Thane. Two hours later, Jason came back in a rare state."

"How are the markets?"

"As stable as when you called an hour ago."

"Give me the rest."

Jasmine loved being the center of attention, even when stressed by unknowns that crowded their space. "All I know is, yesterday Jason came back downstairs shouting and yelling and driving the poor admins crazy. I wouldn't work in that man's office for a million and change. Well, okay, maybe for a million. But I'd want it up front, because if I lasted thirty-six hours it'd be—"

Esther cut her off mid-sentence. "Any idea what got him so hot?"

"Jason spent most of last night poring over the division's personnel files. The *confidential* files. Then this morning he called five staffers at home. Told them to show up pronto."

"You know this how?"

Jasmine dimpled. "Me and Hewitt, we been getting friendly from time to time. I think he might even be a keeper. Long as he remembers to stop playing trader when he's off the floor."

"So Hewitt is one of them. Which other traders did Jason single out?"

"Gavin, Lenoir, Stett, and, let's see . . ."

The MIT newbie offered, "Mandy Charles."

"Yeah, that's right. Her."

Esther held up a hand, thinking hard. The five were all mid-level traders. Each had enough rank to be given their own book, the trader's term for being assigned capital with which they made their own trades and formed their portfolios. Which also meant Esther tracked them. They were fairly successful, but mostly because they followed Jason's lead. Other than that, she could not see an identifiable trend. "Go on."

"Thirty minutes ago, all five of them went up

to the board level with Jason. They're still up there, cooling their heels in the reception area."

"Think Hewitt would be willing to update you?"

"I already asked. He doesn't have a clue . . ." The phone in Jasmine's hand buzzed. She checked the screen. "They're headed into the conference room. Sir Trevor's in there with Reynolds."

Esther turned to her Far East specialist. "The Asian markets are still holding steady?"

"Tokyo up a tick. Shanghai is still closed after the run." He shifted screens. "Hong Kong reopened and is down two percent."

Not important. "When does the portal close on yesterday's trade?"

"Forty-four minutes."

"Okay, let's hang tight." She swept the team together with both arms. "We're after intel, people. Check with your allies inside all markets, see what you can find. We reconnect in an hour."

Twenty-one minutes later, Jasmine stormed into Esther's office and yelled, "The creep just dumped me!"

"Who?"

"Hewitt! He wouldn't even say it to my face." She shoved her phone into the space between them. "Can you believe? A text! 'It's over, ciao.' What am I, chopped liver?"

Esther's alarm bells started jangling. "Phone him."

"I already did. Five times!" Jasmine stuffed the phone back in her pocket. "Voicemail!"

Slowly Esther rose from her chair, crossed the office, entered the division bullpen and looked around. "Anything?"

She got a unified headshake, a chorus of stable markets. Esther said to Jasmine, "Walk with me."

Jasmine fumed beside her as they crossed the skyway and entered the trading floor. Esther stopped Jasmine with a touch to her arm. "How long do we have left on the trade?"

Jasmine looked at her. It was not like Esther to ask a question when she already knew the answer. "Nineteen minutes."

"Right. And assuming the markets don't tank, how much are they going to net?"

Jasmine shot her another look, then walked to the nearest empty station and drew up the Asian markets. She calculated swiftly and said, "Ninety two mil and change."

"Making this the second biggest trade of the quarter." Esther studied the gloomy faces below, none of which even glanced their way. "Do they look excited to you?"

Jasmine managed to see beyond her own distress. "They look . . ."

"Exactly. Go talk to your pals. Find out what they're thinking."

"What about you?"

"I think it's time I paid Jason a visit."

19

Eighteen minutes later, Esther was still waiting in Jason's outer office. She knew the man was not in the building. Jasmine had messaged that much to her ten minutes ago. Esther's response had been five words long: *Locate the five missing traders.* Esther wanted to hustle back to her division, but Jason's secretary had asked her to hang tight.

The portal closed, though only after the markets ticked in their favor. The bank netted $96.3 million. The electronic ticker tape sped on, swallowing the intel and moving on to the next deal, the next risk.

Esther's phone rang. The readout showed a blocked number. She hesitated, then decided to answer. "Larsen."

"Ms. Larsen, this is Talmadge Burroughs."

She sat up straighter. The name fit the older gentleman who had been at the Sunday gathering, then again with Donald Saunders at her university talk. The power brokers who controlled the Charlotte skyline were a small enough group for Esther to know them all, at least by name and reputation. She had never met him but had seen his photograph numerous times. "Yes, Mr. Burroughs."

"I was wondering if I might invite you to lunch."

"Unfortunately I'm caught up in something, sir."

Burroughs spoke with the soft twang of the eastern marshlands. "How about you meet me for a coffee, then?"

"Can I ask what this is about?"

"I got to tell you, Ms. Larsen, your two presentations have really rocked my boat. I shared the data from yesterday's talk with my people. They say you're right on target."

"Wait . . . the university recorded my talk?"

"I thought you knew."

"No, I . . . Never mind."

"I've been worried about this for some time. We're looking at some serious issues here, Ms. Larsen. I'm not talking about blue-sky thinking. This is very real, and very tomorrow."

"I agree."

"I'd like to sit down with you, face-to-face, and see where we're at. And whether we might take the next step together."

"I can get away later this afternoon, sure."

"Three o'clock, City Club. Looking forward to it."

Esther was using her phone to draw up further intel on Talmadge Burroughs when Jason's assistant said, "He's ready for you now."

Esther followed the woman into Jason's empty

office and looked around, confused. "I don't understand."

The assistant pointed to a phone on the credenza. "You don't want to keep him waiting."

The phone was a dullish red in color and fit inside a wooden box. The receiver's weight clued her in. Until that moment, Esther had no idea the bank had a scrambler system anywhere on-site. Esther said, "Larsen here."

Jason was never one for preamble. "I'll be away for a couple of days. While I'm gone, we're putting your best practices to work."

Esther sank into Jason's chair. "You're retreating from the bank's current risk structure?"

"Don't call it a retreat." Scramblers worked either by inverting the signal or inserting an additional tone. The process was then reversed by the receiver. Unless the two phones were directly synched in advance of the call, the conversation remained virtually impenetrable. But it also stripped away most emotion, resulting in a metallic drone. Even so, Esther could tell Jason was irritated by her choice of words. "The traders are already up in arms."

"Where are you calling from?"

"That's none of your concern. You have twenty-four hours to draw up a new set of boundaries in which our group can operate."

"We can do that." In fact, they already had. Esther kept two of her team on that duty pretty much full time. She waited a moment longer before realizing her boss had already hung up.

Esther slowly set the receiver back in place, closed the box's lid. She asked the empty air, "Why this, and why now?"

20

The Charlotte City Club occupied the top three floors of the Interstate Building on West Trade. Four years earlier, the real estate group owned by Talmadge Burroughs had emerged successful from a vicious battle with Esther's bank and acquired the building. The next day Reynolds Thane sent out a blanket order that any executive who maintained their membership was welcome to seek employment elsewhere. Life in the Carolinas was often tainted by such feuds. As far as Esther knew, she was the first CFM executive to enter the club since the acquisition.

Her concerns over Jason's instructions made the elevator feel cramped. Logic told her that the bank had finally come to its senses and recognized no short-term gain was worth the risk of taking down the group. Which could very well have happened. But the simple fact was, the investment banking division was in the black for this quarter only because of those two trades.

As she gave her name to the club's attractive

host, she flashed back to the chummy satisfaction Reynolds Thane and Sir Trevor had shown after the first trade. Reversing course following a second success made no sense.

She was missing something.

Talmadge Burroughs was a hick in a five-thousand-dollar suit. He walked with the tentative motions of a man who remained standing only because of his cane. "I've never been much of a drinker, Ms. Larsen, but I'd surely appreciate it if we could stand at the bar. I'm recovering from a knee and hip replacement. I went against my doctor's recommendations and had them both done at the same time. I tell you what, next time I'll listen to the advice of my betters."

Talmadge Burroughs was the son of a tobacco-fertilizer salesman. At sixteen, two and a half weeks after he earned his driver's license, Talmadge had started a used-car business in Wilson, North Carolina. He mowed a vacant lot owned by his daddy, lined it with brightly colored flags, and displayed his five vehicles behind a hand-painted sign. Burroughs Motors now owned, either in partnership or outright, thirty-nine dealerships throughout the Southeast. They were also majority partners in five NASCAR speed-ways.

Talmadge leaned against a leather-topped barstool while a female bartender in a starched tuxedo shirt served them coffee. "Why did you decide to go public with this, Ms. Larsen?"

"Please, call me Esther."

"I imagine your bank won't be all that happy when they hear about your talk. Which they will."

Esther sipped her coffee and did not reply.

"It's one thing for you to share your concerns after church in the home of a friend. It's another thing entirely for you to put your hard-earned wisdom on display before a gathering of Charlotte's high-and-mighty."

Esther asked, "Why is that a concern of yours?"

Talmadge Burroughs had a farmer's big-knuckled hands. He encircled the rim of his cup and sipped noisily. "I asked first."

Esther was fully aware that he owed her an explanation for why they were here at all. He no doubt realized that also. Even so, she found herself saying, "Sunday afternoon, a friend asked me the very same thing. I've been wrestling with it ever since."

"I'd love to hear what you've come up with."

"I think my friend should be the first to hear my response."

"So make the call." Talmadge gestured with his cup toward an empty back room. "I'll wait for you right here."

Craig answered with, "I'm heading into an exam."

"I need three minutes," Esther replied.

126

"Now?"

"This very instant," she said. "Please."

"What's wrong?"

"Nothing. I just need . . ." She took a long breath. "Being a loner has meant I can indulge a self-centered perspective. Part of answering our question is to accept that I'm doing this for others. This isn't about punishing the wrongdoers, or exposing them, or profiting in any way. None of that measures up to the pressure I feel to *warn* others. I want . . ."

"To work for the greater good," Craig said.

"Yes." Talking with someone who understood her carried an exquisite release. "That's it exactly. But . . ."

"It scares you."

"So much," she whispered.

"It should. You're taking on the concerns of a million families. More. But, Esther, you know what I'm going to say."

"I'm not alone."

"Exactly." The smile was there in his voice. "Can I go now?"

"Yes. I hope you ace your exam."

"Piece of cake. We're still on for tonight, right?"

Esther returned to the club's bar feeling that her feet merely traced over the polished hardwood floors and the Isfahan carpets. Now she knew she had been right. Craig helped her to see the way forward. Her first attempt to speak the words needed to have been with him.

She seated herself on a stool around the bar's corner from Talmadge and gave it to him straight. Calmly, succinctly, one hundred seconds start to finish. When she was done, Talmadge asked a waiter for fresh coffee. "You sure you don't want anything else?"

"I'm good, thanks."

"When you spoke at Patricia and Donald's home on Sunday, you shared an idea on what to do about all this."

"It seems so insignificant in the face of a potential economic collapse," Esther replied.

"Small as a mustard seed." He waited while the waiter replaced the coffee service, then said, "Has your thinking expanded since then?"

This explanation took a little longer, just under four minutes. When she was done, Talmadge poured himself another cup of coffee. "I asked people I trust about you. I wanted a heads-up on who I was meeting. Know what they told me?"

"That I'm intelligent. Good at my job. A dedicated loner."

"And honest to a fault. So I'm gonna respond in kind, Esther. There's only so much a loner can accomplish. No matter how smart. No matter how *right*."

It all came down to that, she knew. "I ask again. Why are we here?"

"Trust," he replied. "Trust and shared motives."

"You want to help people?"

"Oh, I admit I'd like nothing better than to stick it to the bankers who are busy getting us back in the mess we barely crawled out of last time. But, yes, I'm here because I'm worried about our economy. My country, my people, my way of life. I love it all. I want to see it survive."

"So you want to help me."

"You find that strange?"

"To be honest," she said, "I don't see a lot of business conducted out of the goodness of people's hearts."

"This ain't about *business*." His genteel polish cracked slightly. "This is about something *a lot* more important than making another dollar."

Her statement had touched a nerve. She found herself liking him more because of it. "I believe you."

"You know what I thought was the most amazing thing about your talk yesterday?"

She sensed the answer hanging there between them. "Nobody said they thought I was talking foolishness."

He shook his head. "I doubt many folks could watch you write up those fancy equations and call you a fool."

Esther rephrased, "There weren't any objections."

"There you go. Not one single contrary voice

from that audience. And those people, they are plugged in. You hear what I'm saying?"

"They're worried too."

"They're *scared*. Even if they don't know exactly why, they sense something ain't right with our financial system. Down deep in their collective gut." He had planted a fist below his rib cage. "They know something is seriously wrong, and they don't know what to do about it."

"Late at night when I scan the markets, I feel the same way," she confessed. "But I'm also concerned that my plan is too little too late."

"We'll just see about that." He thumped his fist on the bar, sealing the deal. "Will you take some advice from an old man?"

"Of course."

"Don't wait for the hammer to fall. Quit. Resign. Give your notice today. Working at that bank is just slowing you down."

She had all the reasons in her mind before he finished speaking, starting with Nathan and her need for the income. But somehow all she could say was, "I'll think about it."

"You do that, only make it quick. And think about this too." He leaned in close enough for her to smell the coffee and mint on his breath. "Yes."

"Excuse me?"

He leaned back against the barstool. "I think there's more at work here than what you've come up with so far. You need to clear your head of the bank's business to find it. There's something important, just waiting for you to set it in motion. You're the one to do it. I thought that yesterday at the college, and I'm certain of it now."

"I have no idea what you're . . ." Esther jerked back, not from her words but from a sudden thought, a flash of lightning across her internal horizon.

Talmadge saw the change and grinned. "See there? It's already started."

"Sir, you really do have a nasty smile."

"I've been a used-car salesman for fifty-one years. It's part of my job description." He rapped on the bar a second time. "So here it is. Yes. You put it together, I'll agree in advance to back you."

Esther blinked. "Whatever I need?"

"You let me know what it is and I'll put boots on the ground. Matter of fact, I'll start making calls just as soon as we're done here. We don't have much time, do we?"

"I don't think so. No."

"There you go then." He levered himself off the stool, winced, and waved away her offer of support. "You best get to work. Quit. Today. You've outgrown that bank, and the clock ain't on our side."

21

When Craig's daughters emerged from the car, Esther felt as though she were stepping back in her own personal time machine.

The younger daughter, Abigail, wore a softly bruised look, confused and yearning for a different world.

Samantha looked angry.

Just as Esther had at that age.

The pinched mouth, the tight forward lean to her shoulders, the gaze that touched nothing for very long. Esther smiled through the burning behind her eyes and welcomed them inside.

"Got any games?" Samantha asked in a loud voice. The music blasting from her earbuds was audible from where Esther stood.

Craig rolled his eyes. But before he could reprimand his daughter, Esther said, "Sure thing."

Samantha pulled one bud from her ear. "I don't mean, like, checkers."

"I know what you mean," Esther said. "Come with me, please."

She led them up the central staircase and into her office. Abigail spoke for the first time. "What is *that?*"

"It's called a data array. I'm watching the Far East stock markets. Their trading day starts soon."

Esther pointed to each screen in turn. "Tokyo, Shanghai, Melbourne, Singapore, Hong Kong."

She had positioned the screens to be able to see them from the doorway. Her west-facing bay windows were now illuminated by a brilliant sunset. The desk was built from interlocked segments of redwood burl, supported by four hand-carved pillars. Its polished surface reflected the constantly shifting array.

Despite herself, Samantha was drawn forward. "That's not a game. That's work."

"Right." Esther walked over and clicked the mouse. "*This* is a game."

The central screen went blank. The other four thirty-inch screens shifted instantly, all displaying the logo for World of Wizards.

Abigail's eyes went wide. "Whoa."

Craig said, "Their mother will probably not be pleased."

Esther said to the girls, "I've set you up with two access portals. I used your actual names, but you can change that once you log on. The password for both is 'funtime.' Samantha, you're on the two monitors to the left. Abigail, I'll need to bring in another chair from the bedroom."

"I'll get it." As Craig turned away, he said, "Their mother is going to freak out."

"Not if she doesn't know," Samantha said, and poked her sister.

"Ow."

"Just making sure you heard." Another poke. "Tattletale."

Esther said, "You're linked via fiber-optic cable, the fastest access Charlotte has to offer. I signed you both up for unlimited game time."

Craig reentered the room with the chair. "Major, major freak."

Esther went on, "Anything further that you might wish to purchase will require serious negotiations and probably result in a firm denial by the resident webmaster."

Abigail said, "Huh?"

Samantha turned to her sister. "If we want any add-ons, we have to pay for them ourselves."

"Bluetooth headsets are there by the monitors," Esther said. "They're yours to take with you, or keep here if you like."

Samantha looked directly at Esther for the first time. "We can come back?"

"Sure, if you want to. You're welcome anytime. If I need to work, I'll set you up with one of my laptops."

"*One* of them?" Abigail frowned. "How many do you have?"

"I actually don't know. I get a new one every time there's a major uptick in processing speed."

The two sisters looked at each other. Samantha explained, "She's a speed freak."

"Absolutely." Esther pointed to the blank central screen. "If that middle monitor flashes

134

back to the data stream, you need to come find me."

Samantha asked, "How come?"

For some reason, his daughter asking that caused Craig to smile. Esther replied, "It means we're facing a financial crisis, a global melt-down, that sort of thing."

Samantha nodded. "Cool."

Craig followed her from the room. As they entered the upstairs hallway, he stopped her with a hand on her arm. When she turned around, he stepped in close. Esther had time for a single thought, that his eyes looked luminous.

Then he kissed her.

The moment lasted until Esther heard Abigail say, "Eww."

After a dinner of cannelloni and salad, after a fleeting series of conversations with both daughters, and after the girls had been pulled from a final half hour online, Esther spiced her good-nights by asking if the girls might be interested in earning some money. Those were the two bits of advice Rachel had offered—online gaming, and money they did not have to account for. Esther knew she risked Craig's daughters seeing it as a bribe, but she remembered what it had meant for Nathan to slip her cash, so she offered. Esther explained that she was putting her brother's house up for sale, and she needed help going through his things. She would pay them ten dollars an hour. After the girls agreed and plans were put in place, Esther stood on her front stoop and waved good-bye as they drove off in Craig's car. All in all, she decided she could count the evening as a genuine success.

Esther locked her front door, climbed the stairs, and entered the office. The headsets were on a side table, the second chair back in her bedroom. Samantha's place in the office chair still felt warm. Esther switched her monitors back to the data stream and reviewed the global status. The Far East markets were well into the new day. The Shanghai Index was still in government-induced lockdown, while the others had shrugged this off. The currency markets remained stable.

By the time she completed her review, Esther felt like she was back in analyst mode. She regretted the shift, but she also welcomed it.

Because it was no longer business as usual.

She was going into this fully aware, knowing there was a very real chance her old life could actually be demolished in the process. She could argue the point all day long, but what Talmadge Burroughs had suggested meant others could see what was happening as well. Going public with her fears could cost her the only professional life she had ever known. The only job she had ever wanted.

Even so, she knew the time for hesitation and internal debate was over.

As she placed the call, Esther decided it did not feel as if she were simply taking the next logical step. More like the rock was already rolling downhill.

Her friend answered, "Sterlings."

"Keith, hi. I know I probably shouldn't be calling this late, but—"

"Esther? Is it really you?"

"In the flesh, sort of."

"Wow, this is amazing. We were just talking about you . . . when was it, honey?" A voice in the background murmured something. "Carla says you need to fly up for a weekend. The girls are going to forget what you look like."

Keith Sterling had been her closest friend at the University of Chicago, the only member of her class who did not shun the fourteen-year-old freshman genius. Now Keith was a high school math teacher. He had gone on for an education degree, stepped into teaching, and never looked back. To put it simply, Keith loved kids, family, and math in that order. Earlier, Esther had felt kind of sorry for him. Now she envied his ability to remain so buoyant and enthusiastic. Not even six classes of bored teens five days a week could dent his passion. Esther was godparent to their second child. But none of this was why she had phoned him.

Esther said, "I need your help designing a new website."

Keith earned extra money serving as project web designer for a number of local companies. "Sure, Esther. You know I'll—"

"Right now," Esther said. "Tonight."

"Esther . . . it's after ten. I have classes—"

"I'll pay you whatever. But I need the basic structure up and running by the start of business tomorrow."

There was a long pause, and Esther feared he was looking for some way to turn her down. Finally, Keith said, "Okay. This is kind of weird."

"What is?"

"We just learned our youngest needs braces, which our health insurance doesn't cover."

"I'll pay for them."

"No, you won't. But you can help."

"Deal."

Esther heard Keith ask his wife to put on a fresh pot of coffee. Then he said, "So what's so important that it's going to cost me a night's sleep?"

22
Wednesday–Friday

The next two days passed in a relatively calm state. Esther went about her normal routine, though in truth she felt as if she were acting out someone else's life. Her office and the trading floor had never felt more alien. The most real component was meeting Craig for lunch on Thursday, hearing his repeated thanks for her trying to draw his daughters from their shells.

She spent Thursday evening working on her website. Keith had installed a counter at the bottom of the home page, and the small number of visitors mocked her efforts. The site's traffic remained but a trickle. She fired off midnight emails to her allies in DC, New York, and London. She alerted Patricia and Rachel and Craig and Talmadge Burroughs. Then she went to bed.

The next morning, Friday, Esther phoned the office on her way to Nathan's clinic. When she asked how things were on the trading floor, Jasmine replied, "It's like watching a volcano cook. What's the name for one of those experts?"

"There are several different kinds," Esther said. "Seismologist, volcanologist, or a specialist on geological deformities."

"How do you know this stuff?"

"It was on my final at Caltech."

"Girl, are you serious?"

"No, Jasmine, of course not. Now tell me what's going on."

"They got their hands tied, is what. And they do *not* like it."

"You're saying the traders are actually operating within SEC guidelines."

"*Strict* guidelines. As in, do this and don't make any money. While the missing five are probably out grabbing gold with both hands."

"You heard something from your friend?"

"You mean my ex. And the answer is no, not a peep. Which is worse than strange. It *hurts*. Do guys take a secret class in how to break a girl's heart?"

"Something is going on," Esther said. "They're being sequestered."

"What?"

"Thinking." She cast about but could come up with nothing tangible. "Have you heard from Jason?"

"He's not shown up. Three days and counting. My pals in his front office are talking about a weekend cookout to celebrate."

Esther said, "I'm going to take the day off."

"Might as well. Nothing going on around here. Unless of course somebody actually erupts."

"If that happens, you know what to do."

"Take photos and send them viral."

"Jasmine . . ."

"I know, I know. You'll be my first call."

Esther sat quietly for a while. It was the first time she had taken a day off in forever. She half expected the sudden vacuum would be terrifying to face, but instead she felt as though she was getting ready for whatever came next.

After her visit with Nathan, the middle portion of Esther's Friday was spent reviewing the technical content on her website. It was one thing to dash through the math in an auditorium, and another thing entirely to hold up seven years' work to public scrutiny.

That is, assuming anyone who could actually follow her work gave the website a second glance.

The site's logo was Keith's idea. He was big on spiritual meanings and the Scriptures. In their midnight conversation, as she explained her volumes of calculations, Keith had said, "That's it."

"What is?"

"The website's name. 'The Book of Esther.' "

She felt the sudden grip of memories. "Keith, no."

"Hang on a second. Let me check . . . BookOfEsther.info is yours for three hundred bucks . . . Okay, done."

"Keith—"

"You're not allowed to argue with the designer at one in the morning."

"That name carries a lot of painful memories."

"It's perfect. Wait until you see it up, then if you still don't like it, we can argue once we've both had some sleep."

Keith then had Esther pile her tattered volumes on a coffee table and shoot photographs of them. The one he liked best now resided just below the website's headline. Every time Esther read the site's name, she shivered from the impact of events she had not thought of in years.

But she had to admit, the title worked.

Keith had her scan pages from her calculations. He loved the ones with coffee stains and smudged corrections and microscopic notations running down the sides. For the home page he used the first calculation that linked the concept of global risk and interconnected national markets. The formulas were underlined and circled and had shooting stars decorating the top of the page. Keith faded the scan and set a pale rendition to either side of her initial text. This same design became the backdrop to each component of the website. The result was, in a word, impressive.

Meanwhile, she and Craig kept in touch with each other. His end-of-term exams were under way, so for now their conversations consisted of quick snippets, mostly just checking in, each asking how the other was doing. But Esther kept a mental list of things she wanted to discus once his exams were over. The very idea that she remained open to sharing her thoughts with a man was enough to give her the shivers.

Friday afternoon, a half hour after school let out, Esther was standing in front of Nathan's home as Craig drove up. The two girls rose slowly from the car and gave the house a sullen look. Again Samantha's music was turned up so loud that Esther could hear the tinny beat drifting across the front lawn.

Craig approached her and said, "Maybe I should stay."

"Didn't you tell me you had another exam?" Esther saw Samantha hit a button on her iPhone and then heard the music shut off. She found this mildly interesting.

Craig replied, "The last two exams are Monday."

"Use this time to study. I'll drive them home."

"But . . ."

"Go, Craig, and try to get some rest while you're at it."

Samantha muttered, "She doesn't want you to see how she works her slaves."

"You were the one who wanted to come," Craig reminded her.

The girl turned away. "Whatever."

Esther gripped his arm and drew him down the walk. "Put them and us out of your mind."

He sighed. "She and her mother fought last night."

"Craig, look at me. They're my concern today. Now, please, go."

Esther stood at the curb with a smile planted on her face as Craig drove away. Then she walked back toward the house. The girls must have seen something in her expression, for the sullen resentment that had carried them this far began to fade. Samantha pulled out the earbuds and wound the tiny cable around her phone. Abigail took a step closer to her sister as though trying to shield herself from whatever came next.

"I'll be straight with you," Esther told them. "It will be great if you want to work. But you've already earned your keep, just being here."

The girls exchanged a look, then Samantha said, "You're paying us just to hang around?"

"If that's what you'd like to do, yes."

"That's cool," Abigail said.

"No, it's not," Samantha shot back. "It's a bribe."

"You're both right," Esther said. "But the truth is that I really don't want to be alone in my brother's home. I've had a lot of time to get used to the idea that he's never coming back here. I thought I was ready. But I'm not."

Samantha's curiosity got the better of her. "You said he was in an accident?"

"Yes, one that killed his wife. She was expecting a baby."

A bird chirped. A car honked somewhere in

the distance. Finally, Abigail asked, "So, you're afraid it's haunted?"

"Not like you're thinking," Esther replied. "But, yes, there are ghosts inside. A lot of them."

Nathan's house was located in Providence Plantation, an older subdivision off the main southern artery, Providence Road. Like most of its neighbors, the modest home had been built on an oversized lot, among ancient oaks and a magnolia whose limbs stretched out almost fifty feet. Nathan had lovingly restored the place, tearing out many of the interior walls and turning it into an open-plan haven with sweeping views of the back garden, which his wife had landscaped into an extension of the nearby arboretum.

None of this, of course, was why Esther had dreaded today's task.

Nathan's office was the only room on the first floor that was still sectioned off. The windows overlooked his wife's rose garden, overgrown now from lack of care. When Esther opened the windows, the room became filled with the fragrance of spring blooms and the sound of bees.

She took her time, forcing herself to inspect each wall in turn. Getting it over with.

Nathan's office was covered with photographs of their early lives. Many of the pictures she had not seen since childhood. She knew what he had done because he had described the process, ungluing old family prints from their mother's albums, restoring them with the same care and attention to detail as he had shown their home. Then enlarging them to the size of portraits. His walls contained no record of their mother's swift illness or their father's determined retreat. All the pictures here were of happier times.

Esther did not even realize she was being observed until she heard Abigail ask, "Why are you crying?"

Esther resisted the urge to hug the girl. "I found the ghosts."

On Friday evening, Esther deposited the two girls back with their mother but not before she had paid them, and in cash. The pair watched her count out the money with a sense of subdued delight. And perhaps a little guilt from Samantha, who had not done anything the entire day except text her friends and play on one of Nathan's spare computers and listen to music and pretend not to hover while Esther and Abigail talked and packed. Esther watched them walk to the home where supposedly neither of them felt welcome. When they both turned at the door and waved, Esther counted the afternoon as a true success.

She carried the three boxes of personal items into her home. Her plan had been to use an empty corner of her attic and store the items away. Just as she had done with all her memories from that time.

Instead, as she entered her home, the sunset played over the empty walls. She compared it to Nathan's house, where every room had contained a wealth of memories and hope. Nathan's late wife came from a family of seven, and the kitchen and family rooms held testimonies of every niece and nephew. Nathan and his wife had tried for years to have children. The accident had come just three weeks after they learned she was finally pregnant. Esther settled the last carton on her dining table and stared at the room's lone painting, an abstract oil fashioned from mathematical designs.

When the phone rang, she knew it was Craig. She answered with, "I'm so glad you called."

"You know just the thing to say to a guy who's been slaving over books all day. How were the girls?"

"Very well-behaved, all things considered."

"That's not what I heard."

"Abigail's been talking, then."

"Telling on her sister is one of life's great pleasures. Did Samantha really do nothing all day?"

"They kept me company, and they kept the ghosts at bay. Mostly. That was worth the price of admission, believe you me."

"I'm in seminary, remember. We're officially not allowed to believe in ghosts."

"Then you don't want to come around Nathan's place."

"What do you mean?"

She carried the phone back into the dining room and seated herself in front of the first box.

"Esther?"

"Give me a minute." Slowly she lifted the top picture, the one that had brought her to tears. She set it down before her, glad she had company for this moment. "Nathan had a lot of photographs from the lost years. There's one picture in particular. I actually dreamed about it the other night. I'm sitting in my father's lap. Nathan is standing to the left of the chair."

"How old are you?"

"Four, I think. Pop is reading and . . ."

"Esther, hon, what is it?"

"Nothing. It's just . . . it's been a long time since I used that name for my father." Esther traced a finger over the image, smearing her tears across the glass. "He's reading from his favorite book of the Bible."

"The book of Esther," Craig said. "Of course."

"I loved listening to him read. He would stop and talk about what each scene signified, how the world might have looked, and what was going on beyond the words."

"Making it come alive for the daughter he named after the heroine."

"Yes," Esther said. "Pop was a great storyteller."

She sat staring not so much at the picture, but at the two lives that were no more. She had no idea how long she was quiet. Long enough for her neck to cramp. "I suppose I had better let you get back to your books."

"The books can wait."

"Craig . . ."

"Yes?"

"Thank you."

23

Saturday

That night Esther was attacked by a serious case of the doubts. This was the name she had given to midnight worries back in her teens. Demanding that the principal of her middle school allow her to take the SATs five years early, threatening to go to the county superintendent if necessary, fighting because that was how she met every challenge. Only at night had she allowed herself to wonder if she was indeed able to meet the trials she was setting in place.

At three thirty in the morning, she rose and entered her office and scanned the markets. The world held that sort of weekend calm she had always considered false. The risks did not simply disappear for two days. She shifted the data streams, moving from Shanghai to Melbourne to

Rio to Mexico City to Vancouver to Chicago to New York. She recalled Jason's response to her early report, suggesting the bank take a more conservative approach to these dangerous times. Jason had called it following the party line and scorned her for even making the recommendation. That was the day the traders started referring to her and Jasmine as the Downside Twins.

And now, out of the blue, CFM had opted to do exactly as she had proposed? After pulling down over two hundred million in profits in just two trades?

Please.

She sat there watching the markets as dawn strengthened beyond her window. She knew she had no choice but to keep moving forward.

If only she were not so afraid.

Later that morning, Esther visited with her brother, then drove to meet the girls. They opened their front door just as Esther pulled into the drive. The two girls climbed into the backseat. Esther had the impression they both dreaded questions for which they did not have answers.

Esther turned far enough around to face them and said, "I just want you to know, I wouldn't be able to go back there today without you. Yesterday was very hard on me. Having you two there meant the world."

Neither girl replied. Esther put the car into

drive, and Samantha unwound the earbuds. Abigail sat and stared at nothing. Esther had no problem with the quiet, especially since she still felt a little dazed from lack of sleep.

Then Samantha surprised her by pulling out the buds and asking, "So, you and your brother, you didn't get along?"

"No, we're extremely close. We fought quite a bit after our parents died, but that was because I was angry with the world. Nathan was my rock. He kept me sane."

"Where did you go? I mean, after your parents . . ."

"We went to live with my grandparents. Nathan soon went off to college."

The girls must have caught something in her voice, because Abigail asked, "They didn't want you there?"

"They never said so. Well, not in words. But, no, I don't think . . ." Esther sighed. "You want the truth?"

The girls did not speak. Their gazes were intent.

"I think they saw me and my brother as daily reminders of the daughter they lost. It emphasized how silent their lives were without her, how empty of joy and happiness and everything my mother was." Now it was Esther's turn to stare through the windshield. "They shut me out."

Abigail said, "It's awful, isn't it?"

"Is that what is happening in your home?"

Samantha snapped, "I don't want to talk about it."

"I understand," Esther said. "All too well."

Samantha's face grew tighter still, her mouth a tiny pucker in the center, caught in a vise of emotions she was determined not to reveal. "Aren't you going to tell us how it's all in our minds? That they love us and are doing their best by us?"

Esther forced herself to ignore the comment and Abigail's tears, though it cost her. "Can I change the subject?" She took their silence as assent and went on, "I like you both. A lot. And I want you to know I understand. I really, really understand. If you want to talk, fine. If you want to just hole up and use my house as a safe place, that's fine too. I'll make you keys, you can come and go as you like. Because we all need a haven sometimes from life's unfairness."

Of all the responses she might have gotten, the expressions on their faces were the finest part of the day. Esther said, "Let's go kill some ghosts."

Esther and Abigail sorted through boxes and bundles that had not been touched in years. They had cloths wrapped around their noses and mouths, but still coughed from the grime.

Samantha's head poked through the attic

access door. "There's something you need to see."

"Abigail can't come right now," Esther replied. "Whatever it is will have to wait. I can't finish this without your sister."

"There's bound to be asbestos in here some-where," Abigail commented cheerfully. She had spent the past two hours listing all the ailments they were contracting.

"Not Abigail," Samantha said. "I meant you."

"Then it definitely has to wait." The attic now contained two piles. The larger pile was every-thing Esther intended to have the movers dispose of. She slid over one of the boxes they were going to keep. "Carry that out to my car, please."

Samantha protested, "I'm not touching that thing."

Abigail put in, "Not to mention ringworm."

"You can't get ringworm from dust mites," Esther said. She then looked at Samantha. "How about two dollars extra per box?"

Abigail complained, "She hasn't done anything all afternoon and you're paying her *extra?*"

Samantha replied, "You haven't seen what I've found."

"You both get the same bonus," Esther told them. "These keeper boxes are leaving with us today. I'm not coming back up here."

"You really need to see this," Samantha said, then disappeared with the box.

Abigail said, "You can too get ringworm.

Charlotte dust spores carry an extra bonus charge."

"What's in that box?"

"Magazines." Abigail held up a technical journal. "Work."

"Slide it over to the dumpster pile. Please tell me that's the last one."

"We probably won't know what's infected us until it starts eating our brains," Abigail said.

"Okay, we put everything in my trunk that fits, and the rest of the keeper boxes go in the garage. The big pile can stay here until the movers show up."

"I'll probably go blind before you do," Abigail said.

Esther started down the stairs, calling back up, "You are a terrible child. I'm going to tell your father to lock you in a closet and feed you through the keyhole."

"I like that idea a lot," Samantha said, heading back up the stairs for another box.

"Carnivorous flesh eaters," Abigail called down. "Charlotte dust spores especially like young brains."

It was not until Esther brought the last box down, shut the attic door, and entered the master bath for a quick wash that she realized what Samantha had done with her afternoon.

All the personal items—soaps and shampoos and pills and brushes and cosmetics—had been boxed up. And the bathroom was *spotless*. The tile smelled of disinfectant. The tub and sink and mirror were immaculate.

When Abigail walked up behind her, Esther said, "You can't come in here."

"I need to wash my hands."

"Not here."

"But I have ringworms in my hair."

"Me too." Esther turned Abigail around. "We'll find somewhere else to wash up."

"What's the matter with in there?"

"Your sister cleaned it."

"No. Wait. Samantha?"

"Do you have another sister I don't know about?"

"I want to see this."

"Don't touch a thing."

"I won't." Abigail poked her head inside, took a slow look around. "Wow."

They walked downstairs and passed through the living room, which seemed far more crowded with boxes than Esther recalled. Then they entered the kitchen, and Abigail said, "Double wow."

Samantha sat at the breakfast table and scowled at the laptop screen, pretending not to notice as they took in the freshly cleaned kitchen. Esther slowly walked around, viewing the empty cabinets and drawers and the black trash bags lined up by the back door like rumpled soldiers.

Esther turned to Samantha. "Prepare yourself."

"What?"

"I'm about to hug you."

"No, you're not. Eww."

"Rubber gloves and all." She could not have cared less that Samantha pulled away and made a face. "There. All done."

Abigail said to her sister, "Now it's my turn."

Samantha said, "Girl, you come within ten feet of me, I will hammer you like a nail."

Abigail beamed. "My sister hates that stuff."

"From you I do."

"Tough patootie," Esther said. "Abigail, I'll hold her down, you move in for the kill."

"Get away from me, the both of you."

"Treat it like a visit to the dentist. The more you fight, the longer it lasts. Group hug." Samantha squirmed and squealed, but there wasn't much heat to it, and when Esther stepped back, she thought she saw a fraction of a smile. Flickered and gone. But still. Esther said, "Thank you very, very much."

Samantha lifted one shoulder an inch. "You want to thank me, take a look at this."

Abigail peered over her sister's shoulder. "That's just a silly game."

"You didn't think it was so silly when you were playing it until after midnight." Samantha shifted her finger on the touch pad, then turned the computer so the screen faced Esther. "I meant this."

Esther squinted, then realized what she was looking at. "It's my website."

"Well, duh." Samantha scrolled down to the bottom. "Here. Check this out."

Esther stared dumbly at the counter. The numbers kept flipping over. Not the tens. Not the hundreds.

Thousands of visitors. Coming to her website. While she watched.

24

Sunday

Reynolds Thane took the predawn flight from Charlotte-Mecklenburg to Washington-Dulles. His plane was delayed because of fog, and he almost missed his connection to Bermuda. He normally traveled aboard the bank's Gulfstream. It was the first time Reynolds had flown commercial in three years.

Hamilton, the capital of Bermuda, was a teacup fantasy sort of city. Hamilton officially contained 1,100 citizens. There were twice that number of financial establishments. But resident bankers were not counted. The locals did not consider bankers on work visas as, well, real people.

The limo driver was a taciturn islander with the face of a burned prune. Reynolds gave the address of Sir Trevor's secret bank. The journey into Hamilton was pleasant enough. The city was a throwback to a different era, the brightly whitewashed buildings holding to a charming colonial flavor. Reynolds considered it as fake and uninteresting as Disney World.

The correct term for their Bermuda project was *off-book*—no direct tie between the parent bank and the Bermuda operation. Most off-book schemes were paper only. Many international banks used a local attorney to establish a shell company where they parked toxic assets and high-risk ventures that might otherwise raise red flags with the regulatory authorities. It had been a favorite tactic of banks before the 2008 meltdown, and the ploy was now making a comeback.

What made Sir Trevor's operation unique was its size. There had not been an off-book venture this large since Enron tanked.

When the limo halted on Reid Street, Reynolds stepped out and had a look around. Trevor's bank occupied the top three floors of the Perry Building. The traders had a nice view of the Cabinet Gardens and the sparkling blue waters of Hamilton Harbor.

He returned to the limo. As they drove along Front Street to the Hamilton Princess Beach Club, Reynolds watched a sailing regatta in the bay. Tourists lined the park-side walk, photographing the brightly colored spinnakers while a string quartet played waltzes under a Victorian pavilion.

It was a fitting tribute, Reynolds decided, to the current state of affairs. The idle rich looking on as the band played its final tune.

Jason was pacing the hotel's forecourt when Reynolds's limo pulled up. The bank's supposedly missing chief trader had sweated through his starched shirt, though the temperature was barely eighty degrees. He now waited impatiently as Reynolds booked the return journey for noon the following day. Jason then led him into the hotel and up to his bay-front suite. The parlor's French doors stood open to the sea breeze, and a buffet lunch had been laid out on the credenza. "You want anything else?"

"This will do nicely," Reynolds replied.

Jason tipped the bellhop, dismissed the waiter, then demanded, "What are you doing here?"

Reynolds took his time loading a plate, pouring himself a cup of coffee, selecting the chair with the best view. He took a couple of bites, knowing that Jason was about to explode. Timing, he reflected, was everything. Then he said, "If anyone asks, I have heard you are thinking of making this a permanent shift. I am here to convince you otherwise."

Jason settled into a chair. "Works for me."

"How is the operation proceeding?"

"We received the first two billion from Sir Trevor yesterday. It's already in play. Initial results won't be known until Monday."

"Keep all trades on a maximum twenty-four-hour window."

Jason frowned. "That limits our options."

"Even so, we want all the money put out on a very short leash." Which described precisely the best way to handle this man.

Jason shrugged. He would obey because he had no choice. "Was that why you came?"

"Of course not. We could have handled that via the scrambler." Reynolds pushed his plate aside. "We need to talk about Esther Larsen."

That caught Jason by surprise. "What about her?"

"So, you haven't seen her website." Reynolds pulled a tablet computer from his briefcase, drew up the site, then turned the tablet around so Jason could see it.

Jason squinted at the screen. "The Book of Esther? What kind of joke is this?"

"I thought the exact same thing when the chairman of Bradenton Industries brought it to my attention."

Jason lifted his gaze. Bradenton was a six-billion-dollar behemoth that owned eight percent of CFM. "What did he tell you?"

"That the site had gone viral." Reynolds tapped the right side of the screen. "Have a look at her list of sponsors."

Jason wanted to dismiss it out of hand. Which had been precisely Reynolds's first reaction. But the longer he scrolled down the list, the more confused Jason became. "How long has this been going on?"

"Three days. Less."

"That's impossible—"

"But real nonetheless." Reynolds stood and addressed the brilliant day beyond the window. "The site contains three components. First there is the layman's introduction to what Esther claims are dangerous tactics being taken by certain banks. Banks she goes on to name. Sixteen in the US, forty-seven more around the world."

"Are we on that list?"

"Unfortunately not. Otherwise we would already have brought her up on charges."

"The other components?"

"Apparently Esther has developed a series of algorithms for measuring global economic risk." Reynolds lifted a hand, halting Jason's question before it was formed. "These have nothing to do with our own trademarked calculations. Sir Trevor had his analysts work around the clock. They say her structure is, well, astonishing is the word they used. Unique."

"She's spent the past year or so harping about how the national economies are too interlinked to be isolated," Jason conceded.

Reynolds nodded. "I saw the reports."

"And the third component?"

"She has a list of six steps people should make. She urges everyone to withdraw their business from what she refers to as the 'tainted institu-tions.' "

"You've got to be kidding me."

Reynolds watched Jason shove the tablet away and lean back in his chair. Dismissing the news, which was what Reynolds desperately hoped they would be able to do. "Her website has received four hundred and sixty thousand unique visitors. The site includes a counter."

Jason mulled that over, then shrugged. "She could be padding the numbers. Even if she isn't, what difference does it make?"

Reynolds took a long breath of the salt-laden air, made a mental note to book a tee time with one of the island's finer courses. He walked back to the table. "Did you sweep this room for bugs?"

"Of course. But . . . Esther Larsen has you that worried?"

Reynolds was tempted to go against Sir Trevor's edict and tell Jason the truth. That Esther's predictions were too close to the crux of their real strategy. Sooner or later, Jason was bound to realize what their true motives were. He was, after all, a trader. Jason thrived on ferreting out the unseen. But Sir Trevor had been adamant.

Reluctantly, Reynolds held to the party line. "Do you recall the board meeting last week when you requested the additional two billion?"

"Of course. I don't see what—"

"I did not invite Esther to join us because I

wanted her input." Reynolds liked Jason's look of uncertainty. Keeping him off-balance was crucial to their plans. "I did so because I needed to know whether she could be controlled."

"I don't understand."

"Put simply, I needed to know whether Esther could be forced to stay silent. We can't have our in-house risk manager blowing the horn about our endeavors."

"You think she knows?"

"She is bound to suspect. We need to be certain she never utters a word." Reynolds pointed to his tablet, still showing Esther's home page. "Four hundred and sixty thousand visitors in three days. A list of sponsors that already contains six Fortune Fifty companies. What if they do as she says? What if this continues to grow? They could *strangle* us. And even if it doesn't, this is absolutely the wrong kind of attention."

"I should have been monitoring her more closely." Jason slowly shook his head. "When I get back I will personally destroy—"

"You will do *nothing*." Reynolds waited until Jason met his gaze, then added, "Unless I give you the word."

"What exactly are you saying?"

"I want you to develop a strategy for ending this threat. An accident would be best. Keep everything at arm's length." Reynolds kept his voice calm. "Multiple layers of protection between you and . . . whatever you think might be necessary."

"You want me . . ."

"Don't make any moves until I say to," Reynolds repeated. "But if I ask you to reconsider your options, then you have the green light."

25

Esther's Sunday morning began with a series of remarkable events. First, she slept late and woke up so foggy it took her a long moment to bring the clock's numbers into focus.

Esther carried her coffee upstairs and entered her office. The markets were Sunday calm, so she switched all but the central screen to standby. A long breath, another sip from her mug, and then she pulled up her website.

At Keith's suggestion, Esther had included a column down the right side of the home page that read simply, *Sponsors*. If anyone clicked on the headline, they first read in boldface Esther's declaration that she would not accept donations. Rather, everyone on this list had committed to sharing her information with a minimum of five hundred others. They also agreed to withdraw all business from her list of tainted banks within sixty days.

Calling the high-risk banks "tainted" had been Keith's idea, and he used it in spite of her strident objections. "Whatever are you going to call them, Esther? Naughty?"

"Something that doesn't lend itself to taking offense," she argued.

"The entire website is going to offend them," Keith replied. "You might as well get used to the reality that sooner or later they're going to come down on you like a ton of bricks."

She rubbed her forehead. It was going on two in the morning and both their tempers had become somewhat frayed. "I had no idea you were going to be such a trial to work with."

"My first preference for the bad-bank page would be, stinkeroonies."

"Be serious."

"We could put a smiling skunk at the top with its tail curled around the page. Wait, I know, and every thirty seconds a putrid green cloud would—"

"Stop. Just stop."

"Okay. Second choice. 'Confirmed Members of the Evil Empire.' You like?"

"Not even the tiniest little bit."

"Okay then. Tainted Banks. All in favor, say aye."

"No."

"Aye. Tainted Banks has carried by a technical majority. We are moving on."

And move on they did. Next was the question of whether Esther wanted names of new sponsors to be added to the top or the bottom of her column. Esther had suspected Keith was using such an inane decision as a means of diverting her from further argument.

She had phoned Talmadge Burroughs the next morning and wearily explained what she was intending, and been surprised when Talmadge had not allowed her to complete her request. "My company will sign on by lunch today. I'll phone some buddies too. But, Esther, that isn't why I told you yes."

"I'm just getting started."

"Esther, listen to me. How long do we have?"

"You asked me that already."

"I'm just making sure you understand. We don't have time for you to dance a polite little two-step here."

"I have no idea what you are talking about."

"You need to start focusing on the big picture. What should people be doing to protect themselves? How can we raise the alarm while there's still time? Answer those questions, then get back to me."

Now as she sat there, nine fifteen on a Sunday morning, she watched two more names appear on the list. One was a company so large, Esther suspected it was a prank. She made a note to contact them later to ask if they knew where their name had just turned up. But in the back of her mind, she knew Talmadge had been correct. She scrolled down to the bottom of her home page. The visitor-count Keith had installed was clicking steadily forward, the number approaching half a million.

As Esther dressed for church, she could almost hear a faint whir in the background as ever more people came to her for answers.

Craig called her as she was driving to church and said, "The girls can't help you this afternoon."

"Aww, that's a pity. Why not?"

There was a pause, then he said, "I'm sorry, I thought I was speaking with Esther Larsen about not needing to spend another afternoon with my daughters."

"I like them."

"Okay, there *is* something wrong with this connection."

"What is going on?"

He grew serious. "There are several issues. But at its heart . . ." He sighed. "Their mother is pregnant."

"Oh."

"They feel excluded. They're sure now that their stepfather wishes they weren't around."

"I understand."

"He hasn't said anything like that. I'm certain of it."

"He probably doesn't need to, as far as they're concerned."

"He's a civil engineer, works for CP&L. Right now he's supervising the construction of a new power plant. At the best of times, he is not very demonstrative. Right now . . ."

"His focus around the house is on the expectant mother," Esther supplied. "The girls aren't getting much attention from either of them."

"Anyway, Samantha phoned to say they're all going boating on the lake together." Craig hesitated, then added, "I think there's some element of concern about how much they like you."

"The feeling is mutual," Esther replied. "Your daughters are wonderful."

"Can I invite myself over and study at your place this evening?"

She smiled into the sunlight and the quiet Sunday street. "Sure, I'll make us dinner."

Esther carried her smile all the way through church. After the service, she walked down the hall to her classroom but halted at the buzzing of her phone. These days she did not cut it off, even in church. The screen showed a blocked number, but doctors often did that. She turned away from her classroom door. "Esther Larsen."

"Ms. Larsen, this is Emily Waters with ABC Television. I'm calling to ask if you would be our guest tomorrow on *Good Morning America*."

Esther walked toward the end of the hall. "Repeat please."

"Ms. Larsen . . . may I call you Esther?"

"Who is this, really?"

"My name is Emily Waters and I am a producer with ABC." The woman had the briskly intelligent manner of many successful New York women. "This conversation is for real, I assure you."

"How did you get this number?"

"I have assistants who get paid to track down whomever I tell them to find. As for our interest in you, one of our show's advertisers has signed on as a sponsor of your new website. Can you tell me, Esther, is the counter running at the bottom of your home page showing unique visitors to your site?"

"As far as I know, yes."

"And your site has only been up and running for three weeks?"

"No. That's not—"

"Excuse me?"

"Three days." Esther reached the exit and stared through the glass door out at the parking lot. "The website went live on Friday."

"Astonishing. Can you come to New York?"

"That would be difficult in the extreme."

"We would be happy to pay all expenses—"

"An illness in the family makes it impossible."

"I see. In that case, we can arrange for a live feed with our affiliate station there in Charlotte."

Esther heard herself agree to the arrangements in a voice not her own.

26

When Craig arrived that evening, Esther was still coming to terms with the idea of a national television appearance. She fixed a large salad, baked a loaf of frozen sourdough bread, and heated the leftover cannelloni. But she did not mention the phone call from New York. Craig's expression remained clouded by a worry he would not discuss. When she asked, he simply replied, "My girls." Now he worked at the dining table, his books and papers spread out before him. Esther decided her own news could wait.

During the renovations, Esther discovered a pair of solid mahogany doors embedded in the wall between the dining room and kitchen. The doors were drawn back now, making for a wide opening through which she could see Craig frowning over his work. She set two places at the table's far end, away from his books and papers.

They ate in companionable silence until Craig said, "This is truly a beautiful home."

She looked away and mulled that over for a time.

"Why does that make you sad, Esther?"

She toyed with her food. "I've spent every cent I earned making this place special."

"You've succeeded."

"It's a box." Speaking the words brought a lump to her throat. "Just an empty box."

"It's a home," he said. "Your haven against the world."

They finished eating in silence. There was nothing more she could say without weeping. Which was very strange. She rarely felt the lonely emptiness of her house so intensely. Esther stacked the dinner dishes and put on a pot of coffee while Craig returned to his studies.

Esther went up to her office, scanned the markets, then returned with her laptop and a pad and pen. She pulled up her website and spent a few moments watching the counter turn. Just that day, forty-three more companies had signed on as sponsors. There were two unrelated issues she needed to deal with. Watching the counter was her way of focusing, of tightening her concentration.

The first issue was that the website remained incomplete. She felt it in her gut. She wished she could talk about it with Craig, but one glance in his direction was enough to know this was not the time.

The second was, something was not right with the number of visitors. Six hundred thousand visitors in four days? This seemed *impossible.*

No way could word about her site have spread to such a degree. And yet the numbers defied her arguments. Twice she had asked Keith to check and ensure no one was manipulating the counter. Both times he responded that the rising tide of visitors was as real as it was baffling.

She was missing something.

Esther sipped her coffee, trying to wash away the rising anxiety. Why should she be afraid now? She was certain it wasn't the invitation to appear on television. She had been called out to do spots on a local business program any number of times. The bank even had a camera-ready room where employees shot videos or participated in live feeds.

She opened the technical page and ran through her analysis one more time. The structure and the formula, her investigation and conclusions were all sound. She returned to the home page and slid over her notepad. She listed the steps she had laid out, stages she urged her website's visitors to take.

Step One: Get out of debt. In a falling market, debts become anchors that can drag down a family or a company.

Step Two: Withdraw all financial assets from banks now using the same dynamics that brought the nation to the brink of economic collapse in 2008.

While listing those banks she had identified to

Keith, Esther had come up with a warning that now formed a banner over this page: STOP FEEDING THE BEAST.

Step Three: Transfer all accounts to regional banks, which tend to be more conservatively run.

Unlike past recessions, when larger groups were more likely to weather the turbulence, in 2008 the regional institutions were the ones that held up best. Esther was certain the same would prove true the next time around.

Step Four: Make sure all deposits remain below the FDIC insurance threshold, so even if the bank goes under, the family's liquid assets will be protected.

Step Five: Shift all savings and retirement accounts out of the stock market, and move away from funds that deal in stocks and high-risk bonds.

Step Six: Urge all companies and institutions in which viewers have a voice to do the same.

Esther laid down her pen and turned to the night beyond the window. She sighed.

"Esther?" Craig had lifted his head from his book and was watching her.

She felt the nervous tension rise up until it crawled like an electric current through her entire body.

"What is it?"

She looked at him. "I know what I need to do next."

"Do you want to talk about it?"

Slowly she shook her head. "Not yet." Talking about it would only make things worse.

Two and a half hours later, they decided to call it a night. The new page on Esther's website remained only half finished, the blank spaces a silent challenge to everything she had refused to write down. But keeping it bottled up inside did not help either. At some deep and secret level, Esther knew the plans were already in place, the stages worked through, the seventh step simply waiting to be acted upon. She had hoped that by now the electric fear would have diminished. Instead she was certain she would not sleep a wink, which meant arriving at the television station looking far from her best. But there was nothing she could do about it now except call and cancel. . . .

Craig interrupted her futile thoughts. "Can I ask you something?"

"Sure."

"It's about the girls."

"What about them?"

He closed and stacked his books and gathered his pages of notes, his movements as slow and deliberate as a bricklayer's. "Do you think there is validity to their request? I mean, about their not wanting me to be a pastor?"

Dread rose like a giant fist and wrapped itself

around her middle. "Now isn't the best time for such a discussion, Craig."

"It's been on my mind for days. I really need to know what you think."

"With your exams and all the stress you're facing, maybe we should wait and talk about it another day."

"It keeps me up at night. I feel like I can't see my way ahead." His gaze was dark, fathomless. "You're a professional analyst. I need your sense of clarity to help me see how I should respond to my girls. Please."

Esther felt pressure building on all sides. Tomorrow morning would mark her first appearance on national television. She had to complete work on what she now recognized was the necessary next step with her website. And now this. She forced out the words, "Do you want your daughters to come live with you at some point?"

"There is nothing I would like more," he replied. "Not a day goes by that I don't wish I could take them away from a place where they feel so unwelcome and bring them home where they are loved."

"Then that is your answer, Craig."

"I don't understand."

"Being a pastor has similarities to being a politician. You live in the spotlight. And you don't do this alone. Your family will be there too. Your daughters are not thinking about you when they tell you not to take this step. They are being selfish and self-centered teens. They don't want this as the life for themselves."

"So you're telling me to give up my current direction. For them."

"I'm saying . . . is there some compromise? A position where you could wear the less-public persona they want to have in their father and still fulfill this new sense of calling?"

He blinked slowly but did not respond.

"Is there a faith-based organization that needs a firm hand with their finances? Or a company where you could start an in-house ministry? Or—"

"I'll think about what you said."

"Don't be upset with me. You asked—"

"I certainly did."

"Craig . . . please—"

"Good night, Esther."

She watched as he strode across her living room and out the front door. Leaving her gripped by all the fears she felt powerless to do anything about.

Esther locked the door, climbed the stairs, got ready for bed, and lay there in the dark. Surrounded by her elegant and empty home.

27

Monday

Esther's drive to the television station was punctuated by the morning business reports. The news from China was grim. The European markets had caught wind of further turmoil in the Shanghai markets, with two major groups rumored to be going bankrupt. The fact that there was no hard news did not stop the newscasters from predicting another difficult week for the American markets. As Esther turned into the station's parking lot, she shook her head. *Any day but today.*

She had slept only a few fitful hours. Her phone had remained on her bedside, or in her hand, on the dresser, the kitchen counter, now on the console between the front seats. She called Craig four times. At first she did not apologize; she was certain she had done nothing wrong. But when he did not answer or phone back, she broke. Just after dawn she made the last call, apologized profusely, and wished him the best with his exams.

Sunlight glanced through the windshield, irritating her weary eyes. The ABC-affiliate station was housed in a featureless redbrick building surrounded by towers and a fenced-in area filled with satellite dishes. Esther pulled into a visitor's space just as a nervous young staffer rushed over to meet her.

"Esther Larsen?"

"That's me."

"Excellent. We were worried . . . This way, please."

The station director had obviously been alerted, because he appeared five seconds after she entered the building. He introduced himself as Chuck Welton and said, "We'd like to go live with an interview of our own once the network completes its segment. This will segue into our morning business report."

The lobby appeared to have been decorated twenty years earlier. The shag carpet was garish, the furniture scratched and forlorn. "All right."

"Our segment will pair you with our business anchor, Suzie McManning." He flashed his badge at the security portal. "We want Suzie to expand on your comments with *Good Morning America*."

"I understand." People rushed about, radios squawked, and the lights were too bright. The hall was decorated with wall posters of hit shows and local newscasters.

Welton pushed open a door and ushered her into a long, narrow room containing a massive lighted mirror. A waist-high shelf ran the length of the room, fronted by leather-backed stools. "This means your answers will be unscripted."

"I understand."

He nodded to the cosmetician. "Five minutes."

The woman was matchstick thin and smelled of cigarette ashes. She was the one person Esther had seen who remained unfazed by the clock. "Come on, honey. Let's make you look like a star."

The monitor positioned above the main camera served as Esther's connection with the New York studio. The camera itself was massive, almost as tall as she was, and set on a robotic dolly. The screen showed a bright trio seated on a yellow couch in a mock parlor with a color design that could only be described as fluorescent. By contrast, Esther was stationed in a cavernous studio draped in shadows. She sat on a narrow stool with a low back that required her to sit very straight. Other than herself and one technician, the Charlotte studio was empty. She noticed a wide window high in the wall directly opposite her. Esther assumed this was the production booth, though the technician's was the only voice she heard.

That technician stood behind the main camera. He said softly, "We are live in five, four, three . . ."

Then a male voice Esther instantly recognized came through speakers set to either side of her stool. "The term *trending* nowadays is applied to almost anything. But every once in a while, we discover something that genuinely fits the word.

With us today is a woman whose website is actually trending on a national, and perhaps even global, scale.

"At the beginning of last week, Esther Larsen was a risk analyst with CFM, one of the nation's top banks. Then she set up a new website designed to share her concerns about America's economy and financial system." The announcer, a strikingly handsome African-American male, turned to his co-hosts and said, "Maybe we should let Esther Larsen tell us herself what happened next. Welcome to *Good Morning America*, Esther."

"Thank you."

"You put together your website in just one night, is that correct?"

"With the help of Keith Sterling, an excellent web designer. A very long night for both of us."

"But you have been working on the analysis this website contains for a much longer period."

"Seven years and counting."

The younger of the two female anchors said, "So you worked on this project of yours for seven years, identifying the so-called bad banks."

"Not exactly." Esther was beginning to recognize their interview style. The study of such tactics had long been crucial to Esther's work. They did not ask directly. They traded back and forth, which allowed them to probe while pretending the style of a casual conversation. They *observed*. They wanted her to react. They intended for their exchange to keep her off-balance, slightly on a defensive edge.

Esther went on, "Most of the financial institutions that are taking dangerous risks are well known. And a number of their actions are already public. Take for example the nine banks convicted last year of manipulating the global exchange rates. This is far from being the only banking strategy that skirted the line of legality. Nineteen global banks are currently facing new charges involving—"

The other female anchor broke in, "So why go public now?"

"Because it's never been just about the banks. It is about their actions weighed against the economic situation."

The male anchor demanded, "And how do you see the current state of our economy?"

"That is where the problem lies," Esther replied. "It's no longer about *our* economy. We as a nation are impacted by *global* economic trends."

"Okay, so how is that situation?"

"Fragile," Esther said. "And some tactics by some banks are pushing us closer and closer to the brink."

"Let's get back to why we're here today," the first woman said. "Your website. We said at the beginning of this segment that you are trending because of the public response."

"Seven hundred thousand visitors in four days—

is that even possible?" the man seated next to her asked.

"Apparently so," the younger woman responded. "Not to mention over two hundred corporate sponsors, including seven Fortune Fifty companies."

The male anchor asked, "What makes you suddenly so popular?"

"I can only speculate," Esther said. "My guess is that for some time many people have suspected things are not right with our economic structure. I am both clarifying their concerns and giving voice to what worries them most."

The man leaned forward. "Which leads us back to the original issue. Why *aren't* things right, Esther?"

"Because the banks involved in the 2007–2008 crash were never held accountable."

"But the government tried. We've had as our guest the federal prosecutor involved in attempts to bring several major bankers to justice."

"A few individuals, yes. But not the banks themselves. And that has left them feeling bulletproof."

The three anchors shared bright smiles. "That is unfortunately all the time we have today. Esther Larsen, thank you for sharing your thoughts on *Good Morning America*."

Suzie McManning had curly red hair and coppery-green eyes and an economics degree

182

from Yale. She anchored a regional business-news show called CBR, the Charlotte Business Report, and had a sharp, no-nonsense way of getting to the heart of the issue. McManning had irritated more than her share of glad-handing Southern business tycoons, who assumed they could smile their way through any interview done by the pretty lady. Though Esther had never met her before, she entered the second studio of the day already liking her.

Which made Suzie McManning's attitude very jarring. The woman refused to meet Esther's gaze. The carpeted dais was about twenty feet long by ten feet wide. People being interviewed were usually stationed on the sofa, but today Esther was directed to a swivel chair placed to the left of Suzie's desk. The newscaster's first words were, "We're also taping this segment to be aired a second time at the top of the hour."

Esther gave a nod and replied, "Understood. It's nice to finally meet you. I've always admired your work."

"How kind of you to say." Suzie glanced up at the back window and asked, "How is my gain?"

The technician replied, "We're good to go."

Esther frowned. "Is something wrong?"

"Whatever gave you that idea?" Suzie angrily rammed her stack of papers together.

A voice from the back called, "Live in two minutes."

Then Esther spotted the shadow in the studio's far corner. She instantly recognized the man holding the cane as Talmadge Burroughs, the high-powered local business leader. Everything came together in a flash of comprehension. Esther now understood who had been behind her website's sudden rise into the spotlight. "Just a minute."

Suzie snapped, "We don't *have* a minute."

"I said *wait*." Esther rose from her seat. She did not cross the studio because she wanted this to be public, heard by all. "This stops now, Mr. Burroughs. Tell me you understand or I walk."

A young voice said through Esther's earpiece, "Ninety seconds."

Esther turned to the newscaster. "Let me guess. You just heard I'm to be offered a job by this station."

"There is no *offer*." Suzie McManning's Southern lilt sounded odd coming from such a truly Irish face. "The station has been *ordered* to make this happen."

"I refuse any such position." When there was no response, Esther raised her voice. "Mr. Burroughs, tell me you accept this."

"Sixty seconds."

Esther went on, "If we have to win hearts and minds through raw tactics, we have lost even if we succeed."

"We are live in fifteen!"

The man seated in the shadows waved his cane. "All right, all right."

Esther resumed her seat and offered the anchor as much warmth as she could muster. "Okay. Let's go."

Suzie McManning was clearly disconcerted by what she had just observed. She introduced the segment and her guest, then turned to Esther and said, "Let's talk about China."

The production booth was a glass-fronted balcony in the wall opposite from where they sat. Several dimly lit figures stood behind the main console, watching as Esther replied, "We might as well. Everybody else is."

"Why is China important?" The bright lights turned Suzie's arms and hands the color of chalk, which made her freckles more obvious. "I don't mean important in Washington or New York or Tokyo."

"You mean, why should the average listener to your show here in Charlotte be concerned about an economy eight thousand miles away."

The moderator nodded slowly, her expression no longer clouded by her earlier irritation. "Exactly. Help us understand that."

"In every global downturn since the Second World War, the United States has been the engine that brought the world's other economies back to life. After the 2008 downturn, it was China that played the largest role."

"You're saying America no longer matters on the global economic stage?"

"No, not at all. The United States is the largest economy in the world. The issue is growth."

"China's growth rate is larger."

"It was throughout the seven years it took America to return to the employment and output levels prior to 2008. During that period, China's expansion depended on raw materials brought in from the developing world. Following the 2008 recession, those countries and China together generated seventy-five percent of the world's per-capita economic growth."

Esther liked how she and Suzie were now in sync. The initial conflict was gone. Erased. Suzie did not get to where she was today, the only woman in the Southeast anchoring her own daily business report, by carrying grudges. Esther could almost anticipate the question before Suzie said, "But there are problems."

"Three of them. One is directly related to China. One has to do with the developing world. And one is more closely tied to our own future here in the US."

Suzie leaned back, signaling to the audience a dramatic pause. "It sounds like we'll need to have you back on the show again, Esther."

"I'd like that."

"Today let's stick with the original question."

"Why is China important. Right. The issue is that their growth has been fueled by debt. And the problems related to this debt are now reaching a crisis point."

"But hasn't that been the case in the United States? To save the financial system in 2008, we added a trillion dollars to our national debt through TARP, the Troubled Asset Relief Program."

"And another five trillion through quantitative easing," Esther added. "America's debt issue is important to our future. But it is *nothing* compared to what China has done. Since 2008, China's national debt has risen by *twenty-one trillion* dollars. In just eight years, they added debt totaling one hundred and thirty percent of the country's GDP."

"Gross Domestic Product," Suzie explained. "A country's per-capita total output."

"Right. China's central government now owes over *three hundred percent* of its GDP."

Suzie did not smile, but there was a glint to her copper gaze now, enough to assure Esther that she was enjoying the exchange. "But it doesn't stop there, does it?"

"No, China's government has also encouraged its companies and its citizens to borrow at unprecedented levels. Private debt during this same period has nearly trebled."

"Here comes the kicker," Suzie said. "I can feel it."

"No nation in history has reached this level of debt and avoided a major depression."

"Not recession," Suzie said. "Depression."

"Exactly."

"How long does China have?"

"They danced around the cliff edge last winter," Esther said, "but they managed to escape going over. By adding more debt."

Suzie nodded. "Same question. How long do they have?"

"Less than a year," Esther replied. "Perhaps less than six months."

"How will that impact the United States?"

"The trillion-dollar question. And it all comes down to those two other issues."

"Unfortunately, that's all the time we have for today." Suzie turned to face the camera again, but not before flashing Esther with what appeared to be a genuine smile. "Stay tuned for Market Roundup."

28

After the sound engineer had freed Esther of her microphone and battery pack, she thanked both Suzie and the station director, then made her way over to Talmadge Burroughs. Esther did her best to stow away her irritation. She needed Talmadge. Esther seated herself on the base of a mobile camera, which put her a fraction lower than Talmadge's chair. She watched his hands nervously kneading the head of his ivory-topped cane. And she waited.

Talmadge said, "So you're giving the station a definite no, then."

Esther held to her silence.

Talmadge cleared his throat. "I only suggested the station take you on because I thought it would help."

"You *suggested?*"

He coughed. "I might have gone a bit too far."

"A bit?"

He tried for indignation but failed. "What do you want me to say?"

"Start by telling me if you own this station."

"I might have a small interest in companies that have invested in local stations here and there." He coughed again. "I'm on your side, Esther."

"Then act like you are, Mr. Burroughs."

"My friends all call me Cricket."

"There is no way on heaven or earth I will ever call you Cricket," she assured him.

"Talmadge, then." He cocked his head. "You sure can be one ornery lady."

"Let me guess," Esther said. "When I told you about setting up my new website, you contacted the president of the advertising company you have under contract."

"Actually, we own them."

"You threatened the poor man with dismissal if he didn't drive traffic to my site."

"Just so happens my agency is run by a lady," Talmadge corrected. She glared at him, and he quickly added, "I didn't threaten anybody."

"You gave the poor woman a directive, which coming from the owner is as good as a threat." She shook her head. "Shame on you."

He thumped his cane on the slick concrete floor. "Sometimes you got to light a fire under folks."

"You will stop this now," she said. "You will grant me the right to vet any future actions before you put them into play."

"Do that or else, huh?"

"Unlike some," Esther replied, "I don't threaten people."

He thumped his cane again. "Agreed."

"This subterfuge stops now, Talmadge."

"I said all right." He stared at her. "Isn't this when you stand up and storm outta here?"

"I want to. Believe me." She took a hard breath. "But the truth is I need your help with something."

That took a moment to sink in. Talmadge grinned at her. "I bet those words tasted vile coming out of your mouth."

"Awful," she agreed.

· · ·

Twenty minutes later, Esther left the TV studio. She checked her messages while walking to her car. The only item that could not wait came from Nathan's doctor, who asked her to come by as soon as possible. She checked in with Jasmine, then drove to the clinic. When she arrived, the doctor was with a patient, but the nurse introduced Esther to a social worker assigned to the regional mental health facility. The message was clear long before the introduction was over. Esther's time for making a decision on Nathan's behalf was running out.

She phoned Craig from the parking lot as she left the clinic. She needed to talk with him more than she knew how to put into words. Even so, her request that he call her back sounded hollow to her ears. As though she were just going through the motions of what other people might call a normal life.

The realtor was waiting in front of Nathan's home when she arrived. Esther walked the woman through the home, accepted her selling-price estimate, and signed the documents. All the while she remained wrapped in the fog of Craig's silence.

Talmadge phoned her while she was driving toward downtown. "I suppose I should apologize."

"Well, at least on that point we are in complete agreement."

"I have ordered the advertising company to obtain your approval for everything they do."

"And there is no threat of mass firings or any other peril to their careers," Esther said. "I want that made perfectly clear."

"No whip, just carrots," Talmadge agreed.

"Then your apology is accepted." She did not want to let the man go, not when it meant returning to her sorrow and silent phone. "How did your people grow my audience so fast?"

"I don't ask details. I only set goals and make sure the people I hire are the best. Which is why I went after you."

She decided there was no better time to ask, so she pulled into the parking lot of a convenience store, parked, and asked, "Why is this so important to you? I mean, the warning, my concerns, the whole global issue."

Talmadge replied, "My father was raised in a Carolina Depression home. That time meant different things to different folks. Down east it was a decade of making do. Nobody had a cent to their names. If you absolutely had to have something, you either paid for it in kind or in work. If the sellers took only hard cash, it mostly meant you and your family went without."

Esther had the phone linked by Bluetooth to her car's audio system. Talmadge's voice emerged from half a dozen speakers, softened into a buttery Southern burr. He went on, "When I was still a kid, I asked my father what it was like, growing up in them times. Daddy went all quiet, and then he told me he hadn't owned a new pair of trousers for seven years. Hand-me-down years was how he described it. Living off the church poor box. Going to bed hungry, waking up afraid. Seeing his own father worry over losing the farm. Hearing his parents talk about putting him and his siblings in an orphanage just so they'd get a decent meal. Those were terrible times, Esther."

"It shaped him," Esther said.

"Formed us all. My whole family, we carried Daddy's fear of poverty. We were *stained* by this. I'm the only one who made it out. All the rest, they went for safety. Biggest thing they ever allowed themselves to hope for was a government job and a regular paycheck." He was quiet for a time, then continued, "This ain't about *warning*. This is about helping folks avoid the nightmare."

Esther said, "You are a good man, Talmadge Burroughs."

"I told you, call me Cricket."

"Not on your life," she replied, and drove to the bank with a smile.

Jasmine met her midway across the central space, "Girl, you were *cookin'!*"

Esther's reply was cut off by a smattering of applause from her entire team.

Jasmine pretended to whisper, "Can I say that to my boss?"

"What, 'girl' or 'cooking'?"

"Both, I suppose." Today Jasmine wore a denim skirt, a Ferragamo sweater with sparkly buttons, and gray suede ankle boots with three-inch heels. "I should probably say something, you know, more—"

"Respectful," Esther suggested, but she was smiling. "Appropriate."

"Right. Only I don't *care*." She turned to the crew. "Can I get a *hoo-yah* for the boss-lady star?"

This response was louder, especially the whistles.

When the room went quiet, Esther asked, "Any blowback from upstairs? Jason?"

"Nada on both counts. But the redheaded anchor lady called. Like, eleven times."

MIT lifted his phone. "Here she is again."

Esther started to say she'd take it in her office but decided here was fine. She accepted the receiver. "This is Larsen."

Suzie McManning asked, "How did you get past me?"

"I . . . Where are you?"

"First I was in the main lobby downstairs. But my cameraman kept shooting background footage, and the guards grew nervous. So they moved me upstairs to the trading-floor lobby. I'm staring at the elevator doors as we speak."

"I came up from the garage. Different elevators. I don't need to ask what you're doing here, do I?"

"Not if you're half as smart as I think you are," Suzie replied. "Can we please get started?"

29

Esther waited until she was miked and the sound check completed to say, "Okay, explain what you're doing here."

Suzie used the mirror in her powder compact to check her reflection. "There's been some positive feedback from New York." She clicked the compact shut. "Same response to our own segment. We fed it to our affiliates, an action that normally receives little more than a yawn and an automatic reply. Today, they asked for more. So here I am."

They were seated on two stools Jasmine's crew had supplied. The segment was being shot at the back of the trading room floor. Esther had not asked permission because Jason was away and nobody else seemed to care. The traders were too busy fuming.

Suzie ignored the surrounding clamor and said, "I think it will add to the moment if I use a handheld microphone. The one on your lapel will actually pick up your responses, but when I turn the handheld your way, it offers a sense of action and intensity. Also, the sound guy can up the level just slightly to pick up a bit of the background noise."

"Whatever you say." Esther could see the traders pretending not to watch as the cameraman fussed with his three portable lights. Suzie's harried assistant had fielded three calls from the station director, reminding them that the tape was to be fed into the market watch.

Esther said, "I envy you your calm."

Suzie had undergone a distinct change since that morning. She treated Esther as an ally now. She offered a catlike smile, all teeth and sharp eyes. "It's a veneer. I paint it on before I go to work, peel it off every evening. Underneath I'm a bundle of nerves."

"I don't believe that for a minute."

"There's more. Talmadge's communications group owns radio stations throughout the Southeast. They want to try us out for a morning talk show." When Esther did not reply, Suzie added, "We're talking possible syndication."

The sense of arriving at an unseen juncture suddenly crystallized. Embedded in the carpet at Esther's feet was a split in her future path. One course flew further and further away from everything she had strived for—the bank and the position and the safety. Sitting here on the trading room floor, getting ready to declare her warnings over the air was merely the next step.

Suzie scanned the room. "Quite a day. I woke up thinking you were the greatest threat to my career. Now I'm wondering if you might be my biggest break."

"I'm glad for you," Esther said weakly.

The cameraman studied them through his viewfinder, then straightened and announced, "Ready to roll."

"So, Esther Larsen, at the beginning of this morning's broadcast you mentioned there were three issues of primary concern. Together they could push us into the next economic downturn. This morning we discussed the role China might play. What is the second factor?"

Esther could see herself and Suzie on the monitor positioned to Suzie's right. The traders behind them added to the sense of electric tension. All the faces visible on the screen were bleak, angry. They did not speak to one another. They barked. It was perfect.

"We call it the point of inflection," Esther said. "This refers to the moment when the markets change direction."

Suzie drew the mike back. "You're not talking about a temporary downturn?"

"No, this is the third longest bull market in history. The driving force has been cheap money. Low interest rates have meant people and companies with cash have searched desperately for any investment that offers them a potential return. As a result, shares of many companies that have yet to make a profit have been pushed to absurd valuations purely on the basis of conjecture and rumor. Speculative investment has never been at such a high level. One-third of the companies in the Russell 2000 Stock Index do not earn any profits. This is the highest percentage on record outside of a serious depression."

Once more Esther had the sense of Suzie moving into sync. The woman was sharp, perceptive, and she lived and breathed the markets. Which meant she could draw back the mike and make the comment Esther was hoping to hear. "These same investors have been driving up other markets as well."

"Exactly. Again, we are talking about a global event. Because the developing world has shown a faster growth rate, investors have poured in cash, shooting markets around the globe into the stratosphere."

"So walk us through what this might mean."

"There is no *might*. The risk is not just possible, it is *imminent*."

Suzie merely smiled. The professional. Standing at a distance. Letting the audience make up its own mind. "What does this mean for the average American investor, Ms. Larsen?"

"Right now, today, the developing world is in decline. The major economic driver behind the world's recovery from the 2008 recession is slowing. The entire emerging-markets domain, with the single exception of India, is either in recession or decelerating. Russia, Indonesia, Turkey, China, Brazil. These same investors who piled in when the numbers looked good are frantic to get out. That means they're awash with cash and don't have any reliable place to put the money."

Suzie started to respond, but her attention was caught by Esther's team gathered behind the camera. At the outset they had smiled hugely, and Jasmine had given Esther two thumbs-up. But they weren't smiling now. Their boss was giving voice to very real concerns. They might not follow the global trends as closely as she did, but they were smart and market savvy. They shared her worries.

The cameraman said softly, "Rolling."

Suzie said, "Which means the markets here in the United States risk heightened instability."

"Correct. Financial institutions are hunting urgently for any investment possibility that offers a core return and a measurable risk. But where they invest is not driven by corporate growth or predicted returns. It is *speculative* investment. This results in huge swings . . ."

Esther's mind froze on a thought so bizarre, so outrageous, she was terrified it might be true.

Suzie pressed, "You were saying, this results in . . . ?"

"Contagion," Esther said quietly.

"What does that term signify?"

"When panic grips the market, contagion sets in." Esther's gaze locked on Jasmine. The woman's green eyes held the same dread Esther felt. "Everything goes down. Good and bad assets are caught in a spiral."

"Just like in 2008," Suzie said slowly.

"No, not like that. At the onset of the last recession, the US government propped up the economy. This time, the Fed is out of ammunition." Esther found it difficult to swallow. "Interest rates are near zero. Our money cannot be made any cheaper."

Suzie moved even slower this time, pulling the mike over, speaking the words, playing the tension. "What happens, Esther?"

"Deflation," she answered. "Depression. Chaos. That is, unless we do something to rein in the financial institutions. And fast."

30

As soon as the interview was done and Suzie's crew had packed up and was on their way, Esther returned to her office and phoned Talmadge. True to his word, he answered instantly. "Can this wait?"

"No. One question. Did you order your other stations to make room for me?"

"I did not even suggest it. And so we're clear, they are not 'making room,' as you put it. They see the potential themselves and are offering you and your ideas this regional coverage."

"And doing it of their own volition." Esther wanted to be absolutely certain on this point. "No subterfuge of any kind on your part."

"They heard about you, and asked. I told them what I knew. That's it. Now here's a question for you. My ad lady wants to meet with you. She's got some ideas."

"Sure, so long as they are her ideas."

"This afternoon work?"

"Three o'clock," Esther said. "Go make your filthy millions."

"Somebody's got to. Might as well be me."

She put her phone down and sat reflecting on how she could argue with the man and smile at the same time. She scrolled down, saw there were no messages from Craig, and was gripped by that hollow ache once more.

Then as she turned to her screens, an idea struck her. Before she could argue herself out of acting, she made the call. When Patricia answered, Esther said, "Can I stop by after work? I need your advice."

Esther spent the next hour watching the markets and wondering at the utter silence from the trading department. Normally her team would field twenty to thirty analyst requests each day. So far there had not been one. Esther kept a screen focused on the bank's trading activities. Nothing was happening.

She could almost smell the threat of a full-scale mutiny.

She also was waiting for serious blowback from upstairs because of her on-air performances. With a sense of genuine dread she awaited a call from the chairman's office. But it never came.

By lunchtime, though, she had fielded seven calls of a different nature. Friends within the financial community enjoyed telling her the morning performances had gone viral. Several of the top market Twitter accounts had shot out alerts. Keith had set up feeds, which were now available on YouTube, Instagram, Facebook—everywhere. An ally who had left Wall Street to serve as an aide to the Senate Banking Committee phoned to say Esther's talks were being discussed on the Hill. And when she phoned Keith, he congratulated her for reaching her first million hits.

Esther studied the carpet at her feet. The juncture of the road had already been passed. Her course was set.

Esther decided to go over to the trading floor for another look. But as she stepped from her office, Jasmine came racing in from the connecting hallway. "You won't believe what I just heard."

"Tell me." Esther resisted as Jasmine tried to pull her back into the office. "If it's that big, everybody needs to hear."

"The bank is being sold."

The words did not fit. "Which bank are we talking about?"

"Ours." Jasmine loved being first with major announcements. "Gotcha."

"CFM? Are you serious?"

"Totally."

"Is this a rumor or for real?"

"A for-real rumor. Heard it twice. Two different floors."

Esther turned to her staff, frozen and agog. "Not a word to anybody. We don't trade in rumors. We are analysts. Let others spread the half-truths. Clear?" Only when she received affirmative nods from everybody did she turn back to Jasmine. "Details."

"Sir Trevor's group has made a formal offer for a full merger. The board has accepted. Official market notification goes out a week from today."

"And you know this because?"

"My best buddy on the top floor typed up the board minutes." Jasmine beamed. "Come this time next week we'll be working for the sixth largest bank in the world."

"That's the question, isn't it?" This from their MIT guy. "Whether we'll be working at all."

Esther needed to study on this, but first things first. She addressed the group again. "You've all had time to take my measure. Rule one around here is we take care of each other. We watch one another's backs. We are a team. You are here because you are the best. We will get through this, and we will thrive. All of us." She gave that a beat. "Clear?"

She watched the tension and fear ease a notch, then lifted her hand and said, "Now give me a minute to digest all this."

The longer she analyzed, the more uneasy she became. Finally she focused on Jasmine and said, "You need to contact your friend, Hewitt."

Jasmine grimaced. "That's history."

"Listen to me. This is crucial. Whatever it takes, find him."

The dark eyes squinted. "Can I ask why?"

"Everybody is going to assume Hewitt's group was seconded to one of Sir Trevor's divisions. This inactivity we're experiencing is going to be put down to the very same reason. From the instant this news hits the floor, our traders are going to be in full revolt."

"They'll assume the action shifted with the missing people," Jasmine said slowly.

"But that doesn't work. The UK financial authorities are keeping a closer watch on UK investment banking divisions than the SEC." Esther could see Jasmine didn't get it, and to explain her concern meant revealing her suspicions. And like Esther had just told her team, they did not deal in half-formed ideas, no matter how troubling. "Just find him."

Jasmine shrugged. "I'll try. Do you want to hear the rest?"

"Tell me."

"Jason is due back tomorrow morning. He's called a meeting of the whole team, including us."

That sealed it as far as Esther was concerned. "As of this minute, I'm on vacation."

Jasmine's gaze went round. "But . . . are you sure?"

"You are acting head. If Jason asks, tell him I needed to take care of urgent family issues." Which was definitely the case.

"Okay, if you're . . . How long will you be away?"

Probably for good, Esther thought to herself. "A few days, a week at the most."

31

Burroughs Enterprises occupied five floors in the First Union building. The Whitney Advertising Agency was on the floor directly below. Carol Whitney, a no-nonsense woman in her late fifties or early sixties, didn't have a smile to her name. Her iron-gray hair was worn stylishly short, and her beige suit showed off a trim figure. Her large hands were unadorned, save for a gold Cartier watch. The slight hint of a Southern accent did nothing to soften the determination with which she addressed Esther. "My remit, as I understand it, is to maximize your exposure while remaining completely unseen."

Esther was utterly comfortable with her direct approach. "So long as the audience's interest is genuine. So long as the people come because they're confident they'll find what they're looking for."

"Ms. Larsen, I run an advertising company. I do not have a miracles department. If people are not interested, they will not come."

"Understood." Esther glanced at Talmadge, wondering if she needed to emphasize her concerns again.

Talmadge Burroughs was seated in a straight-back chair brought in from the conference room. "Carol and I have reached an understanding."

"I have been instructed to inform you that we are being paid for our efforts," the woman said. "And everything must be passed by you for approval before being implemented."

Esther settled back, satisfied. "So let's hear it."

They spent the next hour running through various elements that Esther did not need to fully understand. Several staffers entered, made swift and professional pitches, then disappeared. Esther asked a couple of questions she hoped would sound interested and engaged. She was rewarded with a complexity of data that would have drawn looks of admiration from her own geeks. She gave it sixty minutes, and then before Carol turned to the next project, she said, "I think that's clear enough. It sounds as if you have everything well in hand. Thank you."

"But we still need to cover your Twitter feed," Carol protested. "Not to mention the dissemination of your upcoming broadcasts, and—"

"Basically what you're telling me is that your team is setting up alerts in as many different places as possible," Esther replied. "But my work is the driver. Either it ignites an interest or it vanishes."

"Well . . . yes."

"Fine. I agree." Esther turned to a grinning Talmadge. "Don't look so smug."

"It does my heart good," he said, "watching you climb down off your high horse."

"I never . . ." She could not quite hide her own smile.

"You were gonna tell me about something new."

"It would form the seventh step on my website," she replied, then glanced at Carol.

"Might as well give it to her now. If I like it, she'll be hearing about it soon enough."

"I want to set up a hedge fund," Esther said. "One aimed at protecting people."

At Carol's blank look, Esther explained that a hedge fund was an investment vehicle that pooled capital from major depositors and invested in securities and other instruments. In most cases, they *leveraged* their investments, paying only a small percentage of the actual investment's total value. This could take the form of short-term debt, or derivatives, or a number of other more complex directions. They also *hedged* their investments by taking positions that limited their potential risk. If a market or industry valuation fell below a certain level, the "floor" went into effect, cutting their losses.

Esther then added, "Hedge funds are largely ungoverned and highly secretive. They charge a flat up-front fee of around seven percent, taking an additional twenty percent of all profits they generate."

"There's bound to be some of them out there already," Talmadge noted.

"There are."

"Yours is different, then."

"In three ways. First, hedge funds generally refuse to accept any investment under a hundred thousand dollars. They also require investors to have a minimum net worth of five million. I want to open this to everyone. Thousand-dollar minimum."

"Ten thousand," Talmadge corrected.

"A thousand dollars," Esther insisted. "And

further investments will be welcome in incre-
ments of five hundred."

"You're gonna be deluged with worried
grannies."

"And secretaries," Esther agreed. "And young
families. Anyone who wants a hedge against
what is worrying us."

Talmadge kneaded the head of his cane.

Esther went on, "Second, we will operate in a
completely transparent manner."

"Which means every Tom, Dick, and Harry can
copy you."

"If they want to, fine. This isn't about making
money. Well, it is. Of course I'll try to deliver a
profit to my investors. But mostly this is about
protection for those who have none."

"And third?"

"All investors under twenty-five thousand
dollars will pay no up-front charge. And if there
is a profit, our take will be limited to ten percent.
Above that level of investment, we charge the
standard fees."

It was the first time she had spoken to Talmadge
about an actual business proposal. She watched
closely as he deliberated. Anything could happen.
He could give her tacit approval and not help her
obtain the required funds, or accept the role of that
all-important first investor. He could condemn
her for setting up a business model that risked
losing money in a variety of spectacular methods.

He looked at Carol. "What do you think?"

"I can definitely sell this."

"No question?"

"Visits to her site are running close to seventy thousand an hour," Carol said. "This hedge fund concept is a logical next step. People are wanting a means to protect themselves, invest what they can, prepare for the worst. This new idea fits perfectly."

Talmadge said to Esther, "Give me a couple of hours."

Esther got caught in rush-hour traffic andrequired seventy minutes to drive the five miles to Patricia's home. She arrived to find Patricia in the kitchen with her sister and daughter. Rachel was making an apple strudel, kneading cinnamon and sugar and sour cream into the dough, which she assured Esther was the secret. Patricia was dressing and sautéing chicken for the grill. Lacy prepared a Cobb salad in a large earthenware bowl. Patricia told Esther, "You can take me away to some quiet corner or you can draw up a stool. But you can't help. There isn't room for a fourth cook."

"I'll quit," Lacy offered.

"You will do no such thing. A good cook never switches serfs in midstream."

Esther only needed a moment to decide. "Here is good." She turned to Lacy and observed, "You're looking better."

Lacy tried for a bright lilt. "I'm staying home for spring break, my mother is fattening me up, and my awful former boyfriend is somewhere far away. Hopefully being miserable and lonely and full of bitter regret."

"I hear the Faroe Islands are especially brutal this time of year," Rachel suggested. "We could send him a ticket."

The kitchen went silent then. Esther knew they were waiting. It astonished her how easy it was to talk with them. After a lifetime of hiding everything away, here she was, seated in a corner of a brightly lit kitchen, on the verge of relating events to three women from very different walks of life. A faint whisper ran through her mind, protesting that they were strangers and always would be. But the voice was stifled within the space of a single long breath.

As she recounted the events surrounding Craig and his daughters, Esther thought she sounded dry and utterly disconnected. But there was nothing she could do about that. She did not try to describe her inner tumult because she did not know how.

Even so, when she finished, Rachel said, "I could kill that guy."

"You can't do away with a pastor," Patricia warned. "It's written somewhere in the church code of ethics."

"He's not a pastor yet." Rachel pounded the dough. "If he doesn't watch out, he never will be."

Esther asked, "So you don't think I did something wrong?"

Lacy shook her head. "I've been humming that same dirge a lot recently. Mostly late at night."

"No, honey," Patricia said to Esther. "I think you told Craig exactly what he needed to hear. His girls don't want to be part of a pastor's family. Regardless of everything else they're facing, this is not going to change. We can all see that."

Rachel sprinkled flour over the dough. "You answered his question honestly and from the heart. You didn't insist. You didn't order. You didn't criticize."

Patricia said, "You know what I like best? Your first thought was for the two girls who have been struggling with a very difficult situation."

"Those girls have needed an adult to be on their side," Rachel agreed.

"Craig is on their side," Esther pointed out.

"He's also *involved*. You asked him to see *his* life from *their* perspective." Rachel pounded hard enough to shoot a cloud of flour into her face. "Craig should have seen that and *thanked* you."

"Why, Aunt Rachel," Lacy said, "you've gone all white."

Esther felt the moment crystallize inside her. The flash of realization went far deeper than just the issues with Craig. Up to that point, she had been involved in the public warnings mostly on a mental level. She understood her motives. She analyzed the events and knew she had to act. She was objective. She was . . .

Removed. Distant.

This was different.

Craig's earlier question came alive in her mind and heart. *Why was she doing this?*

Esther said softly, "I understand."

"I wish I did," Rachel said.

This was what it meant, to care for one another. To lift one another's burdens. To offer light in a dark hour. To counsel. To . . .

To *care*.

Esther wished desperately for Craig to be here now. So she could share this realization with him. She confessed, "I miss him."

Patricia asked, "Should I call him?"

"Sure can't be me," Rachel said, with a last punch at the dough. "I'd only yell at him."

Patricia flicked a strand of hair from her eyes. "Would you like a cup of tea?"

"That would be nice, thank you."

She watched Patricia wash her hands, set the kettle on the stove, and stretch aluminum foil over the tray of chicken. Internally she observed the various strands of her life coalescing and weaving and binding. Her fears, Craig, these people, Talmadge, Jasmine, Keith, her years of study, the books of calculations, even her splintered childhood. She had the sense that she had been on some odd form of pilgrimage, one that had lasted from her parents' funerals to this moment. It was only now, as she smiled her thanks and accepted the steaming mug, that it made some kind of sense. The knowledge of what she needed to do next was so clear, so vividly simple, Esther knew it was simply the next stage. "There's another problem I need your advice on," Esther said. "It has to do with my brother."

When she finished explaining the situation, the calamitous choice she faced, all three women had stopped work. They stared with a unified expression. Patricia needed a moment to find her voice. "Esther, honey, how long has this been going on?"

"The accident was seven months ago."

"Why haven't you *told* us?"

The truth, so simply asked, left her unable to stop the tears. "It's how I've lived my whole life. Alone."

32

Patricia insisted that Esther stay for dinner. Five minutes later, Donald pulled into the drive, followed by Rachel's husband and daughter. The evening was warm enough for them to sit outside and dine by the sunset's glow. After dinner Esther took a seat by a side wall somewhat removed from the family. The others left her alone, accustomed as they were to her quiet reserve. Then Lacy settled on the bench beside her and said, "I've been assured that it gets better. Well, not better. Easier. And then after a while the pain backs off, and we'll be able to breathe and think like human beings again."

Esther wondered at this poised young lady who had no difficulty offering advice on romance to a woman a dozen years older. "What if I don't want it to get better?"

Lacy's smile seemed forced. "What tiny portion of this has anything to do with what we want? Please tell me. My parents keep going on about how it's probably all for the best."

Patricia walked out to the deck and said, "Donald wants to ask you about your brother . . . I'm sorry, what's his name?"

"Nathan."

"I hope it's okay that I told him about it."

Esther rose from her chair. "Of course."

For a specialist who had just returned from twelve hours in surgery, Donald showed remarkable interest. Esther explained the decision she faced, assuming that would be enough for anyone. But he gently insisted she start at the beginning. She relived the awful night of the accident, how she had arrived at the hospital only minutes after the two of them had been brought in. She had held Nathan's hand as he was rolled from the ER into surgery.

Esther's mind remained caught by the flash of horror that still brought her out of the deepest sleep some nights, the female ER doctor coming out of the other alcove with one shake of her head at the chief resident, her gown still stained, her face creased with the futile battle for a life she had just lost. . . .

Donald waited her out, then pressed forward. The others had stopped pretending not to listen by this point, which in some odd way actually made the telling easier. Patricia had seated herself beside Esther and now held her hand. Donald asked if she remembered the specific injuries the surgeon had treated. Esther replied that she remembered everything.

Donald had very little to say about it all, except to ask if he might drop by and speak with the rehab clinic's doctor. Esther almost wept at the thought of being able to put off the dreadful decision about moving Nathan. He smiled at her gratitude and pretended not to notice her tears.

She returned home an emotional wreck. She had talked more about herself that afternoon and evening than . . . well, forever, really.

She spent a futile half hour studying the markets, but the screens might as well have been showing a message from Mars for all the sense they made. She finally admitted defeat and got ready for bed. But she knew she wouldn't sleep. All the memories and emotions were still there, crowding her bedroom.

She returned to her office and pulled her Bible off the bookshelf. She settled into the bed and read from the book of Esther. When she finally shut off the light, she continued to hear her father's voice, reading the passages and then describing what it might have looked like, what Esther might have felt and experienced. As she drifted off to sleep, she could almost feel the touch of his hand.

Tuesday

Esther overslept for the second time in a week. She awoke in such a luxurious obliviousness, she needed a moment to realize . . .

She was due on air in thirty-three minutes.

Esther bolted from bed and raced through dressing herself, skipped cosmetics entirely, blessed the automatic timer on her coffeemaker, took a single insulated mug with her, and was out the door in twelve minutes flat.

When her phone rang and she saw that it was the clinic, she almost let it go to voicemail. But the sense of obligation was too ingrained. She answered with a hurried, "Can I call you back in an hour?"

For the first time ever, the clinic's doctor had lost his assertive rush. "Ah, perhaps it would be best . . ."

Dr. Carter Cleveland was a man ruled by an utterly unflappable confidence. The hesitancy rang Esther's alarm bells. "What's the matter with Nathan?"

"Nothing . . . That is, nothing more than usual."

"What aren't you saying?" When he remained silent, she almost shouted, *"Tell me."*

"I've had a word with Dr. Donald Saunders."

"And?"

"He wants to arrange for your brother to undergo several more tests."

Esther wished she could reach through the phone and shake him. "I'm driving at near sixty on city streets because I'm due on air in eleven minutes. Either tell me why you called or—"

"We can't do these tests here. It means transporting your brother to the hospital."

"Are you saying he can't come back?"

"Well, no. But any movement of your brother carries risk."

"I don't understand. You're worried about transporting my brother down the block when you are *forcing* me to move him to another *city?*"

"We're not . . . Look, I just wanted to make sure you were in agreement here."

"The answer is *yes*."

"After all, you are his guardian."

"That is correct." She raced through a caution light and took the final corner far too fast. "I have to go. I'll stop by the clinic later."

The same harried aide was pacing outside the station's main door. As Esther cut her motor, he shouted, "You're on in three minutes!"

Esther did not waste breath on a response. Together they rushed across the foyer, aiming for the door the receptionist had already buzzed open. They passed the station director who said something Esther did not bother to hear. Onto the sound stage, across the darkened cement floor, halting behind the central camera.

A voice called over the intercom, "Ninety seconds break."

Suzie McManning gave Esther a serene smile. "I told them you'd show up, and on time."

The makeup lady straightened Esther's hair and decided, "I'm not going to do your face. You'll only sweat it off."

"Dab a little powder over that sheen on her nose and forehead," Suzie said. "She'll be just fine."

"Thirty seconds," the techie said.

Suzie asked, "Are you ready?"

"Not a bit," Esther replied.

Suzie's smile only broadened. "This is going to be fun."

• • •

"We're back with Esther Larsen, senior analyst with CFM here in Charlotte, and soon to become our very own financial guru. Welcome, Esther."

"Thank you."

"We have been discussing three issues impacting our nation's economic prospects," Suzie reminded her audience. "First was China, second, the declining economies in the developing nations, and third . . ." She nodded to Esther.

"The financial institutions," Esther supplied. She wished there were some way of slowing down her heart so it didn't cause tremors in each word.

"Are we speaking about our local banks and investment funds, or all of the US, or . . . ?"

"There is no longer any such boundary," Esther replied. She took a quick breath, let it out. "Every major bank in Charlotte now has significant presence overseas. Their investments take place wherever they see a potential profit."

"This is particularly true with the institutions that have investment banking divisions?"

"Correct." Esther felt her breathing ease. She was back on her own turf. They were in sync once again.

Or so she assumed. Thankfully, it was not often that one of her analyses was so far off target.

"Your website contains a great deal of useful

information on the role banks currently play in today's economy and tomorrow's potential decline. So rather than deal with it here, I'd suggest the audience take a careful look at your online data."

The comment caught Esther completely off guard. She had expected the entire on-air discussion to center on the banks. She felt a swooping dive of fear, which was only heightened by Suzie's knowing smile.

The newscaster said, "Esther, if you had the opportunity to address our nation's leaders, what would you say?" Suzie waited through a ten-second silence, then pressed, "I assume there is something."

Into the frozen tundra of Esther's scrambling mind rose one coherent thought. She said, "In one of the last speeches before his death, President Abraham Lincoln told Congress, 'I see a crisis approaching that unnerves me and causes me to tremble for the safety of my country. . . . Corporations have been enthroned, and an era of corruption in high places will follow. And the money-power of the country will endeavor to prolong its reign by working upon the prejudices of the people, until all wealth is aggregated in a few hands, and the Republic is destroyed.' "

It was Suzie's turn to pause. "You think that time is now?"

"Perhaps. If nothing is done to stop it. Yes."

34

Esther arrived at the clinic, but the doctor was nowhere to be found, and Nathan was still off-site being tested. She phoned Donald only to be told he was in surgery. She walked down the hall and stood in the doorway to Nathan's room, staring at the empty bed, trying to acclimatize herself to the idea that he soon would be permanently elsewhere. She simply could not see how Donald's assistance and any amount of testing could do more than put off the inevitable.

On the drive home, the realtor handling Nathan's home called to say she had a prospective buyer. They were expected to make a formal offer that afternoon, as soon as the bank approved their loan application. Esther tried to put some enthusiasm into her response, though the news left her both thoughtful and sad.

As she pulled into her driveway, Talmadge phoned to say, "I'm putting together a start-up fund of seventy-five million."

Esther cut the motor and tried to fit the words into her mind. "Say that again."

Talmadge chuckled. "Shaking your tree really is a dandy way to spice up my day."

"Suzie McManning already did that, thank you very much."

"Yeah, I saw that. I thought you recovered well, for somebody who got sideswiped. That quote from Lincoln was a nice touch."

"Let's return to the subject at hand."

"I never left it." Talmadge was enjoying himself enormously. "I talked with a few cronies. They share my concerns. They're near-bout committed to a seed investment of seventy-five big ones."

She found Talmadge's easy manner and down-home strength reassuring enough to ask, "Is near-bout a word?"

"Is where I come from. Two things. They want to meet you for dinner tomorrow. Sit down, eyeball to eyeball, watch how you respond to a dose of Carolina barbecue."

"Done. And the other?"

"They want you to start immediately. I'll have my lawyers draw up the papers. Soon as the money comes in, you put it to work."

She had a dozen reasons to argue, starting with how such a move could threaten her position with the bank. There was nothing in her contract that forbade her from offering outside advice, so long as she did not divulge bank secrets. Otherwise even her conversations with the television station could be classed as a fiduciary breach. But Esther was not interested in excuses, or delays. She could almost hear the counter whirring at the bottom of her website. Counting up the number of people relying on her to get it right and help them stay afloat. So all she said was, "I can do that."

He chuckled. "City Club tomorrow, six o'clock."

She was unlocking her front door when Craig's car pulled in behind her own. The sight was so jarring, the images did not want to fit together. A beaming eleven-year-old skipped up the sidewalk toward her, waving a blue banner over her head. She was followed by her older sister, who for once did not appear to be carrying her burden of rage.

And behind them was Craig.

Esther had imagined various responses to his reappearance. Her reactions altered to fit her mood. Angry, defiant, pleading, sorrowful, hurt . . .

Anything but this.

Abigail stopped directly in front of her, lifted the banner with both hands, and shrieked, "They're all over town!"

"We saw three on the way over here," Samantha agreed.

"Four! I saw four!"

"Whatever."

Esther forced herself to focus on what Abigail held. "It's a bumper sticker."

That caused both girls to laugh. Abigail said, "It's *your* bumper sticker!"

The background was chalk blue, the classic

type done in fluorescent white. The bumper sticker read, *STOP FEEDING THE BEAST.* And underneath in smaller type, *BookOfEsther.info*.

"I wish you could see your face," Samantha said.

"I wish you could see *yours*. You have such a lovely smile." Esther pretended not to see Samantha's blush and turned to their father on the front walk, waiting. "Hello, Craig."

"Hi."

Esther said to the girls, "Why don't you go blast some evil warlocks."

"Evil wizards," Samantha corrected.

"Whatever," Esther replied. "Go."

Craig remained ten feet from her front steps, the penitent struggling for words. "I owe you an apology, Esther. Your words really rocked my world. I didn't handle it well. I'm so sorry."

"It was the wrong time to have that conversation. For a number of reasons."

"Which you tried to tell me." His hands fumbled by his belt, for all the world like he was spinning an invisible cap. "I talked to the girls. They both cried. I never . . . I just wish . . ."

They moved toward each other. She couldn't wait any longer. The strength and goodness of Craig's embrace felt, well, exquisite. Esther whispered, "I've missed you so much."

"I've missed you more," Craig said. "I can't tell you—"

His reply was cut off by an eleven-year-old. "Ew."

Her father said over Esther's shoulder, "I thought you two were inside."

She released him slowly, taking time for a long look into his wonderful eyes, sharing another smile. Then she heard Samantha say, "There's something wrong with your computers. They've all gone blank. And it's not my fault."

35

As Reynolds left the bank, he reflected on how there was a certain electric dread attached to the prospect of shedding someone else's blood.

He walked to his BMW 7-series, slipped behind the wheel, and started the motor. He turned the a/c to high. His was the only space in the bank's parking garage with a view of the outside world. The wall curved down here, allowing him to look eastward, out over the green border of First Ward. Reynolds knew many bank employees assumed he had ordered the dip in the wall as an act of vanity. The amount of time people spent on minutiae never ceased to amaze him.

Reynolds Thane had been born in the Appalachian community of Mountain View, a region of poverty-stricken valleys and roads that went nowhere. The Interstate connecting

Asheville to Tennessee ran forty-seven miles to the north. It might as well have been on the other side of the moon.

His father had run the county's only bank. The old man's greatest legacy had been to die young. Reynolds inherited the bank at the ripe old age of twenty-six. His first big decision as CEO was to sell it to Carolina First Mercantile. His father had been dickering with them for years. Reynolds sealed the deal in a week, but with one new proviso. He was to be made a senior vice-president of CFM. He negotiated hard, insisting the position be hammered out before the deal was signed. He was not after being stuck in another backwater like Mountain View. He was aiming high.

The great mistake made by many of his fellow executives was to discount Reynolds because of his heritage and personality. He had the quiet manner and fierce independence of his Appalachian forebears. His burning ambition, however, was all his own. At the age of forty-nine, Reynolds Thane was named CEO of the eleventh largest bank in the United States.

Reynolds reached into his briefcase for a new disposable cellphone whose number matched the code for that day. He had returned from Bermuda with a dozen of them. He set it on the divider between the front seats and checked his watch. Sir Trevor's call was scheduled to begin in two minutes. He settled back and resumed his walk down memory lane.

His father had been terse with his emotions. The old man had dressed like an undertaker and usually wore an expression to match. Every now and then, however, he had offered his only child a true gem of banking wisdom. The one that came to mind now had followed the old man's heart attack. Reynolds had been seated by his father's hospital bed, wondering if he should reach out and hold the man's hand. Signs of affection between them had been as rare as gold dust.

Then he realized his father was awake and watching him. Reynolds straightened in his seat. He had no idea what his father might say. A final note of pride, perhaps. A message for the man's long-suffering wife. Instead, he coughed weakly and whispered, "Board meeting tomorrow."

Reynolds replied gamely, "I've put it off a week, so you'll have time to recover."

His father lifted one finger from the bedcovers and waved that away. "To rule the world, first you have to rule your lieutenants."

Reynolds leaned forward in his chair. He had never confessed his personal aspirations. Mountain View tended to frown on people who sought to rise above their station.

His father said, "You understand what I'm saying?"

Reynolds cleared his throat. "Choose them wisely."

The old man gave a fractional headshake. "Select the one most disposable. Find his weakness. Make sure he knows you know. Take him down. Make it public. Make it slow."

Reynolds had still been recovering from that little gem when his father swiveled his gaze to the bedside table. Reynolds lifted the water glass and fit the straw into his father's mouth. The old man swallowed once, coughed, and said, "Make no mistake. So long as the money is parked in our vault, it's ours. We might tell the public we hold it in trust, but that's nonsense."

Reynolds repeated something he had often heard the old man say. "Possession is ninety-nine percent of the law."

His father's eyes flashed with what Reynolds hoped was approval. "Never is that more true than with somebody else's cash. We pay them a fair market return. That's the end of their involvement. It's ours to do with as we want."

Now, as Reynolds sat in his leather-lined car, he wondered what his father would think of all this. Merging CFM with a global behemoth. Doing it to mask another tactic. Taking these risks. All so he could join the most exclusive club on earth. The handful of people who could attach the word *billionaire* to their names.

By the time his phone rang, Reynolds had

decided his father would be absolutely comfortable with the recent turn of events.

"I'm ready," he said into the receiver.

And he was.

Sir Trevor demanded, "Have you heard about yesterday's outflow?"

"I have. Yes."

"The sixteen US banks your Larsen identified as high risk lost six hundred million dollars. In one business day."

"There's no way reporters could be certain of that figure," Reynolds said. "That information is highly confidential and—"

"Ah, but there *is* a way." Sir Trevor clipped off the end of each word. Like he carved them from a block of ice. "All it requires are allies inside each of the sixteen banks. People who are willing to break corporate rules and volunteer this information. To the *Wall Street Journal*, no less."

"All sixteen institutions have denied the information is true."

"What other choice do they have? Confess to the world that your Larsen's efforts are impacting their balance sheets?"

"She's not *my* anything," Reynolds countered.

"Only because you don't control her." Sir Trevor gave that a frigid beat, then continued, "I hear those bumper stickers of hers are *every-*

where. I spotted several this morning even here in *London.*"

"I've cut off her access to our system, a warning shot across her bow."

"I don't want her warned. I want her *gone.* She must be *eradicated.*"

"Understood." Reynolds leaned back in his seat, satisfied. His sole aim for this conversation had been for Sir Trevor to take ownership of the action. Reynolds already knew this was to be their course. "This line isn't secure. Maybe we had better—"

"We don't have time for that. This is *most urgent.* I fielded a call this morning from my ally at the *Financial Times.* They have heard rumors of our merger."

This was news. And most unwelcome. "We have to move things up."

"I agree."

"So we go public," Reynolds said. "Tomorrow."

"Which means we have no choice but to accelerate our other actions," Sir Trevor added.

"The markets are stable," Reynolds said. "We don't have the lever."

"Ah, but that is where you are wrong. You are hardly the only friend I have in high places."

"I haven't heard a thing—"

"Because *your* allies are focused on *your* markets, correct?"

"Tell me what you've heard."

Sir Trevor swiftly related two items.

Reynolds's mind swirled. "Are these for real?"

"I do not bandy in rumors. Not at this stage."

"I'm going to go shake a few trees," Reynolds said.

"You do that. And just so we are perfectly in sync . . ."

He nodded to the sunlight. The adrenaline rush was exquisite. "Larsen is all but erased."

Jason Bremmer called ten minutes later. They had arranged for a daily check-in to follow the call with Sir Trevor. Reynolds wished his senior trader a good morning and then waited patiently as he was given a summary of their secret trading arm's current positions, scarcely hearing a word.

When Jason was done, Reynolds said, "It's time for you to reconsider your options."

Reynolds heard the quick intake of breath, the tight swallow. Then Jason asked, "You mean . . . ?"

"Exactly what I said," Reynolds replied. "Exactly what we discussed."

"I'll need thirty-six hours."

"Then there's not a moment to lose." Reynolds ended the call.

36

Esther had never been more thankful for Talmadge's support than when she called to report, "CFM has severed my home access to the bank's system. My data array has gone blank. I feel like I can't breathe."

"Explain that to me in words my grandkids might understand."

But ninety seconds into her explanation, Talmadge cut her off and said he had no idea what she was talking about or why this was so important, except for one thing. "This means the bank is worried."

"Upset is probably a better way to describe it. Irritated. Like swatting a fly."

"Did you see today's article in the *Journal*, the one talking about the six hundred million outflow from your enemy banks?"

"They're not my enemies, but yes, I saw it." She hesitated, then added, "I heard from a friend in New York this morning. The ante is over a billion now."

"I got an office with your name on the door."

"I have an office, thank you very much."

He laughed out loud. "You best jump while you still can. Before they shove you off the cliff themselves."

"I'm thinking about that."

"You do that. Stay close to your phone. I'll have somebody who speaks geek call you right back."

Less than three minutes later, a young woman phoned, breathless from having just received a call from the company owner. Yes, she understood what Esther needed. Yes, Burroughs Motors had access to a financial data array. Their provider was far less sophisticated than the one the bank used, but the technician assured her that Talmadge had already signed off on anything extra she might require. The young woman did not try to hide her envy when Esther mentioned that her home was linked by fiber-optic cable. Ten minutes more and Esther's screens came back to life.

Samantha and Abigail were offered two of Esther's laptops for their e-game, but the girls preferred watching Esther learn to navigate the new system. Craig went to a deli and came back with sandwiches, and they ate a late lunch in her office. Esther described her new hedge fund and explained her need to have it all in place before close of business the next day. She knew the girls did not understand much of what she was saying. But both of them seemed to like how she spoke to them as adults, introducing them to a different world. Craig said little, though his eyes rarely left her.

After the meal, Abigail helped Esther clean up

while Samantha returned to her game, which she assured them with teenage intensity was an extremely serious matter. Craig moved to the dining room table to work on a talk he was delivering at church that evening.

Abigail helped wrap the remaining sandwiches and pickles in plastic and stowed them in the fridge. As Esther rinsed the plates and loaded the dishwasher, Abigail put the wrappings in the garbage, then accepted Esther's offer of Häagen-Dazs Rocky Road, which Esther explained was her emergency comfort food.

Midway through the bowl of ice cream, Abigail declared around a bite, "My mom and her new husband never hug each other."

Esther's movements became slow as she sorted through her thoughts, looking for the proper response. "You mean, your stepfather."

"I don't like that word."

"Okay, fine."

"I call him Hank. Samantha too. That's his name."

"Understood."

Abigail inspected her reflection in the spoon. "Hank says affection should be kept private."

Esther closed the dishwasher and quietly settled onto the stool opposite Abigail. The doors leading to the dining room were slid shut, but Esther had the distinct impression that Craig was listening.

Abigail went on, "Hank says how a couple express their feelings is between them alone."

Esther asked, "Do you understand the word *diplomatic?*"

Abigail took another bite. "Sort of."

"Diplomatic is like a big suitcase. You open it up and all sorts of things come out."

"I was talking about Mom and Hank."

"I know you were. And I'll listen carefully to whatever you want to tell me. But it would not be diplomatic of me to respond, except to say that I understand. And that I care for you."

Her response caused Abigail's lower lip to tremble. She said to her bowl, "Daddy told us what you said to him. About what we want being important."

Esther simply nodded.

Abigail said, "It made Samantha cry."

A voice from the hall said, "You did too."

"Yeah, but you never cry."

Esther rose and walked to the doorway. She took Samantha by the hand and pulled her into the kitchcn.

Samantha said, "Not one of those hug things again."

"You betcha." Esther embraced the girl, then reached out one arm and gestured for Abigail to join them.

Samantha squirmed at her sister's approach, but not too hard. "Yuck."

Esther held them as tight as she could, breathing in their fresh scent. "You two are so special it makes my heart full just to be in the same room."

They stayed like that for a long moment, until Esther felt Samantha's arm encircle her waist. Then the doors leading to the dining room slid open, and another pair of arms enfolded them all.

Esther closed her eyes and thought how the house was finally becoming a home.

37

At 2:47 that afternoon, the markets hiccupped.

Esther was busy adjusting her new data stream and preparing her presentation to the hedge-fund investors. Then the news ticker crawling across the top of her central screen caused her to gasp.

Craig was seated in the padded chair brought in from her bedroom. "What's the matter?"

Esther remained focused on the screens and waved him quiet.

Samantha and Abigail had fashioned a corner alcove from throw cushions and quilts. They rose from their game and came over to see what was going on. Abigail said, "Can you really understand all those graphs and—"

"Hold that thought." Esther sensed Craig step up beside his daughters. She scrolled back on the news item. " 'Spain has called for snap elections.' "

Craig asked, "Why is that important?"

Esther checked the wall display to her left, six clocks in global array. It was eight o'clock in the evening in Europe. That might give the markets time to digest the news before tomorrow's opening.

"Esther, what's wrong?" Craig asked.

"Spain is the EU's largest debtor nation. As a percentage of total GDP, their national debt is still considered by most experts to be manageable. But it is a huge burden, and a growing percentage of the nation is in revolt against the required austerity to make the repayment schedule. This has been imposed by the other EU nations, especially Germany." She looked up at him. "Spain's most recent municipal elections have brought in two new political parties. One is intent on seceding Spain's richest province from the nation. The other is demanding debt relief. It looks like they will be able to form a majority alliance and take over the national government."

"Like Greece?"

"No, Craig, *not* like Greece." She could hear the tight edge in her voice, but couldn't do anything about it. "Spain is *ten times* the size of Greece's economy. If a new Spanish government invalidates the debt agreements, Europe hits the wall."

Samantha said, "So this is bad, right?"

"At this point, it's just another news item." She switched two screens to view the US markets.

The controls were slightly different from those she was used to, and the time lag of several seconds only heightened her concerns. "Elections are set for seven days. Hopefully the markets can hold steady until . . ."

When the second news item slid across the screen, she felt the breath lock in her throat.

"Esther?"

"No, no, no, no."

"What?"

"Japan's government just announced it's gone back into recession. That means their last public growth estimate was *three percent* off."

"Why has the ribbon at the bottom of your screen gone all red?" Samantha asked.

"The US markets responded to the news by going into panic mode." Esther pointed to the graphs on the central monitor. "This shows the Dow ticking downward. To have a visual shift in the entire market, within the space of less than a minute, means only one thing: a huge sell-off."

When the phone rang, Esther put it on speaker without taking her eyes off the screen. "Larsen."

Jasmine asked, "Are you watching this?"

"Yes."

Esther's rock-solid number two actually stammered, "Is . . . is this it?"

"Not yet."

"For real, or are you saying that just to get me down off the ceiling?"

"Analysts are not allowed to climb the walls. It's in our contract. Is Jason in the building?"

"He was this morning."

"Go tell him to hedge the downside. Aim for nine hundred points below the market's opening position."

"You really think the market will stabilize?"

"Yes. Which means the bank can still profit from this turmoil. If they act immediately."

Jasmine said slowly, "You know the traders are barking that the bank should liquidate their positions."

"That would only add to the decline, and the panic, and the loss. Hedge is better."

"Nine hundred point floor. Got it."

"Hurry." Then the previous day's fears struck with the force of a hammer. "Wait! Are you still there?"

"Yes."

"Have you located Hewitt?"

"Have I . . . ? Esther, we're in crisis mode here. I can't be worrying about some—"

"This is *important*. You have to *find him*."

"Okay, okay."

"*Now,* Jasmine. Once you speak with Jason, locating Hewitt is your absolute number-one priority." Esther had not pulled her hand away from the phone when it rang again. "Larsen."

Suzie McManning asked, "Can you come in?"

"What, right now?"

"Our session this morning has gone national. Bloomberg played it twice. We want to lead as soon as the market closes."

"On my way." Esther swiveled her chair around. Three sets of staring eyes watched her as she asked, "How would you like to see inside a television studio?"

38

Esther had disliked the feel of the cosmetician's fingers on her face. The smell of cigarette ashes had lingered through much of the first broadcast. So Esther took time now and did her best job. She would touch up with powder before going on, if she had time. Otherwise she was fine.

When the phone rang and she saw it was the clinic, she answered, "Is this an absolute emergency?"

"Esther, this is Dr. Cleveland. I have—"

"How is Nathan?"

The doctor was clearly not accustomed to her taking control. "Nathan is, well, there's no change. But—"

"In that case, this needs to wait until tomorrow."

"I'm afraid that's not—"

"Listen very carefully. I have a stock market in full panic. I am scheduled to be on air in twenty-six minutes. This conversation is over."

"But—"

She cut the connection. Samantha, seated on the padded cushion of the front window box, said, "You look nice."

"Thank you." Esther checked her reflection in the glass. She wore a midnight-blue Lauren suit with a silk blouse cut like a man's tuxedo shirt. Ferragamo pumps. "I think I used too much hair spray."

"I can't tell." Samantha pointed at the phone on her bed. "Are you always so . . . ?"

"Bossy," Esther finished for her. "Hardly ever. But that doctor . . . I don't know. I think he likes to bully people."

"He treats your brother?"

"*Treat* is not the right word. He runs the rehab clinic." She picked up her purse. "Is it okay if we don't talk about Nathan right now?"

"Sure."

"It's just . . . talking about him makes me sad, and I need to focus."

"Hey, you don't *ever* have to explain that to me." Samantha rose to her feet. "You're sure it's cool, showing up with your posse?"

Esther waved her toward the door. "I think it's great."

They quickly decided to all go in Esther's car. Once they were under way, she connected the hands-free and made a call. "Talmadge, it's Esther."

"Of course it's you." His voice filled the car.

"I don't give out my private line to so many folks, I can't recognize their number."

Abigail said softly, "He's rude."

"He thinks he can get away with it," Esther said, "because he's rich."

Talmadge demanded, "Who's that listening in on what I thought was a private conversation?"

"Friends."

"And what does that make me, fried catfish?"

Esther loved having a reason to smile on such a dark afternoon. "I assume you're aware of what's happening."

"Watching and sweating. Is this the big one?"

"I don't think so. No."

He actually sighed. "Okay, I can fit my heart back into my chest again. Long as you're sure."

"Call it eighty percent certain."

"That'll have to do. Where are you now?"

"On my way to the station. They want to do a live feed after the closing bell."

"Yeah, Chuck already passed along that news flash. Looks like they'll want you on every evening."

"In that case, we need to postpone tomorrow's dinner with your investors."

"I got a better idea," Talmadge replied. "Let's have our meeting at the station. We'll come on over and watch you scare the living daylights out of folks."

Esther did not know how she felt about more

people observing from behind the cameras, but she just said, "I'll see you there." She said good-bye, then glanced over to Samantha in the passenger seat. "Anything?"

The girl was busy scrolling through the news feeds on Esther's tablet. She said, "There's another thing here about Japan."

"Read it to me." In truth, Esther did not need to hear it. It was only the pundits responding now. There would not be anything real until the Far East markets opened. But she liked having the girl feel engaged. Craig was seated behind his daughter, Abigail beside him. Esther liked having them all together in one car. She was certain someone from the station could drive them home if necessary. After all, she was doing a daily show now. They had not even discussed a paycheck. The least the station could do was provide her posse a lift home.

Abigail crowded forward between the two seats and shrilled, "There's another one!"

A maroon Nissan in the next lane had a *BookOfEsther.info* bumper sticker. Samantha said, "Blue on a purple car? Puh-leese."

"You are too much," Esther said.

"That makes *six*," Abigail said. "On *this trip* alone."

Esther said, "Check the market."

Samantha's nimble fingers found it easily. "Down another three eighty."

Craig asked, "Is that bad?"

"It's not good. But at least the downward slide isn't as fast—" Her phone rang. She hit the hands-free button on her steering wheel. "Larsen."

"Ms. Larsen, this is Emily Waters with *Good Morning America.*"

Esther saw Samantha's eyes go round. In the rearview mirror Abigail mouthed a silent *Wow!* to her dad. Esther said, "Yes, Emily."

"We'd like to invite you back again for tomorrow morning's show."

"I'm more than happy to participate," Esther replied. "So long as Suzie McManning handles the session."

"I'm afraid that's not possible."

"Then I can't accept. Sorry."

Emily Waters was clearly not accustomed to being turned down. "Ms. Larsen, there could not possibly be a greater boost to your publicity efforts than appearing on *GMA.* Our presenters—"

"Are the best in the world at infotainment," Esther said, cutting the woman off. "I absolutely agree. And that is *precisely* why I will work only with Suzie."

Emily Waters revealed a terse New York edge. "We design our program to appeal to the largest possible audience. A *national* audience, Ms. Larsen."

"But this is *not* entertainment. You're calling because the market has taken a serious nosedive, and people are afraid. I want to respond to this in a businesslike fashion. Suzie is part of the package."

There was a moment's silence, then, "We could perhaps offer to carry the feed on our affiliate business-news channels."

"Same answer as before," Esther said.

The woman's voice had lost all hint of civility. "I'll have to get back to you."

"Great." Esther cut the connection, then added, "You do that."

Samantha stared over at her. "That was so totally *ice*."

Esther liked having a reason to grin. "Glad you approve. Now check the markets one more time. We're almost there."

39

Wednesday

Reynolds Thane spent six long hours reviewing accounts and income figures with the bank's various divisions. It was all for show. On Monday he was scheduled to make his final quarterly report to the market analysts. But if their plans unfolded as they should, the world's attention would be elsewhere come Monday morning.

Running the numbers and building a prediction of the next quarter's profits was normally one of his more pleasant responsibilities. But today was different, and not just because of the events he and Sir Trevor were putting in place. As expected, the previous afternoon's turmoil in Spain and Japan continued to impact Wall Street. The markets were initially down, including CFM's shares. But by midafternoon it appeared that a floor had been realized. The fact that this was precisely what Esther Larsen had predicted, in contrast to most of the other on-air pundits, was repeatedly mentioned by the banks' senior executives. They intended their comments as compliments. After all, Larsen was CFM's top analyst. They assumed Reynolds would be delighted. Reynolds pretended to enjoy their banter.

The meetings finally ended just as Wall Street halted the day's trading. Because of Esther Larsen, the bank actually realized a profit over the two days of turmoil. Reynolds invited the senior executives from each division to meet with him on the investment bank's trading floor. Jason was at the back of the giant cube when Reynolds arrived. He followed his boss as Reynolds slowly made his way among the traders, shaking hands, thanking them personally, promising each trader a substantial bonus for their loyalty through a difficult period, watching the scowls and the resentment wilt beneath the force of his charm. By the time he arrived at the front, the open space at the back and the aisles were crammed with people from other divisions.

He stood beneath the massive flat-screen monitors. Above his head was displayed the intel from markets all over the globe. He had started to suggest the screens be shut off, then decided the data stream made for a fitting background. They were, after all, entering into a global venture with one of Europe's largest and oldest banks. So Reynolds began his presentation with a smile and sweep of his hands, taking in the markets and all the opportunities they represented.

His announcement drew no surprised murmurs, which confirmed the need to do this now. Draw in his troops by affirming the rumors were indeed facts. Show them how this magnified their opportunities. Assure them that everyone present was part of the new future.

Start to finish, it required only seven minutes. He could see a few questioning expressions, but then some of the bank's older employees had entered the firm expecting lifetime employment in a bank with steady if unimaginative growth. Reynolds pitied them. They belonged to a bygone era. Banking had moved on. There was really no place for them now.

In the midst of what should have been a successful conclusion to his singular performance, every eye rose to the monitors overhead. Reluctantly he turned and found himself watching an alert for another session from Esther

Larsen and Suzie McManning, due to start immediately following Market Roundup.

Reynolds dismissed the image with a sweep of his hand and a smile. Most eyes were on him, so that few saw Jason savagely order the nearest trader to switch channels. When Larsen's picture was replaced, Reynolds made his way back down the central aisle, shaking hands, taking it slow, keeping his simmering rage down where it did not show.

When the executives departed, Reynolds gave the bank's head of PR the green light to alert the press. Then he and Jason stood isolated by the normal trading clamor. Reynolds said, "I assume there's no need to ask about our conversation yesterday."

Jason shook his head, tight as a boxer throwing off sweat. "As of tonight, there won't be an issue that requires our discussion at all."

"Glad to hear it." Reynolds kept his smile in place for all the watchful traders. "Between now and then, Larsen needs to understand how vital it is for her findings to remain in-house."

"Agreed."

"I'll have my assistant track her down. I will then lay it out in black and white. Those on-air chats end now."

"You sure you don't want me to handle this?"

"What I want," Reynolds said, "is for you to get ready for the arrival of more funds."

The senior trader glanced at the monitors. "The markets are down substantially, which means we can reap the whirlwind."

Reynolds reflected that the man had never spoken truer words, only not for the reasons he thought. All he said was, "I want you to hold everything in cash until tomorrow."

Jason turned to him. "You have word of something?"

"I do indeed," Reynolds said.

"Big enough to impact our secret trades?"

"Without question."

"Will you tell me?"

"Soon. You'll receive your team's marching orders by midnight tomorrow."

Jason nodded. "You're certain these events will create upheaval?"

Reynolds smiled at the screens on the side wall. "Be ready to move as soon as word comes in."

"How much more are you putting on the table?"

"Another four billion."

"In that case," Jason said, "it's important I leave for Bermuda. Right now, as a matter of fact."

"Have a pleasant flight." Reynolds bore his bland smile back through the corridor and into the elevator. Not even then did he release his rage. These days, cameras were everywhere. He stared at his reflection in the mottled bronze doors and took comfort in his absence of remorse.

There was a blithe satisfaction to the act of murder by proxy. Besides which, the woman had intruded upon his moment in the spotlight. She deserved her fate.

40

Esther spent most of Wednesday sequestered with Talmadge's attorneys, jumping through the legal hoops required to set up her hedge fund. Talmadge had instructed them to have the project up and running by close of business, and as a result the process moved swiftly. Even so, it made for a long and tiring day.

Added to this was the need to watch the markets. Wall Street opened down, fell further for the first hour and a half, then began to steadily make up at least some of the lost ground. By midday Esther was fairly certain her predictions had proven correct. Jasmine called an hour later to congratulate her for, as she put it, boosting the bank's bottom line.

Esther drove straight from the lawyers to the clinic, where the duty nurse told her that Dr. Cleveland had been called away on a personal matter, but that he very much wanted to speak with her as soon as he returned. Esther counted the doctor's absence as an unexpected gift. She spent time with Nathan, then spoke by phone with Craig, who promised to stop by later. He actually laughed out loud when Esther asked if the girls were free to join them.

Then the realtor for Nathan's home called to say she had received the formal contract. Esther drove to the realtor's office and signed the papers, both relieved and saddened. Next it was time for her to leave for the television studio.

Esther was parking her car when the phone rang again. She answered it, and Jason's assistant said, "Glad I caught you. Reynolds Thane would like a word."

She waved to where Craig and his girls were climbing out of their car. "Sorry. No."

"I know you're on vacation, Esther, but you really need to take this call. Jason was on the trading floor with Mr. Thane when the wall monitors flashed an alert about your doing another televised interview. I saw them. Reynolds did a better job at hiding his reaction, but I can tell you they were both extremely displeased."

She turned toward the west. The late-afternoon sun cut silhouettes from a stand of tall pines. "Tell them I resign."

"Excuse me?"

A flood of reasons and logic poured in now. "It's time."

"I'm sorry, I don't . . ."

"It's very simple," Esther said. "I quit. Effective immediately."

She put her phone away and stood studying the trees turned luminous by the descending sun.

"It had to be done," she said softly.

Craig had overheard her side of the conversation. To his credit, he did not question her actions. He merely asked, "Are you all right?"

She turned to face him. "I'm fine."

And she was.

Suzie McManning watched Esther seat herself under the lights and greeted her with, "Some of the pundits you proved wrong with your analysis yesterday are not pleased."

"I suppose that's inevitable."

"They want you drawn and quartered, burned at the stake, and made to walk the plank. In that order."

A man behind the cameras said, "We are live in three minutes."

Suzie checked her reflection in a hand mirror from the pocket of her jacket. "Sure you don't want makeup to check you over?"

"I'm good. Besides, you're the star." Esther liked the woman's smile, smooth and confident, a glow about her that served as a magnet on camera. "Are you going to hit me with another unexpected shot today?"

"If I can. It brings out the best in you."

"I'm not sure about that."

"I am." Suzie straightened the lapels on her

jacket. "That suit looks great on you. What is it?"

"Ralph Lauren."

The man in the shadows behind the cameras wore a single-ear headset with a plastic mike. He lifted the clipboard and said, "Sixty seconds."

Suzie shot her a look, and Esther had the impression it was the first time she'd gotten a glimpse beneath the professional veneer. "Everybody around here is talking about what you said to New York. We're still waiting for their decision. Just so we're clear, either way, I owe you."

The man said, "We are live in three, two, one . . ."

"We have experienced another turbulent trading period," Suzie McManning began. "At its lowest point, the Dow plummeted 1,114 points in heavy trading. But by today's close it had regained almost 400 points. With me now is Esther Larsen, senior analyst with CFM. Esther, how can you help our viewers make sense of this?"

She started to correct Suzie, to explain she was no longer employed by the bank, but then realized she should have mentioned it before-hand. Now it would have to wait.

Suzie caught her hesitation and smiled. "Hard to know where to begin."

"Actually, it's tragically simple," Esther said.

"Since yesterday's dive, most analysts have been pointing at the situations in Japan and Spain. But they are merely the triggers. The real problem is what has been growing in the shadows."

Suzie nodded, which surprised Esther. "You are speaking of the electronic trading system that operates outside Wall Street's traditional boundaries."

Esther leaned forward slightly. "You're worried too, aren't you?"

"Anyone who studies the markets would have to be," Suzie said.

"I'm not talking about just the past two days."

"And neither am I." Suzie's smile remained comfortably in place. "Answer the question, please."

Esther supposed some people would find Suzie's methods to be offensive. But she liked it. Two concerned women, discussing issues for which there wasn't enough time.

"Over the past nine years there has been a huge upswing in electronic trading," Esther said.

Suzie interpreted that. "Trades that happen between one financial institution and another, with total disregard for Wall Street's system of controls."

"That is correct. It's not just the size of these trades that has created concern, but the speed. Market overseers now know that a growing number of financial groups are applying algorithms originally developed for the derivatives trade to the stock market."

"To remind our viewers, algorithms are formulas used to interpret mathematical data in real-time situations, such as linking us to our computers."

"Nowadays these electronic trades are referred to as *algos*," Esther said. "The growing trade in algos has become a real enemy."

The seven men and six women Talmadge had drawn together were seated in two rows of folding chairs at the studio's far end. All Esther could see of them were fourteen motionless shadows. Craig and his daughters stood clustered to their right. The Exit sign illuminated Craig's arms draped over their shoulders, holding them close. Esther found it far easier to direct her words to the girls. If she could make it clear to them, perhaps the audience would understand the urgent need. And then act while there was still time. Perhaps.

Esther went on, "Every major investment banking division now operates computer-driven stock trades. Their algorithms are designed to respond to set conditions. For example, they might say if the stock market declines fifteen percent in one trading day, the computers will then sell every share the bank owns."

Suzie asked, "Can you give us a real-world example?"

"Sure. Some of these highly secretive actions have become public knowledge through court documents. For example, four years ago Citigroup devised a program they called Dagger that compared the price difference between identical shares of the same company on two different markets, say, Tokyo and New York. Whenever a discrepancy was identified, the program immediately bought hundreds of thousands of shares on one market and at the same time dumped these shares on the other. The difference in price was a matter of pennies. But the result was a wild swing in the company's value. And no one knew what was going on until it was over."

Suzie asked, "How fast would such trades happen?"

Esther nodded. That was the issue. "Too fast for a human to counteract the order."

"You're saying that, in a crisis, these computer systems might dump shares in a heartbeat?"

"Oh, no," Esther replied. "A heartbeat is far too slow a measurement."

Reynolds drove the sunset streets toward his home in Myers Park, listening to yet another discussion between the bank's former chief analyst and Suzie McManning. Esther Larsen's casual rejection of his command to appear had shocked him. Reynolds tried to tell himself that Larsen had merely become addicted to the limelight and saw herself building a public profile. But in truth he thought it was something else entirely. Larsen had sacrificed her position with the bank in order to speak her mind. She was passionate about her concerns. She felt this was her duty.

There was nothing so dangerous as an individual with a cause.

Reynolds listened as Esther Larsen drew closer to his and Sir Trevor's true aims with every word she spoke. He clenched the wheel at the sudden sensation of her breath on his neck.

He jerked in surprise when his phone rang, cutting Larsen's next comment off in mid-sentence. The car's screen showed a blocked number. "Yes?"

"It's Jason. I thought I should check in." The man's normal air of aggressive fury was gone, replaced with an uncharacteristic uncertainty. "You know, just in case . . ."

"Nothing's changed."

"You're absolutely sure. Because once this thing gets set in motion—"

"Jason, I want you to listen very carefully. Do. It. Now."

Jason breathed hard, twice, three times, then said, "They are putting things in place as we speak."

"Good." Reynolds cut the connection and then turned off his radio. Punch the right button, silence the pesky woman for good. It was that simple.

41

Esther felt more intensely than ever the audience beyond the cameras. She told Suzie, "When investment banks started their algorithm-based trades, they instantly discovered that the standard fiber-optic communication systems slowed them down."

Suzie emphasized, "The fastest communication systems in the world were too slow."

"They *were* the fastest, but they're not any longer," Esther replied. "Remember what we talked about earlier, the defining trait of all investment banks?"

Suzie was ready for that. "They operate cross-border."

"For these financial institutions, national boundaries *don't exist*. That is why downturns like today's are no longer restricted to one nation."

"How does this tie to algo trades?"

"The trader who gets in and out first makes the biggest bucks. For these computer-driven algo systems to operate, the banks needed faster communications. The fastest bank to act was the one making the biggest profits from each trade. So they laid their own undersea cables. Then these owners were beat out by banks who bought satellite bandwidth."

"Which I assume most of these big traders are now using," Suzie said. "What is faster than that?"

"Nothing. Yet. That is why some algo traders started cheating. Circumventing the standard system with its checks and balances, inserting their algorithms into the communication links between markets, telling their computers to respond *instantly* to shifts in market trends."

Esther could hear the tension building in her voice, the acceleration of her words, the intensity of her fears. Suzie caught it as well. Her own voice dropped an octave. "Tell our audience why this is so crucial."

"Speed," Esther repeated. "The time frame has become so small, there's no room for human input. Which means there are no brakes."

Suzie moved in tight. "That is the crux of the matter, isn't it? The speed."

"The banks have put in place a system that interacts with other systems. Independent of humans. Free of legal checks and balances. All this is kept highly confidential. Investment banks and hedge funds don't want outsiders interfering in their profits. But the few non-bank mathematicians who have had a chance to study these algorithms say they have now taken on symptoms of what is known as emergent behavior."

Suzie nodded once, but did not speak.

"Emergent behavior is one component of a

biological system. An *independent* system. In this case, one system will structure its algorithms around the command that if blue-chip stocks sink by, say, five percent, it sells all high-risk stocks. This sets up an alarm in a *second* system, which then sells all the bonds in their portfolio holding junk status. This alerts a *third* system, which sells every European stock the bank holds. Then a fourth, and a fifth, and a sixth."

Suzie asked, "And all this happens how fast?"

"All six events can take place in the span of three seconds," Esther answered. "Perhaps less."

"And these trades hold how much value, Esther?"

"Billions."

Suzie nodded. "Can you give us at least one example, sort of put flesh to the bones?"

"Right. Court records recently revealed that in 2011, US banks made fifty-five billion dollars from credit swaps, a form of derivative trading that relies on this kind of speed. That sum represented thirty-seven percent of all the profits made by the banks during that period."

"So what you're saying is that these trades are now large enough to create the sort of downward spiral we viewed today." Suzie leaned back. "We're almost out of time. Esther. What measures can our viewers take to halt the next downward spiral?"

"Write to your congressman and senator and our

president," Esther said. "Urge them to institute three new laws. First, regulate the hedge fund industry just like they do banks. Second, establish caps that limit the speed and scope of the algo-trading system. Insulate the economy from these institutions and their absurdly dangerous behavior. Third, require all financial institutions to spin off their investment banking arms. This was proposed after the 2008 recession and championed by two recent presidential candidates, Mike Huckabee and John McCain. In response, lobbyists representing the financial industry spent over a hundred million dollars pressuring Congress. The proposals were quashed. The bills never went forward."

"A hundred million," Suzie repeated.

"In a good week, they make that back."

"In a bad week?"

"We only need to look back to 2008 for that answer," Esther said. "We all pay. And one thing more."

"Yes?"

"Stop feeding the beast," Esther said. "Do no business with *any* financial institution that trades in derivatives."

"But wait a minute. Your own bank has a huge derivatives portfolio."

"It's not mine anymore," Esther replied.

"Excuse me?"

"Before coming on the air, I resigned."

• • •

Talmadge's staff had set up a catered buffet in a disused studio. When they entered the vast windowless chamber, Esther found starched tablecloths covering banquet-style tables, comfortable chairs, even some tall standing lamps. A trio of monitors showed the nightly market report. The buffet contained a delectable array of choices. Most of the station's employees drifted in also, filled plates, and returned to their work. At Talmadge's invitation, Craig and his daughters and Suzie and the station manager joined them at the central table.

The room went silent when the Far East markets again opened sharply down, but Esther was not worried. At Talmadge's request, she stood and explained how the markets responded to panic first, reason second. As she fashioned the words, her tremors returned, as though she were resonating to a concern that her brain had not yet managed to fully shape.

Esther pointed out how the US aftermarket trading remained stable, meaning the floor established by the major hedge funds had not been breached. The nation's markets were not entering free fall. They were safe. This time.

The entire studio went quiet when the news channel re-aired Esther's earlier comments. Both times the program switched from her to gatherings of financial pundits, who responded furiously.

Their voices were caustic, their comments vicious. It sounded to Esther as though they were mortally offended. As though she was personally liable for shaking the markets. They called her deranged. Deluded. Spastic in her knee-jerk responses to what they considered normal trends.

Three seats away, Abigail sniffed loud enough for Talmadge to notice. As Craig hugged his younger daughter, their host leaned forward and said, "Don't you worry about them, missie. It's part of being right."

"They're just so *nasty,*" Abigail said.

"They're afraid of the lady here."

From Abigail's other side, Samantha was fuming. "They don't have to talk like that."

"They got on air by being spiteful. And you know what? The louder they shout, the more folks they drive our way."

Abigail stared at Esther. "But what if they're right?"

Esther's own response was cut off by Suzie McManning speaking from the table's far end. "They're not. I know those people. I've listened to them for years. And one thing you can say about them all. They got where they are by looking backwards. They base their analysis of tomorrow on what happened yesterday. Esther is saying something different. She's saying the old model doesn't work anymore. There's a new structure in place. And it's putting our nation's economy in real danger."

"There, you hear that?" Talmadge leaned back in his seat. "That's why we're here. To try to stop that train before it runs us all over the cliff."

Esther knew Talmadge had used the young girls' concerns as a means of stifling protests that might have arisen from their would-be investors. She knew he was strategizing with every breath. She also knew if it were possible, he would profit from any coming downturn. But it did not impact her growing affection and admiration for the man. He was cantankerous, conniving, and manipulative. But he also possessed a good heart.

Esther faced the two girls. "When I first discussed this issue with your father, he asked me why I was so concerned. Why did I want to become involved? Who was I doing this for?"

Gradually the table went quiet. Esther kept her gaze focused on Samantha and Abigail as she said, "The answer is, I'm doing this for you."

Craig smiled briefly, first at her and then at his daughters, and settled his arm around the back of Abigail's chair.

Esther went on, "I can't focus on a million families out there who have been put in danger. Doing this for the right reasons has meant doing it from the heart. And you've taught me that."

Abigail said, "We didn't do anything."

"You were there when I needed you," Esther

replied. "I've lived by the law of self-sufficiency. What I need, I buy. What I have, I earn. But this action is taking me on a completely different course. You and your sister are helping me come to terms with what that means. I'm doing this because I care for people I'll never meet. I want to help them. I want to keep them safe."

Esther turned to the rest of the group and wondered at the changes in herself. Allowing her to be open to strangers. She finished, "Even when that means doing what comes hardest for me."

42

At the close of the gathering, Esther embraced Craig and his daughters before one of the studio staffers drove them home. She then shook hands with each of her new hedge-fund investors. Last in line stood Talmadge, wearing that canted grin on his face.

It seemed totally natural to hug him as well. She could feel the strength Talmadge required to hold himself erect. He kept his grip on the cane, which meant he could hold her with only one arm. When she stepped back, he showed her a rare defenseless moment, cleared his throat, and said, "Well, now."

"I have the feeling you're an excellent friend," Esther said, "and an even better partner."

"I try to be," Talmadge replied. "On both counts."

Suzie was watching on the periphery, looking pleased. When Esther approached, the newscaster drew her into the studio's shadows. Well removed from the others, Suzie said, "Several times over our on-air sessions, I got the impression you had started to say something, then held back."

Esther found herself fighting the urge to reveal her deepest fear. "I always tell my team that analysts don't deal in rumors."

"I have contacts," Suzie said. "Maybe I could help."

Again she fought against sharing it. "It's too big. If I'm wrong, I could be spreading panic."

"And if you're right?" Suzie waited, then said, "Insisting on evidence is what brought me to this position."

"That and the fact that you're extremely good at your job," Esther added. She knew a genuine pleasure in reaching out and hugging this woman. Only then did Esther realize how tightly wound Suzie was. "Thank you so much."

"Evidence," Suzie said. "Let me help you find it."

Esther carried an uncommon force of calm during the ride home. There was a distinct sense of rightness to the night. She could even reflect on her resignation without regret. She started to think on everything the next day would bring, then just let it go. It drifted away like smoke in the wind. The peace she knew was that strong.

Then her phone rang. Esther quickly realized she had not called the clinic or even cast a thought in Nathan's direction. She pulled to the curb. The phone number was blocked. Carter Cleveland was probably phoning on his private line.

But it wasn't the doctor. Instead, Jasmine's first words emerged so broken that Esther thought she had misunderstood. Esther said, "Say again."

"I've. Just. Been. Fired."

Esther cut off the car's motor. The main road bordering Dilworth streamed behind her. But here on the street leading to her house, everything was quiet. She was parked beneath one of the giant elms, the branches forming a canopy that blocked the streetlights. Esther was hidden in plain sight. "That doesn't make any sense."

Jasmine might have huffed, or she might have sobbed. "Since when does anything that man does make any sense?"

"Jason fired you? Personally?"

"His assistant did."

Esther felt the night slow further. As though the darkness and the minutes and the quiet street all congealed into a liquid mass through which her thoughts and impressions could be dissected. One at a time. Thoroughly. "Jason's secretary phoned you. At nine forty-three in the evening. To say you've been canned."

"She said Jason had called her from the airport. Told her to deliver this message." Jasmine blew her nose. "At least she had the decency to apologize."

"I resigned today."

"I saw you tell Suzie on the show. Thanks for the heads-up, by the way."

"It happened just before I went on air. Reynolds Thane wanted me . . . Never mind. It can wait."

"So Jason figured he'd get rid of both Downside Twins in one afternoon? Or maybe this is revenge?"

Esther shook her head. "He needs you now more than ever. Who'll be in charge of our department?"

"MIT."

Esther couldn't help but laugh. "That geek couldn't lead a hamster to the feeding tube."

"Glad you find some humor in this."

Esther used the electronic controls to lower her seat back, settling further down in the vehicle. She stared out the windshield, beyond the tree limbs, to the crescent moon rising over the rooftops. "Do me a favor. Walk me through what's happened since you and I talked yesterday."

Jasmine took a steadying breath. "Soon as I got off the phone with you, I went to Jason's office and told him what you said. He kinda froze. He was—"

"What?"

"He looked distracted. Which I thought was strange, you know?"

"With the markets in free fall." Esther felt the night condense further. "Go on."

"Right. I told him what you said about building a hedge. He looked at me like he couldn't place me, then picked up the phone, called his number two, said exactly what I told him. Afterward he thanked me. I thought, well—"

"That you had done a good thing and he'd be pleased."

"Right. So I went back to the team, and we held our breath until the markets finally stabilized this morning." Jasmine's voice held a deeper timbre than normal, but her emotions had steadied. "You and Suzie did a good job, by the way."

"Thanks. What happened next?"

"The team took off right as the Eastern markets opened stable. When I was alone, I went back to what you'd told me to do, you know, before."

The answer was clear as lightning across the sky. Esther said, "Hewitt."

"I still don't have any idea where he is. I was searching when Reynolds Thane called us to the trading floor to announce the merger. Promised the moon and the stars. An advert for you and Suzie's report popped up on the monitors just as he finished. Reynolds was not the tiniest bit pleased about that. He dismissed the troops, had a quiet word with Jason, and vanished. Ten minutes later, I heard from my pals that Jason had left on another of his mystery trips."

Esther nodded slowly. The answer was there in the moonlight. "Hewitt is the key."

"To what?"

"To everything. You have *got* to find him."

"Did you hear a single thing I just said? It doesn't matter anymore. I've been *fired*."

"Jasmine, listen carefully. You have a job."

"I . . . What?"

"I'm starting a hedge fund. Talmadge Burroughs is putting together a group of initial investors. I want you to come work for me."

"That's why you quit?"

"No, not exactly. Look, right now there is only one thing you need to focus on."

Jasmine said, "Finding Hewitt. Got it."

"This has never been more important. Does his phone still work?"

"Straight to voicemail."

"But the number is still valid. Call and tell him what's happened. Tell him you need him. Give him the works."

"You mean, beg."

"Sob, plead, whatever will get the man to contact you. Tell him it's his fault. You were so desperate to find him, you rocked Jason's boat and the man fired you. Tell him he owes you a call. And when he does—"

"If," Jasmine corrected.

"No, when. How can he possibly resist you?"

"A joke. That's good. I could use a reason to smile. So when he calls, what?"

"Have him call me," Esther said. "That very instant."

43

Esther set her phone on the center console, lowered her window, and sat listening to the night. She drove a Mercedes mini-SUV called a GLK. The GLK was boxy and functional and utterly lacking the pretentiousness of most Mercedes-Benz vehicles. Esther discovered she loved its higher elevation almost as much as she did the legendary Mercedes efficiency. Everything about it worked brilliantly. And unlike many SUVs, this one was designed with women drivers in mind.

She lowered her seat to the floor, so she could see a slice of night sky between the rooftops and the lower branches. It meant only the top of her head was visible from the outside, and even that was masked by the tree's shadow. She could have driven the half block to her home and walked around back, but an unanswered question held her fast.

Jasmine had been dismissed in a futile attempt to stifle her search for Hewitt. Which meant the bank was desperate to hide something. The question was *what?* The only answer Esther could come up with was, something highly profitable.

In the current market, that probably meant the deals Hewitt and the other hidden traders were putting secretly into play were also stepping over the boundary of legality. But there was a chance, the very slight possibility, that something far more sinister was at work.

Esther needed to determine whether her deepest fears were in fact happening. And if she was right, she needed to structure a platform that would serve as proof to the outside world. And for that to work, they needed a witness. It was essential that they locate . . .

Directly in front of her, the night altered course.

Esther's car was positioned on the left side of the street about a block from the main road bordering Dilworth's eastern boundary. Her home was five houses down on the street's opposite side. Her front lawn contained three cherry trees and a magnolia, all over a century old. They formed a fragrant veil between her home and the street.

Between Esther's position and her driveway, nine cars were parked along both sides of the street, indicating someone probably was entertaining. The house directly across the street from her own was a mock Tudor with lead-paned windows. The owners had planted a yew hedge that now stood almost eight feet high. Some neighbors complained about how this created a barrier to the street's open look. But Esther thought it suited the home. The hedge had three openings, two for the curved driveway and another carved into a living arch framing their front walk.

A man stepped out of the central arch. He was definitely not the homeowner, who was a wispy retired architect in his early seventies. This man was tall and massive, but he moved in utter silence. Esther's window was wide open and she heard nothing. When he passed within range of a streetlight she saw his skin was dark and his features sharply defined. He slipped to the right with a dancer's grace and reentered the shadows, as though he could feel the light's presence.

He stepped into Esther's front yard.

She was still coming to terms with what this meant when a second figure rose from a crouched position by the hedge separating Esther's home from her neighbor to the east. This person was slightly built and most likely a woman. Her hair was hidden beneath a scarf or maybe a knit cap.

Then a third person appeared from behind her magnolia. Another man.

Esther did not realize her hands were shaking until she pulled her phone from her purse. She crouched down into the footwell, the steering wheel digging into her ribs. She started to dial

911, but the readout showed that her last outgoing call had been to Talmadge. She hit redial.

When Talmadge answered, she whispered, "I think someone has come to kill me."

Talmadge stayed on the phone with her while he used a second line to wake up the world.

Six minutes later, the first police car arrived. Never in Esther's life had those flashing lights meant so much. While the police approached her property on foot, Esther called Craig. The need to hear his voice overcame her reluctance to disturb him at a quarter past eleven. Four minutes after that, Talmadge arrived with his attorney, who also happened to be on the city council. Talmadge's embrace was fierce enough to threaten Esther's first tears of the night.

Because of the councilman's presence, a deputy chief arrived with a senior detective. As she watched the flashlights play off trees and the walls of her home, Esther tried to tell herself it was all a mistake. That the three shadowy figures were somehow components of a normal night. She wanted desperately to pretend that the fabric of her safe haven had not been ripped apart. But the analytical portion of her brain would not be stifled.

Just as the police completed their initial survey, Craig pulled up in his car. His hug helped heal the night more than Esther thought was possible.

The detective was a stocky woman named Sanchez, whose dark eyes reflected a coppery glint in the streetlights. She told Esther, "The forensics team should clear your home shortly. I need to ask you a few questions."

Esther handed Craig her phone and stepped away. "All right."

When the councilman approached, Sanchez said, "Give us a minute, please."

"I am here as Ms. Larsen's legal representative," the councilman replied.

The detective was then joined by the deputy chief. Sanchez did her best to ignore them both and told Esther, "Walk me through what happened tonight."

Esther could not quite keep her voice steady as she described the events. Sanchez stopped her repeatedly, asking questions that forced her to proceed more slowly. The detective's questions drew up details that Esther would otherwise have dismissed as unimportant. When she finished, Sanchez asked, "What made you certain this man was a threat?"

The lawyer protested, "Oh, come on, Detective. Three strangers gather in the middle of her front lawn for a confab?"

"No, it was before that," Esther said. "He scared me the very first moment he became visible."

"Come with me, please." Sanchez led her down the street. "You say he was hidden here?"

"Inside the hedge. Right. He must have been stationed there for at least an hour. That's how long I was parked."

"And you stopped the car where you did because . . . ?"

Esther had already been through this three times. She could see the lawyer was about to object. But she lifted her hand, stifling his protest. She liked how the detective was using the repetition to bring out new details. "My assistant phoned me with the news that she had been fired."

"From the same bank where you resigned. Are the two events linked in any way to tonight's disturbance?"

"I have no hard evidence to suggest this," Esther said.

A hard-edged humor shone in Sanchez's eyes. "Now you sound like a detective."

Esther stepped into the alcove carved from the hedge. A cast-iron gate blocked her entry. The detective's flashlight showed where it had been dusted for prints. Esther unlatched the gate and pushed it open. The gate squeaked loudly. Esther rocked the gate back and forth, listening to the noise. "My car window was open. I would definitely have heard this."

"So the man was standing right here the entire time you were in your car."

"I stayed there because I was trying to sort through tonight's events," Esther said. "I'm an analyst. It's what I do."

"And did you come to any conclusions?"

"I need to uncover several more elements before I can determine whether my former employees were involved."

"If they were behind the incident, your search might cause them to try again."

Esther liked how the hedge offered them a semblance of privacy. She felt safe enough to reveal her tremors. "I understand."

"Do you really?" Sanchez motioned Esther out of the alcove. "Walk with me."

They proceeded down the driveway and around to the rear of Esther's home, trailed by the deputy chief and Talmadge's attorney. A trio of portable lights had been set up near the large birch tree in her backyard. A man was on his knees, waiting for a plaster cast to dry. Sanchez showed how an individual had stood here for quite some time and then held out a small plastic bag containing six cigarette filters.

"Here's what I think might have taken place," Sanchez said. "This is all conjecture, so don't hold me to anything. But it looks like there was a five-man crew."

"Three in front, plus the rear observer." The

sight of the cigarette butts dangling from Sanchez's fingers left Esther feeling nauseated. "Where's the fifth?"

"He or she played mobile observer. They parked outside the television station. They knew you were there because they caught your act or were told about it by whoever ordered the hit."

The casual way Sanchez said the word *hit* opened the night like a great gaping maw. Esther said weakly, "They waited for me."

"You described how you exited the station with several others. That probably saved your life. There might have been two in the car, a driver to help spot you and the hired killer. Or maybe they'd already decided to go for you here at your home. In either case, I'm thinking they only had one car. They didn't want to risk you noticing you were being trailed. So they followed long enough to be sure you were heading home. Then they called ahead. And team two got into position. Three in front, one in backup position right here." Sanchez slipped the plastic bag into her pocket. "Only you didn't pull into the drive. You stopped far enough away for them to be unable to identify your vehicle. And there were others parked along the street."

The deputy chief said, "You are one very lucky lady."

45

Esther walked back to where Craig met her. "How are you doing?"

"Not great, but I'll be okay. Thank you for being here."

"I'm glad you called." Craig returned her phone. "Talmadge left while you were with the detective. His hip was bothering him. He asked you to call as soon as you were free."

"Can you tell him I'm okay and that I'll connect up with him tomorrow?"

"I already did. He wanted to tell you—"

"Later. Please. All right?"

"Sure thing." He pointed to where Patricia and Lacy Saunders were stepping from their car. "I called them. I hope that's okay."

"It's better than that." Esther stepped forward to accept their embraces. "Thank you so much for coming."

Patricia held up a thermos. "I've always found hot cocoa to be a soothing balm to every calamity."

"That sounds nice."

Patricia unscrewed the cap and poured. The fragrance of steaming chocolate filled the night's empty spaces. Lacy looked around, asked, "All these police came for an attempted break-in?"

"Must be a slow night," Craig agreed.

Esther realized they did not know any details. She asked Craig, "What did Talmadge tell you?"

"That there'd been an attack on your home," Craig said.

She sipped from the cup and felt the warmth spread through her. "This is great."

"See?" Patricia studied the two men talking with the detective. "Is that Councilman Edwards?"

"Talmadge called him," Craig said. "He thought having an attorney here might help."

"And he did," Esther replied. "A lot."

Detective Sanchez walked over, declined the offer of chocolate, and said, "It's okay for you to enter your home."

"She won't be staying here," Patricia declared. "She's going home with us."

Lacy said, "Mom, maybe Esther would rather be alone."

"She's had a shock. The last thing she needs tonight is to stay here by herself."

Esther hated the necessity of correcting either of them. And the truth was, she dreaded stepping inside her house just now. But she could not accept their invitation without first clearing up the situation. "Actually, that's not entirely correct." She handed back the cup. "They invaded my property. But it appears they did not enter my home."

She found it interesting that only Lacy seemed to understand. Craig and Patricia both stared at her in confusion. Patricia said, "You caught them *before* they broke in?"

"Mom . . ."

"What?"

Esther said softly, "It was a hit squad."

Craig swung toward the detective. When Sanchez did not respond, he turned back, now reflecting Patricia's confused expression. "How . . . ?"

"I spotted them because I parked down the street a ways to take a phone call. Otherwise I'd be . . ."

Lacy said, "Oh. Wow."

Esther nodded.

"We'll assign a patrol car to stay near your home and keep watch," Sanchez said. When the three people remained frozen from the shock of what they were hearing, she went on, "Another will be serving as your personal escort. You shouldn't drive anywhere."

Esther asked, "Is that really necessary?"

Sanchez nodded. "Your would-be assailants are still out there. Maybe you should think about having us move you into a hotel."

"No," Patricia said, more quietly now. "She's coming home with us."

For the third time, Lacy said, "Mom . . ."

"What?"

"Don't you think you should talk this over with Dad?"

"Your father is in surgery until who knows how late. He'll sleep at the hospital. He has rounds tomorrow morning. He'll come home and find Esther in our guest room and a cop car on our doorstep. Isn't that right, Officer?"

"Detective," Sanchez corrected. "Long as Ms. Larsen is in residence."

Craig said, "Talmadge has also arranged for private security." All eyes turned his way. He shrugged an apology at Esther. "Talmadge wanted to be the one to tell you, but you said to put him off. I thought you should know that it's happening."

"There, you see?" Patricia said. "Craig, go home and get some rest. Esther, come with us."

Esther started, "I'm not sure . . ."

"Well, I am. Good night, Detective."

Craig embraced her once more and said, "The girls are going to be furious they missed all this."

"All right, you two can hug on each other tomorrow." Patricia made a shooing gesture. "It's like herding cats."

46

Thursday

Esther awoke to the smell of fresh coffee. She dressed in her clothes from the previous day and went downstairs to find Craig and his daughters seated at the dining table. Their chairs were placed so they could look around the open-plan chimney and carry on a conversation with the pair in the kitchen. Abigail rushed over and hugged her tightly. No words were required. Esther lowered her face so as to take in a huge lungful of the girl's fresh scent. "I didn't know I needed that until just now."

Samantha made a great drama of rising and walking over and taking her sister's place. Which made the deed all the more special. After Esther released them, Craig was standing there, smiling and ready. "My turn."

Abigail said, "Daddy wouldn't let us wake you."

Craig asked, "How did you sleep?"

Lacy said, "How do you take your coffee?"

Abigail said, "We drove by your house. There's a *policeman* parked out front."

And from Samantha, "I thought this was going to be just another boring spring break."

Esther just buried her face deeper against Craig's chest.

Patricia insisted on making oatmeal. Five minutes later, Esther was spooning cinnamon and raisins and shaved almonds into her bowl. Patricia seemed happiest when she had a cooking spoon in her hand. Esther remembered how happy her mother had been, filling their home with light and chatter. Patricia was nothing like the memory Esther had of her mother, the tall willowy woman who was incomplete without a song. But there was a similarity in the way Patricia met every need with an embrace and just the right dish.

Esther's cellphone rang while she was enjoying her second cup of coffee. Patricia said, "That's probably Donald. He wants to speak with you about your brother."

Esther stopped in the process of answering. "Is Nathan okay?"

"He didn't say."

But when she answered, Suzie McManning said, "I'd be furious with you if I thought it would do any good."

"I should have called the station," Esther said.

"Well, duh."

"It didn't even occur to me."

"At least it did to Talmadge. Only he left his message far too late. Our crew managed to inter-view the councilman and the deputy chief. We'll roll footage again before you and I go on camera. We want to run a midday report."

Esther shook her head to the watching group. "I don't think—"

"You don't have a choice," Suzie interrupted. "We let you sleep in. That's all the breather you get. When can you be here?"

Esther heard the determination in Suzie's voice and accepted defeat. "A couple of hours."

"Make it sooner."

"Wait, how are the markets?"

"Stable," Suzie assured her. "The world is still spinning. Which is the only reason I didn't insist they wake you."

Esther cut the connection and was about to ask Patricia for her husband's number when her phone rang again. The readout showed a blocked number. "Larsen."

A man's voice spoke softly, "Jasmine said I had to call."

Esther was up and out the rear door in a flash. She was alone on the deck, but still whispered, "Hewitt?"

"If anybody here finds out I made this contact, I'm finished."

She did not bother to tell him how true that was. "You've taken precautions?"

"This is a throwaway phone. I'm on my lunch break. Is it for real, Jasmine got fired because of me?"

"It's my fault, really. I told her to find you."

The man had a honeyed voice, strong and warm,

even when scared. "Why couldn't you just leave it alone?"

"You know the answer to that. Where are you?"

Hewitt was silent for so long that Esther feared he was going to turn her down. Then he replied, "Bermuda."

"Will you tell me what you're doing?"

"We've made all three of the deals your team suggested. Our take was four hundred million. In a week."

"On how large a portfolio?"

"Seven big ones. More coming in today, so I've heard."

"Where did the funds originate?"

"That's why it's all so secret. CFM and the Brits are taking advantage of a short-term window. Because of the merger."

Esther said, "It's a ruse."

"What are you talking—?"

"They tried to take me out. Last night. A professional hit squad. Five, maybe six attackers."

"Is this a joke?"

Esther pulled the detective's card from her pocket. She read off the number. "Ask for Detective Sanchez. She'll confirm everything I've just said."

Hewitt mulled that over. "Okay, so they over-reacted. But we're talking about huge profits. My take is five million bucks."

She saw Patricia standing in the kitchen's open

doorway and waved her away. "And you may be right. Maybe they're just skirting the edge of illegality. But what if it's more than that?"

"It's not," Hewitt said. "I'm one of the frontline troops, remember?"

"It's not *so far,*" Esther countered. "But is a take like this, no matter how big, worth risking the two bank charters? Not to mention serious jail time for everybody involved?"

Hewitt was slow to come back. "What else could it be?"

"Maybe nothing. In fact, I hope I'm wrong. But what if they're putting all this in place for something else entirely?"

"Like what?"

"I'm an analyst. I might not be working for CFM anymore, but I still don't deal in rumors. Tell me one thing. How many of Sir Trevor's traders are there?"

"Five, same as my group. The ten of us are supported by just three staffers."

"Has Sir Trevor's group put forward any deals of their own?"

"Not yet. But I keep hearing they're preparing some big transaction. Huge."

Esther's gut churned with a grim certainty now. "So long as you keep on this tactic, we don't need to talk again. But if Sir Trevor's project shows intent to destabilize the markets, *you have to call me.*"

Hewitt's response came out slow and measured. "Get. Out."

"No, Hewitt, that's what *you* have to do."

"They're paying me five mil to stick around."

"Listen to me. They sent a hit squad to my house because I asked the wrong question. Do you really think they'll leave you alive to spend your take?"

Hewitt went quiet.

"Do it for Jasmine," Esther said. "The minute you hear *anything,* call me. Then *run.*"

47

Five minutes later, Esther spoke with Donald Saunders, who insisted that she come by the clinic. He refused to say anything more, responding to her questions with what she considered a doctor's typical terseness. Esther thanked and hugged her friends, then asked the security detail to drive her home. She needed to shower and dress for the day ahead.

She disliked going anywhere in someone else's car. She loved to drive almost as much as she liked the private time to think. She understood the logic in being accompanied everywhere, but in the light of another lovely April morning, all the reasons for the tight security flew out the window. Even so, the first phone call she made once they were under way was to Talmadge. "I owe you more than I can ever say."

"Careful now." He sounded enormously cheerful. "I might insist you come to work for me."

"I don't owe you *that* much."

He laughed and said, "You do a cranky old man's heart a whole lot of good, young lady."

"This morning I feel about a million years old."

"I imagine watching a passel of killers stalk your front garden would do that to a body."

"I have another request."

"Name it."

"Yesterday my number two at the bank was fired. I told her she could come work for me on the hedge fund. But Jasmine needs reassurance that the job and the project are actually happening."

"She needs a real office in a real company," Talmadge agreed. "Give me her details. I'll make the call myself."

When Esther had done so, she hesitated, then said, "Can you meet me at the studio?"

"Nigh on impossible. I've got back-to-back meetings all morning. I interrupted a conference with my tax accountants to take your call."

Esther decided she did not want to rush through an explanation that amounted merely to suspicions. She did not have enough hard evidence to call it anything else. She especially didn't want to lay out here what she was thinking, as the two strangers in the front seat were within earshot. So she said, "I'll check in with you later."

Esther reviewed her incomings and saw she had thirty-seven voicemails and almost twice as many texts. There was no time to deal with them all, so she quickly scrolled through the messages for anything urgent and spent the remainder of the journey surveying the markets on her cellphone. Suzie's description of their status as stable went too far. Esther could almost feel the tremors resonate from the charts, up through her hands, as if they were shaking the car and the earth beneath the asphalt.

All the markets needed was one hard shove and they would tumble off the cliff's edge. But that had been true for weeks now. They were merely one step closer.

Even so, when they pulled into her drive, she could almost feel the cold wind blowing up from the abyss.

The female agent asked Esther for her house keys and security code. Esther refrained from pointing out that the police had kept a car parked out front all night, since her protest would only delay her getting upstairs and into the shower.

The two security agents were fairly easy to ignore. Both were quiet and somewhat nondescript, as though they had developed a persona that allowed them to vanish in plain sight. The woman was a couple of inches shorter than Esther and wore a navy blazer over gray slacks. The driver was male and wore an identical jacket and trousers with a white polo shirt and Ecco lace-ups. They both wore pistols in shoulder holsters under their jackets.

Esther decided to use the moment to phone Detective Sanchez. When the woman answered, Esther thanked her again for coming to her rescue, then described her phone conversation with Hewitt and what this represented. As she talked, the male agent turned around in his seat and watched her. His eyes were a smoky brown, his expression tight. He did not seem to even blink.

Esther hit the phone's speaker button so her security could hear the detective say, "You're thinking that these two banks consider you enough of a threat to their illegal activities that they targeted you. What did you say their take was?"

"Around four hundred million for the first week, minus commissions."

The male agent spoke for the first time that morning. "Four hundred million dollars is a big impetus."

Sanchez asked, "Who said that?"

"The security driver. And I don't think you understand. An investment banking division can make that much in a month of normal trading. Less. Everything they've done, setting up this off-book project, siphoning in secret funds, none of this makes sense."

"Same answer," the driver replied. "Four hundred big ones."

"I agree," Sanchez said.

"Not when you look at the risks they're taking," Esther insisted. "They would lose their bank charters. Their merger bid would be crushed by the financial authorities. Both company presidents would be fired. Not to mention public humiliation and serious jail time."

"So what are you suggesting?"

"I want you to check and see if any Bermuda-based criminals have recently flown into the US."

The driver nodded slowly. Sanchez replied, "That's good thinking."

Esther went on, "If the two banks are behind this attack, it means they're planning something much bigger. And everything they've done to this point is just part of the ruse."

48

They left her home forty-six minutes later. Esther continued scanning the morning positions on her cellphone as security drove her to Nathan's clinic. US markets were nervous but relatively stable. Still, the jumps were huge, an 874-point shift just in the previous half hour of trading. The movement was within a defined range, however, and prices were now anchored by electronic hedges.

Analysts working for other investment bankers had arrived at the same conclusion as Esther. The problems faced by the global markets were vast and growing bigger still. But for the moment, there was no reason to panic. So their traders had set up a system known as bottom-feeding. Whenever a stock moved below a threshold calculated by both the company's profit level and its year-on-year share price, the computers were set to buy. This created a base below which the market could not move without a shift larger than the bankers were capable of handling.

Esther stared up at the female security agent holding her door.

The woman asked, "Something wrong?"

Esther opened her mouth, but did not know what to say. So she rose and followed the agent past the three dogwoods bordering the parking lot. Another of Talmadge's guards stood by the clinic's entrance. He exchanged hellos with Esther's security and held the door open. Esther waited while the duty nurse phoned the clinic's doctor. She went back over the mental steps that had brought her to the portal now looming before her. The one that opened into all her midnight terrors.

The nurse replaced the phone and said, "Dr. Cleveland is in a meeting and asks that you wait."

"I don't have time this morning." Esther started toward the rear hallway.

"No, please—"

"He knows where to find me." She signaled for the agents to remain in the lobby, walked down the corridor, and entered her brother's room. "Hello, Nathan."

The pleasure and sorrow over seeing him again were equally intense. Nathan had already shifted his head away, so his closed eyes were pointed toward the window opposite the doorway. Only a slight lifting and lowering of the covers over his chest showed that he lived at all. His features looked far more flaccid than the last time she saw him. Or perhaps the harrowing hours had granted her a distance she previously had not realized.

"Esther. Good morning." To her surprise, it was not Cleveland who greeted her, but Donald Saunders. He asked, "How did you sleep?"

"Fine. Thank you again for your family's hospitality."

"Please take your seat. Carter?"

Carter Cleveland positioned himself in the doorway, only partway inside the room. He refused to look Esther in the eyes. "I'm good here."

"Excuse me a moment." Donald stepped out and returned with a chair from another room. During his absence, Cleveland neither moved nor looked her way.

Donald Saunders seated himself by the foot of Nathan's bed. "The description you gave me of your brother's condition made me wonder if perhaps we might need to look in a different direction. Which is why I asked permission to run a few tests."

"What did you find?"

But Donald was not to be rushed. "An accident serious enough to kill Nathan's wife suggests the possibility of serious head trauma to the survivor."

"There was no indication of any such injury in the patient's records," Cleveland snapped. "The spine and head were inspected via X-ray and MRI. Nothing was noted."

Donald did not give any indication that Cleveland had spoken. "Recent developments in scanning procedures have revealed that even when the skull and spine have shown no direct harm, it is possible for the brain itself to be injured. Think of it as an extremely severe bruise. Soft tissue can sometimes mask such trauma from noninvasive imaging. Even so, the injury can be so acute that healing is never complete."

"Again," Cleveland interrupted, "no swelling. No indication of any kind that this occurred."

Donald smiled thinly at Esther. It was just the two of them now. Carter Cleveland was nothing more than a minor interference. "I injected a very sensitive dye into Nathan's system, one designed to pass through the blood-brain barrier. What

I discovered is not conclusive, but it suggests—"

"Conjecture," Cleveland said, cutting him off. "Supposition, and highly objectionable."

Donald waited him out, then continued, "It suggests that your brother has suffered a series of mini-strokes."

Cleveland snorted and crossed his arms.

"We won't know for certain until or unless an autopsy is performed. But Nathan's condition contains a textbook collection of related symptoms."

Esther heard herself ask weakly, "What does this mean?"

"What we know," Donald said, his voice growing gentler still, "is that such minor strokes rarely if ever are solitary events. They form a repetitive pattern. These mini-strokes can impact a single capillary, an incident so small we have no way of tracking it. There is no direct evidence to any one stroke. All we can see is a gradual decline, a collection of symptoms that together show us that the first stroke has now been followed by others. In your brother's case, it suggests he has suffered a large cluster of mini-strokes."

Cleveland snorted again, scowling at the floor between his feet.

Donald pointed at the other doctor with his chin, his eyes conveying a message that Esther caught, despite her growing distress. She nodded once and asked, "You're saying he has been experiencing these mini-strokes repeatedly since the accident?"

"That is my professional opinion, yes."

Cleveland snorted again, more softly this time.

"If we had recognized this earlier," Esther said, "is there a possibility that Nathan might have been treated and his symptoms corrected?"

Donald leaned back, satisfied that she understood the deeper significance. "The evidence is inconclusive. But in some cases . . . yes, there is that possibility."

Esther looked directly at Dr. Cleveland. "Do I need a lawyer?"

Cleveland pushed himself away from the door and stormed down the hall.

Esther turned back to Donald, who replied, "I can introduce you to an attorney who specializes in medical issues."

"I don't want to sue anybody. All I want is for Nathan to be allowed to stay here for the rest of his days."

Donald leaned forward, silent.

Again, Esther understood what he was restricted from saying. "For free."

Donald nodded and jerked his chin at the same time, as though hearing words she had not yet spoken.

She added, "And be repaid for what I've already spent here."

"Some of it," he responded. "Perhaps."

She drew in a hard breath. "How long does he have?"

"Impossible to say. But given what we are seeing, and assuming my diagnosis is accurate, I think we should measure Nathan's remaining life-span in terms of a week or two." Donald rose to his feet. "Perhaps you'd like a few moments alone with your brother."

Esther stood and hugged the doctor. "I can't tell you what this means."

She shut the door after he departed and drew her chair in closer to the bed. Esther took Nathan's hand in both of hers, leaned her head on his arm, and wept. Hugs were not the only thing coming far more easily these days.

49

Esther left the clinic for the station less than twenty minutes later. She was surprised at her response to the news that Nathan's treatment had been based on a false premise. Esther had no doubt that Donald was correct in his diagnosis. Looking back, she could detect subtle indications of Nathan's decline that she had chosen to ignore.

Esther stared at the passing cars and recalled moments that she had misinterpreted because, just like the clinic's doctor, she had not seen them through the right lens. It would be so easy to blame Dr. Cleveland and his air of superiority. Drag his clinic through the courts. Bleed him. Make him pay.

But Esther felt no desire for revenge. Nothing she did would bring Nathan back. And from what Donald said, the entire issue of mini-strokes was mostly conjecture. There was no way to tell for certain without an autopsy. Cleveland was not wrong. He had simply been conveniently blind.

Despite this, her mental dialogue was not the full reason for her calm.

She simply did not have any desire to take the path of rage and retribution. It was like listening to thoughts from someone else's life. Her entire focus was not on punishment. It was on saving others.

Her phone rang. Once again, the number was blocked. "This is Esther Larsen."

"And *this* is your one and only warning."

There were moments in her professional career when a flash of unexpected data sent her into hyperdrive. When she felt as though her mind could actually compete with the algo trader's supercomputers. She now parsed the seconds in a manner that left the entire concept of physical time unimportant.

She raised her voice and almost shouted, "Sorry, I can't hear . . . You're breaking . . . Who is this?"

While she spoke, she hit both the phone's speaker button and its recording app and jammed the device in between the front seats. When the voice returned, the man was much angrier. His accent was a smooth lilt turned sour by his fury. "You *listen.* You have *one* chance to live."

"Hello?" Esther raised her voice higher.

As Esther yelled her response, the driver slipped across two lanes, eliciting honks from several cars, and parked by a hydrant. The female agent turned so she could crouch over the phone. Esther said loudly, "It's very hard to understand—"

"If you don't stop with all this talk and the interviews, you are *gone.* You and your brother and your pals, *finished.*"

"Look, I'm sorry, but whoever this is, I'm not hearing . . . Could you please call back? Hello?"

The man cursed and cut the connection.

The woman said, "You handled that like a pro."

The driver asked, "What accent was that?"

"Bahamian, Bermuda, both sound similar at times. I've vacationed in both spots."

The female agent was already dialing. She said into her phone, "Detective Sanchez, please. It's urgent."

Twelve minutes later, Sanchez reported, "Three members of the Bermuda mob, such as it is, passed through customs at Dulles Airport the day before yesterday."

Sanchez had called back on the security agent's phone, which she had already connected via Bluetooth to the car's stereo system. Their driver asked, "Bermuda has a mafia?"

"Small but fairly active. Bermuda is a focal point for shipping brokers and insurance groups. The mob plays a significant role in drug and human trafficking. These three recent arrivals are known to the authorities, though their records are clean. Bermuda lists them as very violent. Esther, I'm emailing you photos as an attachment. See if you recognize any of them."

They pulled into the station's parking lot. Nine of the cars sported bumper stickers urging the world to stop feeding the beast. One of them was Suzie McManning's Audi. Under different circumstances, Esther would have found that mildly thrilling. "I will."

The woman agent said, "We think additional protection is required, and Talmadge agrees. We've put a security detail on the Saunders family and doubled the agents handling Nathan."

Esther nodded. "What about Craig Wessex and his daughters?"

The woman took out her phone. "I'm on it."

As she left the car, Esther heard a faint hiss, like a distant kettle letting off steam, or perhaps the charged emission of a high-voltage power line. Only when the hiss followed her into the building did Esther realize the sound was internal.

She knew she was amped. She could feel the sense of urgency like a force building in the air around her. When they passed the makeup room and Suzie McManning called her name, Esther had to resist the urge to ask if the newscaster heard the sound as well.

Suzie asked, "What took you so long?"

"Meeting with doctors."

Suzie pushed away the cosmetician's hand. "What's wrong?"

"It's my brother. Last year he was in a bad accident. He's . . ." Esther stepped fully into the room and shut the door. "He's dying."

The two women shared the same grave look. The cosmetician said, "You poor thing."

Suzie asked, "Are you okay?"

"Look at the woman," the cosmetician said. "She's anything *but* okay."

Esther tasted the words as they were formed, measuring how it felt to be so open. "I keep waiting for something to kick in. Guilt. Recrimination. Anger. Sorrow. Something. I've been living with this for seven months. All I feel right now is . . ."

Suzie waited, then pressed, "What?"

"I feel ready," Esther said. "Is that terrible?"

In response, Suzie rose from her chair, stripped off the napkin draped around her neck, walked over, and embraced Esther. "You are a better woman than you give yourself credit for." She released Esther and turned around. "Doris, do your magic."

She patted the chair back. "Let's get started, hon."

Esther glanced in the mirror. She looked washed out. She said to Doris, "The smell of cigarette smoke makes me nauseous. It always has. I'm so sorry."

"For what? Hon, my daughter's been after me for years. She won't even let me set foot in her kitchen until I wash up and change tops. I'll put on a fresh jacket and gloves. Now come sit down."

Esther did as she was told. "Do you mind if I check my messages?"

"Long as you use the speaker, it's fine by me. I can't work with your hand by your face." Doris finished snapping on the latex gloves, then extended them toward Esther. "How's that, hon."

"It's fine, thank you." Esther could still smell ash, but the odor was fainter now. Her reflection showed an undeniable need for Doris's help. She looked as fragile as a china cup. She said to the woman in the mirror, "I have to be strong today."

"No, hon." Doris brushed her hair back with strong, sure strokes. "You have to *look* strong."

Esther pulled up the emails on her phone. The first was from Jasmine, reporting that she was settled into Talmadge's office complex. His techie had duplicated Esther's data stream on the system in Jasmine's new office. She even had an assistant.

Esther then opened the email from Sanchez and downloaded the three photos. The instant she saw the second photo, she placed the call.

"Sanchez."

"The second picture. It's him."

"Hold on. Okay, I'm recording this. Say again." When Esther did so, Sanchez asked, "How certain are you, on a scale of one to ten, ten being as sure as you are of your own name."

"Eleven."

"Tell me why."

"His features. When I saw him in the streetlight, I was reminded of old photos of Plains Indian warriors. He is that striking."

"Okay, that's good. He is in fact part Carib. His name . . ."

"Do I really need to hear this now?"

"No. But you *do* need to be aware that he's extremely dangerous. He's never been convicted, but he's been questioned in regard to several murders."

Esther felt Doris's hands tremble slightly. "Understood."

"What about the other two?" Sanchez asked.

"I can't be certain. He was the only one who stepped into the light."

"Never mind, this is still very useful. I'll speak with your security. Take care, Esther, and stay in touch."

50

Esther switched from email to her voicemail. It was good to use this as a distraction, as it kept her from visualizing the killer's face. Keith Sterling had called seven times. The last two included reminders that he was on spring recess—a quiet means of urging her to call him without delay. Esther looked at Doris in the mirror. "Can I hold the phone to my ear now? This might get personal."

"Use your right side. When I touch your shoulder, shift hands."

When Keith came on the line, he asked, "Are you aware of the traffic on your website?"

Esther tried to keep the impatience from her voice. "I don't have time for that right now."

"Well, you need to *make* time. Esther, you've had almost four million unique visitors."

She wanted to ask him what *unique* actually meant. Then she decided this was another of those details that would just have to wait. "That's amazing, but why is it urgent?"

"Have you looked at the account you set up for your hedge fund?"

"Different question, same answer," she replied.

"Because they deposit through the online

system, we've got a fairly accurate measure of the first investments."

Esther spoke so he would know she understood. "If they invest again and go directly to the account, your system doesn't register."

"Right. Esther, your followers have deposited more than one hundred and eighteen million in the escrow account."

That explained the nine calls from her bank manager. "Say that again."

"Wait, it's just topped one nineteen. You've had a cluster of really large chunks, then the rest comes in at mostly between five and twenty thousand per investor, some fifties, a few up to a quarter mil." Keith was clearly enjoying this. "The counter just keeps clicking along."

Talmadge answered on the first ring. "How are you holding up?"

"Fair. I look worse than I feel. I have a makeup artist making a lie of my face."

"That assistant of yours is a firecracker with the fuse lit."

"Jasmine is also a good friend."

"Yeah, I got that much. She asked me if I thought she needed to worry about you. I said not just yet. Was I right?"

Esther felt the lump develop in her throat. "I'm surrounded by people who care."

"Glad you got that memo."

"Starting with you."

Talmadge was clearly enjoying this exchange. "You ready to start calling me Cricket?"

"I would rather have a root canal." She relished the sound of his laughter. "Talmadge, how much have your investors put in the fund's escrow account?"

"Hang on, let's have a look . . . Ninety-three mil."

"Don't I recall you mentioning something about twenty-five?"

"That was before you talked them through yesterday's roller coaster. They've been scrambling ever since, hunting down their loose pennies."

"But it's not just them, is it?"

"I might've mentioned it to a few more folks. I had to, since your security is costing me an arm and my good leg. Either I upped the ante or I started renting rooms in my home."

"I'll pay you back."

"Lady, you already have. You just concentrate on saving the world. Leave the rest to me."

Esther cut the connection and cradled the phone with both hands. She planned a little, but mostly she sat listening to that same inner hiss. She knew it was her imagination, but she also had the sense that it represented something much greater than her own internal musings.

The station director came in and asked Doris how much longer she needed. The cosmetician said something in response that Esther did not bother to hear. When the door sighed shut, Esther placed a call to Craig. "Where are you?"

"I'm driving my two spring-break beauties for a pancake extravaganza. Their mom is driving them to dance afterward. After I bring them home, I plan on popping over to the local television station and visiting with this famous person we know. We're traveling with an armed escort. Two of them, in the car behind us. Seriously, is that really necessary?"

"Maybe. Better safe than sorry."

"Abigail thinks this is the coolest thing since they invented Häagen-Dazs. She can't wait to show off her security detail at school. Samantha can't decide how she feels about it. And their mother is definitely worried about the company I'm keeping."

Esther had no idea how to respond except to change the subject. "What are you doing now that your exams are finished?"

"I've got four and a half weeks off. I have a paper to write. Otherwise I was mostly planning on keeping three sophisticated ladies entertained. Why?"

"Do you want a part-time job?"

"I wouldn't say no. Do you have a lawn that needs cutting?"

"My hedge fund now holds a hundred and nineteen million dollars. I put initial trades into place yesterday, but that was only for the first twenty-five. I have an assistant who will coordinate the actual deals. But I need somebody I can trust to handle the books. I was wondering if you would be able to help out. Call yourself a temporary external auditor, consultant, whatever—"

Esther did not realize Craig had her on the car's speakerphone until she heard the girls reply together, "Please, Daddy! Tell her yes!"

Esther found a calm reassurance in the transformation Doris was making to her face. The ashen weariness was gone now, replaced by a woman who looked extremely alert. Esther knew there was nothing that could be done about the sense of bruised fragility. In fact, she decided it actually fit the day. "Your work is amazing."

Doris flashed a smile at the mirror. "Had a good canvas to work with."

"How much longer?"

"Five minutes."

"I'm not rushing you. I just wanted to know if I have time for another call."

"Then give me ten. I want to try something new with your hair."

Esther hit the speed dial for Jasmine. Her assistant answered with, "It's a crying shame I'm so honest. Otherwise I'd waltz outta here with a few million and vanish like a hungry ghost."

"Ghosts don't exist, and you're the most honest person I've ever met."

"Must be why I spend so much time alone. I don't know when or how to lie."

Esther did not have time for Jasmine's version of casual conversation. "You're monitoring our accounts?"

"Hundred and thirty-one million."

"I was told one nineteen."

"Just got another ten-five. And Esther . . ."

"What?"

"Talmadge passed along a call from the fund managers for state employees. They wanted to discuss an investment."

"How much?"

"Two hundred and fifty million was mentioned. There. I said it out loud, and I didn't crash to the floor."

Esther breathed in and out. Getting used to the idea of handling not simply a very large amount of money, but the trust that the money represented. "I want you to start putting the funds into action."

"Wait. Okay, I'm recording."

"You have traders on call?"

"Standing by."

"Not with CFM, I hope."

"Oh, puh-leese."

"All right." Esther shut her eyes and focused on the data stream in her brain. "Here goes."

51

When Esther finished passing the trading instructions to Jasmine, she cut the connection and opened her eyes to discover that Doris had done her hair in a French twist. The effect was astonishing. Her neck looked like an alabaster vase rising to a surprisingly strong jawline. Her eyes looked enormous. "Wow."

"That's the reaction I like," Doris said, applying a final mist of hair spray. "Nothing beats a good wow factor."

"Thank you so much."

"You are most welcome." Doris pulled the paper bib away. "Got to take care of my investment."

Esther rose from her chair before she realized what the woman had said. "You put money into my fund?"

"Twenty-two thousand, three hundred and eighteen dollars. Everything I could get my hands on."

"Wow again."

Doris had the cantilevered smile of a woman who had seen more than her share of hard knocks. "You really struck a chord around here. Everybody's in."

Her morning had been too full of shocks. That

was the only reason for the sudden desire to weep. "Suzie too?"

"Hon, that lady has given you every cent she has."

Esther thanked Doris once more, then stepped from the room to find Suzie standing in the corridor. The newscaster was having an intense conversation with Chuck, the station director, punctuating every few words with a tap on his forearm. Esther walked up and wrapped her arms around her.

When Esther released her, Suzie asked, "What was that for?"

"Trusting me."

Chuck cleared his throat, "Actually, I could use one of those myself."

Other than anger, Esther had never been comfortable with public displays of emotion. Yet this had been a season of change in a whole host of new directions. She reached out and hugged the smiling station manager. "There. Better?"

"Oh, yeah."

Suzie asked, "Ready to go on air?"

"Not at all."

"Tough." She pushed open the studio door. "It's show time."

Not ten minutes into the interview, Suzie signaled to the production booth. She swept a hand back and forth in front of her neck, then turned to Esther and said, "This isn't working."

Esther nodded glumly. "I sound awful."

"You sound flat," Suzie corrected. "You've always had a spark that ignites even the boring bits. Today you're—"

"Disconnected," Esther said. "I agree."

"What can we do about that?"

"A week off would be nice. Sleep in my own bed. Arrest the hit men from Bermuda."

"I mean," Suzie said, "what can we change about things under our control."

Esther stared at the microphone on the table. "That is the big question."

"What do you mean?"

"Why are we here?" Esther replied. "It can't be just to wave a red flag in the bull's face. We need to focus on what we can change."

"So let's start with the obvious," Suzie said. "What do you need to change here in the studio?"

The answer could not have been clearer if it had been scripted on the monitor. "Are we going to be doing this on a regular basis? I don't mean for the next couple of days."

"Chuck and I were just discussing that. We got over three hundred calls and maybe two thousand tweets this morning alone. We need to make this a semipermanent structure. The number of other stations feeding—"

"Let's table that discussion. What I mean is this.

If we're going to be doing this for a while, I'd like to take over an empty studio. You have one here, right?"

"This station dates back to when a lot of on-air programming was local. There are several that haven't been used in years."

"Let me lease one. Set up our hedge fund's office here. Hook into your satellite feeds. Run our data stream through this place. When we do a broadcast, we show the trading office in the background."

Suzie's expression changed to highly engaged. She glanced back. "Chuck?"

"I'll have a word with Talmadge. Sounds good to me."

Suzie asked the station manager, "What about bringing in monitors and setting them up behind us? Show the markets while we talk?"

"I like that," Esther said. "A lot."

They immediately rearranged the set so the monitors played behind them. Then they taped one long session that Suzie said could be split into several segments. Suzie paused the cameras a number of times, coaching Esther on her responses, then repeating the question and having Esther respond again. Doing some takes four, five, six times. Esther found she did not mind. They helped her to stay focused, to push away all the unknowns and deal with the immediate.

After an hour they took a break. When Esther

came out from under the lights, Craig was at the back of the studio, smiling a welcome. "You done?"

"Not even close. Will you do something for me? Go to Talmadge's office. Meet Jasmine, my number two. Start building a formal accounting structure. Bring in Talmadge's people if you want, especially on the tax side."

"Esther . . ."

She rushed over whatever protest he might have been forming. "I know you haven't agreed to work with us yet. But this is moving at the speed of sound. I desperately need—"

"Yes."

"—somebody to . . ." She stopped. "Yes what?"

"Yes, I'll help you. Yes, I'll get started this afternoon." He grinned. "I wish you could see your face."

"I can't kiss you now," Esther said. "There's probably a camera on us somewhere, and Doris spent hours on my face."

Suzie called, "Esther, we're on in two."

"I don't mind being owed a few of those," Craig said. "I'm an accountant. I'm good at keeping records."

"Esther!"

"Go," Craig said. "I'll go meet . . ."

"Jasmine."

"Right. And see what a mess I can make of your accounts."

The rest of the taping took almost four hours. When it was done, Esther felt burdened by the fatigue and banked-up stress. She almost fell asleep in the makeup chair while Doris cleaned her face. She returned to the lobby to find her security detail waiting for her by the front entrance. Esther asked, "Do you think we could stop by the clinic again?"

The woman said, "We can go wherever you want."

"In that case, I'd like to visit with my brother."

Once in the rear seat, Esther leaned her head back and watched the sunset play through the trees and buildings as they drove. Her thoughts came and went in a blur. She could still sense that looming threat just beyond the horizon. She knew she needed to work out what that might mean. She needed to do a hundred different things, but just then she was too tired.

Thankfully, the doctor's office was dark when she arrived. The duty nurse offered her the standard professional greeting. Esther entered her brother's room and shut the door.

Nathan was turned away. His closed eyes and slack features were painted with the sunset's rosy pastels. For the first time, Esther saw his body's position not as a response to her presence, but rather as his search for the light. At some core level, perhaps this was all he could react to now.

She picked up her chair and settled it on the bed's opposite side, so that her back was to the window and the gathering dusk.

Esther found herself talking softly to Nathan about their early days. About the times when they were a family. When happiness was a normal part of their existence. She talked about how she had started remembering things from those times, especially before she went to bed. She confessed that for the first time in years, she was not waking up in the middle of the night from dreams she couldn't remember, her pillow wet with tears she didn't recall shedding. She told him about the dreadful experience she had just endured, then falling asleep in a strange bed, and waking up from a dream of laughter. Her own, as a child. She and Nathan playing in the back garden. She remembered it like it had happened yesterday.

Then she began talking about the bad times. She apologized for never having thanked him. Because he had been a great brother. The best ever. And she should have been a better sister. She should never have raged at him like she had, as though all the bad things were his fault. She thanked him for forgiving her. For understanding even when she did not. She talked until she wept, then she leaned over and settled her face on her arms, there on the bed beside her brother. And she slept.

She had no idea how long she remained there.

When she finally lifted her head, the room was dark except for the medical monitor's faint glow. But the light was enough for her to see that Nathan held her hand.

A single glance at her brother's face was enough for Esther to know her brother was gone.

They all came to be with her.

Craig arrived with his daughters, who were sleepy but crushed by the weight of sharing in their new friend's grief. Patricia came with Lacy. Donald drove over from the hospital. Talmadge brought Jasmine. Rachel and her husband. Suzie and the station director. All of them lining both sides of the clinic's hallway as Nathan's body was brought out. They each talked with her, held her, supported and cared and wept with her.

Then Patricia and Lacy took her back to Esther's own home. Esther assumed security was there somewhere, but they had the grace to remain unseen, on the periphery of this shattered night.

Patricia settled Esther into her own bed and stayed there in the rocking chair as she drifted away. Esther carried the sound of the rocker into her dreams. Comforted by the knowledge that her home was empty no longer.

52

Friday

Another day, another disposable phone. Reynolds had lost count of the number of phones he had used once and then tossed. He was parked in the guest lot of his golf club. To his right, dew glistened on the emerald-green ninth tee. The trees shielding him from the clubhouse swayed gently in the dawn breeze, as though nature saluted his audacity.

Sir Trevor was fretting. "I heartily dislike moving forward with that Larsen woman still in the wind."

Reynolds had never heard Sir Trevor in this condition before. The man sounded as nervous as a groom before his wedding. By contrast, Reynolds was flooded with an icy calm. He decided this was how a professional sniper must feel that instant before he pulled the trigger. All the world receded to a vague distance. Everything became focused on the point at the center of his target.

Sir Trevor, on the other hand, was frantic. "I fail to see how it could prove so difficult to dispose of one troublesome female."

"Her partner in the hedge fund is a local business leader by the name of Talmadge

Burroughs," Reynolds replied evenly. "He and I have had our previous run-ins. Burroughs can be difficult in the extreme. He's surrounded Larsen with professional security. Ditto for her brother and various friends."

"So the shooter's failed attempt has raised his risk level. Tell him to try harder. The man is certainly being well paid."

Reynolds waved the air before his face, a silent urge for them to move on. "The police now have an APB out for him. We can't risk an arrest. He knows Jason. Besides which, he and his crew are essential to cleaning up our loose ends in Bermuda."

"Surely something can be done. We're almost out of time!"

Reynolds allowed a hint of the lash to enter his voice. "Which is *precisely* why we need to *move forward*."

"But Larsen—"

"Forget about the woman!"

Sir Trevor must have tried for outrage, but failed. "How dare you speak to me in that tone—"

"How dare *you* endanger *two years* of planning with your last-minute jitters!"

"I would hardly consider—"

"Let's review what we actually know. Larsen has resigned from her position at the bank. She has parlayed herself into a local celebrity status with a regional television business report."

"One with national reach. She has even been mentioned in the UK!"

"Yes, she has a growing audience. But for what? She predicts a severe downturn. So do a dozen more well-established pundits."

Sir Trevor went silent.

"She actually plays to our hand. Let's set aside our fears and focus on what we know. She has not come *close* to uncovering our aims. She is predicting—"

"I am well aware of what she is predicting!" The petulant tone had returned.

"—that the global economy is going to enter meltdown and drag America with it. Which is *precisely* what is going to happen. So she predicts it. So what?"

"But what if she realizes our aims?"

"She won't."

"How can you be so certain?"

"She's an analyst. She calculates risk. But she's also limited to reality. We're not. We're *manipulating* reality. She might comprehend our actions later, but by then it will all be after the fact." Reynolds gave that a beat, then continued, "Our take, as of this morning's positions, will be just shy of two billion dollars. Each. I would say that justifies the risk one woman might or might not—"

"All right." Sir Trevor sighed. "You win."

Reynolds smiled. "Timing is everything. You

will confirm the plans with your ally in China's central bank?"

"Yes, yes. They're standing by. You're certain about Brazil?"

"I received confirmation from our source an hour ago," Reynolds said. "His final payment is dependent upon holding to our agreed-on schedule."

Sir Trevor turned silent again. Reynolds watched the clock set into the walnut-burl dash. The second hand clicked softly, each tiny movement bringing him one step closer to his ultimate aim.

Sir Trevor said quietly, "This is it, then."

"It is indeed."

Trevor cut the connection without further comment.

Reynolds placed a call to Jason and ran through the final set of instructions. Then he started his car and drove to where the club's valet waited to greet him. He was struck by something his father had once told him. Back in the savings-and-loan debacle of the eighties, his father's bank had almost gone under. Afterward, he told his son that in times of crisis there were only two alternatives to abject and crushing defeat. Either you are first off the starting block, his father had said, or you cheat.

Reynolds tipped the valet and entered the club, wondering what his father might have said now, when Reynolds had found the third option. Which was to combine the two.

Reynolds smiled at the greeting from the club pro and decided his father would be very proud indeed.

53

Whenever Esther looked back during the days and weeks that followed, she had the distinct impression that she had known what was coming before she even opened her eyes that morning. Before the first alert arrived. Long before the initial phone call.

Esther knew this was the day.

Of course, she did not perceive the actual events that would hammer the globe. She had not learned how to peer around the bend of time.

But looking back, it seemed to her as if her subconscious had worked through the dark hours, compiling the data that had been lost to her during the tumult and danger and loss.

In the moment between drawing her first waking breath and opening her eyes, she sensed that the world faced a false dawn. Global events were set on a course toward the brink. And because her friends had helped her gain the rest she so desperately needed, she was ready for today. Which was vital. Because she was fairly certain the events she had both expected and dreaded were about to unfold.

Esther lay in bed, smelling coffee from downstairs, and knowing the security people were up and doing their job at keeping her safe. She also knew she needed to go by the funeral home and start making arrangements. She needed to step away somewhere quiet and allow the loss and the grief to overwhelm her, at least for a little while. She knew she needed to spend a few hours just sitting in her backyard being held by a pair of good strong arms. She knew all these things, and she knew they were not going to happen.

Instead, she rose, slipped on a bathrobe, and stepped into her office to check the markets.

Which was when her phone rang.

Jasmine sounded weak with worry. "Hewitt called."

"All right. Wait." Still in her pajamas and robe, Esther rushed down the stairs, waved a frantic hello to the agent seated in her kitchen, and poured herself a mug of coffee. She added milk, sipped, then asked the agent, "Do you sweep this house for listening devices?"

"Every morning and evening," he confirmed.

Esther took her cup into the dining room and slid the doors shut. She seated herself and said, "It's bad, isn't it?"

"Yesterday afternoon they received another tranche of funds."

"How much?"

"Four billion."

Esther took another sip, then said to Jasmine, "Tell me the rest."

"This morning Hewitt and the other traders were handed new instructions."

"And?"

"He wouldn't tell me. I begged. All he said was the trading orders don't make sense."

Esther's calm state remained disconnected from her racing heart. "You need to call him back."

"He says he can't talk."

"Jasmine, you have *got* to get that man on the phone. Tell him it is *absolutely vital* that we know what they're planning. Then he must leave. Get on the next plane. Flee while he still can."

"Hewitt says his payoff is coming Monday. He says—"

"They are not going to let them live through the weekend!"

Three things happened in the same instant. The sliding doors opened, and the female security agent peered through. Patricia appeared at the bottom of the stairs, clothes rumpled, hair in disarray, and her eyes round with worry. And Esther's strong and capable assistant broke down and wept over the phone. Esther saw no reason to tell the others to leave her alone. They were all in this together.

Esther said softly, "Jasmine, I want you to listen to me."

"I-I love him."

"I know."

"Should I go out there to Bermuda?"

"No, definitely not. You wouldn't arrive until this evening, possibly tomorrow. Once you arrived, you wouldn't know where he is. By the time you found him, it would probably be too late. And more important, it would only put you in their line of fire too."

"W-what do I do?"

"Call Talmadge. Ask for his help." Esther gave her Talmadge's private line.

"But it's just past six."

"He won't mind. Ask him if he can identify a private investigator based in Bermuda. If so, can he track Hewitt down? Explain the urgency. Tell him . . ."

"What?"

"Tell him it's happening. Today."

Jasmine took another ragged breath. "Are you sure?"

Esther took internal stock. The conviction lodged in her gut grew until it filled her heart and mind. The static charge she had been hearing all the previous day now had a source. She was moving into the eye of the tempest.

She said, "I'm absolutely certain."

As soon as she cut the connection, Patricia asked, "What can I do to help?"

Esther stared at the stocky woman, her features worn by the same hard night. "Maybe you should get back to your family, get some rest—"

"Don't even start. Tell me what you need doing."

"All right. I could use your help clearing the decks. Everything that can be set to one side has to wait. Can you begin on Nathan's funeral arrangements?"

Speaking her brother's name almost undid her. Esther took an extremely hard breath. Another. But when Patricia started around the table, Esther halted her with an upraised hand. This was not a day for more embracing.

Patricia said, "Leave it with me."

54

Esther did not have a television upstairs. If there was some newscast she wanted to see, she either fed it through her office system or she did what she was doing now, which was to carry her tablet from room to room.

As she showered and dressed, she switched back and forth between the morning business reports. The Far East markets continued the previous day's wild swings but within established parameters. The morning e-trades were nervous, yet positions remained within the bounds of reason. On the surface it was just another day in a period of tension and concern. But Esther knew otherwise. Her certainty was not dependent upon Jasmine's news. That sort of external evidence would prove useful in convincing others. No, her confidence went far deeper.

When the next phone call came, she was ready.

Though the number was blocked, she did not hesitate. "Esther Larsen."

A voice she instantly recognized asked, "Is this line secure?"

"Hold one moment." Esther raced across the hall and flung open the door to her guest room. Patricia was brushing her hair and froze in mid-stroke. Esther said, "I need your phone."

While Patricia rummaged through her purse, Esther rattled off the number from memory. The person on the other end of the line repeated the number back, then cut the connection.

Patricia asked, "What's going on?"

"I have a call coming in that needs a secure line. Secure as in it's not possible to use a parasite software and listen in. I've given them a number that isn't linked to me."

The woman's eyes could not have gone any more round. "Who is it?"

As the phone rang, Esther replied, "One of the good guys."

Rob Wright's first words were, "How certain are you of this line?"

"It belongs to a friend. Even if listeners were aware and intended to invade the conversation, they'd need fifteen, twenty minutes to set it up. The house has been checked for bugs by pros. We're good to go."

Rob Wright had started his career as an analyst in the foreign exchange department, known as forex, of Goldman Sachs. Esther had met him at an industry gathering her first year with CFM. Unlike Esther, Rob had wanted nothing more than to become a trader. When he finally gained his chance, he succeeded in magnificent fashion. And his success almost did him in. The man spiraled into the chasm of drugs and late nights and women offering electric highs. But he woke up in time, turned his life around, and then realized that the trading life was built on lies that did not hold him any longer. So he went to work as a lowly Washington aide to a Missouri congressman. Within two years Rob Wright had risen to the post of senior staffer to the Senate Finance Committee.

He asked, "Are you doing another broadcast today?"

Esther glanced at the bedside clock. "We go live in ninety-eight minutes."

Rob Wright said, "This is off the record."

"Understood."

"Now and in the future."

"This conversation did not happen," Esther assured him.

"Last night the president's chief of staff received a call from his counterpart in Brazil."

Esther stood at the window in her guest room. She knew Patricia was in the bathroom doorway, listening to her side of the conversation. "Tell me."

"Brazil is going to renege on its national debts."

Esther traced a finger over the sunlit glass. Trying to freeze every fragment of this moment.

"You there?" Wright asked.

"Yes." The word felt caught in her throat. "The timing makes sense. They have a six and a half billion interest payment due . . ."

"Tuesday. And a forty-billion-dollar bond repayment at the end of the month."

"But with the recession, their tax receipts are way down," Esther said. "When is the public announcement?"

"Monday. The cabinet minister is a personal friend of the president's aide, and the call was intended as an informal heads-up."

Esther nodded. "Giving Treasury and the Fed time to prepare contingencies."

"Right. But there's a problem."

Esther did not need to ask. "Word is slipping out."

"At this stage, it's just rumors. But, yeah, we're tracking a couple of tweets with solid South American sources. All they've got so far is that Brazil is in serious trouble."

"It won't hold through the weekend," Esther said, "which means the electronic traders will wreak havoc."

"Unless the news comes out while there is still time for a normal trading day," Rob added. "That's the purpose of this call."

The impact of what Rob was proposing slammed her. "You're asking me to release the news?"

"Correction. I'm *offering* this to you. On a strictly confidential basis."

Esther did not reply.

"Like I said, we need to remain utterly disconnected to this alert. Your links to Washington are still a mystery. Plus, you're getting a lot of attention right now. This fits into your scenario."

"Rob . . ."

"What?"

"I owe you."

"You got that right. Big time."

"There's something . . ." She stopped.

"The clock is ticking, Esther."

"I need to call you back. On the record."

Clearly that was the last thing he expected. "Are you serious?"

"Yes. And right now. Give me a number, and be ready to tape."

"Okay, here's my office line." Rob Wright read it off, hesitated, then said, "Esther, are we talking about what I'm afraid we're talking about?"

"Let me give you what I have, then you decide."

Esther clicked off and handed the phone back to Patricia. "I'm going to call him on my office number. You might want to listen in."

"Who was that?"

Esther was already up and moving. "His name is Robert Wright. He's the Senate Finance Committee's chief of staff." She entered her office and dialed the number. When Rob came on, she said, "Ready?"

"Fire away."

She started with the previous two events, Japan and Spain. Then the attempt on her life. This morning's call from Jasmine needed longer to explain. When she was done, she stopped and breathed and listened to the electric sizzle grow louder by the minute.

Rob said slowly, "Wow."

"Can you move against them?"

"Are you kidding? The seventh largest bank in the US conspiring with the third largest in Europe? Accuse them of pushing the global economy over the brink? I can't even take this to my boss without hard evidence."

"You'll get that," Esther said, "but only when it's too late."

55

Four minutes later, they all left for the studio. Patricia insisted on following. She told Esther she wanted to see what the eye of a hurricane looked like. Lacy rolled up as they were pulling out of the drive and waved at Esther and slipped into her mother's car. During the drive, Esther placed a call to Suzie. The newscaster reported, "Technicians have been here all night, putting together your idea."

Esther said, "Talmadge?"

"The man is amazing. He walked through here just after midnight, complimented the workers, then told Chuck, 'Ain't it amazing what you can accomplish if you throw money at the right people?'" Suzie hesitated, then added, "I'm really sorry about your brother. But I have the feeling it would be better to wait on that."

"Definitely," Esther said, swallowing the sudden lump in her throat. "Can you get Chuck on the line?"

The station director surprised her. Within the first few moments of her warning, his normal nervous tizzy simply vanished. In its place emerged a totally different guy. Not just intent, but on target. He said, "We need to expand coverage."

"I think so too."

"New York won't want to believe a local station has come up with the goods. But I'm going to call them because I have to. Once they fob me off, I'm going to start calling other regionals. I'll link with as many as I can. Feed into their morning news shows."

"And all your radio affiliates," Esther said.

"You bet. How far out are you?"

"Fifteen minutes, maybe twenty depending on traffic."

"We'll be ready."

Esther phoned Jasmine and issued a set of terse instructions. Then she started calling her allies. She offered each person the same brief message. It was happening. Today. There was no time for details. Either they prepared for the worst, or they didn't. It was their call.

The studio parking lot was as full as Esther had ever seen it. A trio of vans bearing an electronics company's logo were parked alongside the entrance. The pavement between the vehicles was littered with cables and tools and plastic bubble wrap. Esther watched two frantic techies race out of the studio, grab another massive flat screen, and hustle back inside.

As Esther rose from the car, Lacy ran over and handed her a note. "Something to carry you through the tempest."

Esther unfolded the paper and read silently,

"Who knows whether you have not come to the kingdom for such a time as this?"

Lacy said, "It's from the book of Esther."

"This was one of my father's favorite passages." She cleared her eyes and smiled at the younger woman. "Would you like a job?"

"You mean, today? Really?"

"I need someone to key in a record of all our hedge trades onto the website. That was part of my promise, making this information available to everyone." Esther pulled a pad and pen from her purse as she spoke. "Call Keith Sterling, my resident web guru. He'll walk you through what needs to be done."

Lacy accepted the paper. "This is just so totally cool."

"Good. Let's get started." Together they walked into the studio. As she slipped Lacy's note into her pocket, Esther felt as though her father and brother had managed to join them. And found the sensation very fitting indeed.

Suzie walked Esther into makeup and told Doris to take her time, explaining the techies needed another few minutes. Through the closed door Esther heard the sounds of drills and frenzied shouting. While Doris worked, Esther and Suzie walked through a scenario for the initial segment. It was the first time they had ever prepped in advance. But Esther could see that Suzie shared her sense of gravity. They had to get this right.

Just as Doris was finishing up, Jasmine rushed in with three sleepy traders in tow. "These are all their company would let me borrow."

Esther greeted the traders and interrogated them long enough to be certain they knew what was required. She then asked everyone but Jasmine to leave the room, Doris included. She drew her assistant into a fierce embrace and said, "This is going to have to last us both through a very long day. You understand what I'm saying?"

Jasmine nodded. "I'm sorry about—"

"We won't talk about it now," Esther said. "Today is all about focus and helping as many people as we can."

Jasmine turned away, took a trio of jagged breaths, wiped her face and said, "Tomorrow."

"Right." Esther had never been prouder of her friend. "Now let's go save the world."

56

"Analysts have different names for economic issues that negatively impact the world's economies," Esther said, her face angled so that it appeared she was looking straight at both Suzie and the nearest camera. "They generally prefer names that sound explosive. Blasts, IEDs, barrel bombs. After the tidal wave that struck Japan, such events were called tsunamis. Over the past couple of years, a new name has come into vogue."

They had made the announcement about Brazil defaulting on its national debt forty minutes earlier. Suzie and Esther spent five minutes doing a quick overview of what this might mean. Then they took a break. It was now coming up to the opening of the American markets, and they were back for round two.

"Black swan events," Suzie offered.

"Correct. The name was penned by a Lebanese American economist, Professor Nassim Taleb. It refers to the assumption during the era of Victorian explorers that all swans were white. But then a black swan was discovered in Australia. In finance, the term refers to a totally unexpected event that upends the assumptions underpinning markets."

Suzie said, "Please explain to our viewers why this is so important."

"A black swan event carries the potential to create utter havoc. Never has this been more probable than now. Remember what I said earlier. In order to stay ahead of the electronic game, e-traders have already set their algorithms in place. These computer-driven trades are linked to very tight boundaries. If the markets appear ready to shift outside these parameters, it puts these electronic trading orders into motion. Once that occurs, the speed is beyond our human ability to halt the process. A landslide is inevitable."

Suzie leaned forward. "If the markets only *appear* to shift."

"Correct. Computer algorithms cannot tell the difference between appearance and reality. This means any activity that seems to indicate a crisis will be *treated* as a crisis."

They were seated behind a slightly curved desk, so she and Suzie could face each other as well as the cameras. The wooden desk was empty except for two mikes on stubby stands, similar to the ones formerly used on the *Larry King Live* show, and a pair of coffee mugs. Esther's contained green tea. Her stomach would not accept any more acid. During their first break she had tried to eat a bagel and barely managed to get down a few bites.

Technicians still worked setting up more trading desks. But six were functional now, four of them staffed by Jasmine and her three traders. They worked the phones and the e-markets, establishing positions for Esther's new fund. Beyond them and to the right sat Craig, his desk piled with the forms required by the SEC for registering such trades. Many hedge funds used legal loopholes to avoid disclosing their ongoing positions. Esther considered that just another symptom of a critically ill trading system. At the desk beside Craig, Lacy typed furiously, feeding onto the website each transaction as the paper was passed to her by Craig.

Technicians scrambled around the perimeters, laying cable and unpacking more workstations. Suzie had insisted they go ahead and film from their new positions with all this activity taking place behind them. Esther liked how the scene added to the dramatic tension of the moment. They were not just sitting back and playing observers. Instead, she and Suzie McManning were deeply involved in the unfolding events, entrenched in the action. Today's tension was good.

Lining the far wall were three large flat screens. As they talked, the third went live, bouncing from matte gray to a display of the South American markets. Suzie said, "It is now fifteen minutes to Wall Street's opening bell. Let's take a moment and examine the current electronic positions. Esther, it looks to me as though the Brazilian markets are stable."

"They're not stable, they're static." Their desk was backed by a low credenza. On it, five flat screens had been lined up like electronic soldiers. Esther traced her hand along the graph representing the morning trades. "A static market means far more than an absence of movement. This signifies an unnatural break in the action. What you see here is only a fraction of the normal number of electronic trades."

"Everybody is waiting," Suzie said.

"Right. The trading divisions of major investment banks are holding their collective breath, like runners on the starting block. All they need is the gun to set them off." Esther turned from the unchanging screen. "Right now the intel we shared this morning is nothing more than rumor. Traders around the globe are waiting for confirmation that our information is on target. When that happens . . ."

Suzie started to ask her to complete the sentence. But the simple fact was, at this point, Esther couldn't. She gave her head a fractional shake, just a single but faint tremor. But Suzie was alert and they were in sync. The newscaster caught herself and turned to face the camera. "We'll be back after a short break."

Five seconds later, the cameraman said, "And we're off."

Chuck came down the stairs from the production booth and said, "Every major network has carried a report of our announcement. Most name you specifically."

"What's our next topic?" Suzie asked.

Esther rose from her chair. "I don't know."

Chuck jammed his glasses up his nose and stared. "You don't . . . What are we supposed to do now?"

"We wait." Esther walked between the cameras and left the studio. She knew what they were thinking. That perhaps she had it wrong. Maybe the markets would use this announcement and stabilize. Yet she knew this wasn't going to happen. It was more than knowing about the hit men. It was more than Hewitt's news about the banks' secret trading arm in Bermuda. It was more than the current tumult. She felt certain that her worst-case theory was correct, but she could not go public. Not yet. She needed one more piece to her puzzle, one more item. She was an analyst. She did not deal in half-completed investigations.

Esther stepped into the empty makeup room, shut the door, and leaned her head against the mirror.

"Come on, Hewitt," she muttered. "Talk to me."

57

The US markets opened and held steady. Esther could feel the tension mount throughout the station as Wall Street trended only slightly downward. Trading remained very light through the first two hours.

Esther waited for someone among the team to express doubts over her announcement. They had every reason to suspect that her news about Brazil's default was off, or that her analysis remained skewed by an inbred pessimism. Which was what the pundits on other networks were saying. Most simply dismissed her announcement out of hand. They called it the ramblings of a regional wannabe analyst, who was using her ninety seconds of on-air fame as a lever to spout total nonsense.

But Esther was not wrong.

Perhaps her own calm certainty in itself was enough. Or perhaps no one wanted to be the first to question their direction. Esther had no idea. She had never been in a position of leadership before. All she could tell is that whatever doubts they might have felt were kept well hidden. To her careful eye, it appeared that everyone remained with her. The feeling of being trusted to get it right was . . .

Exquisite.

All morning, the global markets remained trapped in the amber of indecision. Brazil's own news sources remained utterly silent. The world held its breath.

One o'clock came and went. Europe started shutting down for the night. England's post-market reports carried a mention of Esther's claim, delivered with a proper amount of derision.

By two o'clock on Friday afternoon, the financial pundits were calling for Esther Larsen's head.

At two forty-one that afternoon, she and Suzie took another break. The monitor showed a woman happily applying a stain remover to her children's clothes. Chuck stepped onto the dais, his shirt rumpled, a pair of headphones slung around his neck, his glasses askew, his hair a mess. He smiled at Esther and handed Suzie a note.

Suzie read it, paled, and passed the page to Esther.

Its impact slowed time. Esther felt the crystalline quality to every frantic heartbeat.

Suzie's voice shook slightly as she asked, "How do you want to play this?"

"You make the announcement, I'll comment."

"Got it."

"Hang on, there's more." Chuck then handed Suzie a second note.

She read it, and offered them both the day's first smile. She asked the station director, "For real?"

"It's nice to know this day holds some good news," Chuck said. "They start the feed at the end of this break."

Suzie's first on-air words were, "This is Suzie McManning, coming to you from the newsrooms of WFPX in Charlotte, North Carolina. We are now being carried live nationwide by ABC. So, hello, America. We have just learned that the White House has called a press conference for three o'clock local time, which puts us nineteen minutes out. With me is Esther Larsen, who this morning broke the news of a pending default by

344

the Brazilian government on its national debt. Esther, I think it's safe to say . . ."

Suzie's voice trailed off. She had no choice. Jasmine stepped into the camera's view, her face stricken. She planted her phone on the desk beside Esther's coffee mug. And stood there. Too broken to realize she was on air.

The phone's screen carried a message of one word. The single word was all that was required.

Dollars. H.

Esther looked up, said to the camera, "Yes, the White House will confirm the Brazilian event. Yes, this has seismic potential to rock the global markets. But no, this is not the worst that we can expect."

"Explain to us what that term 'cascade' means," Suzie said.

It was the fourth time Suzie had repeated the word. Esther had used it in the run-up to the announcement by the White House press attaché. The press conference was still under way, and the central wall monitor showed the attaché speaking on C-SPAN. But all attention was now centered on the market's reaction, which was massive.

Jasmine and their new chief trader were bouncing back and forth now, shifting from the trading stations to Esther's desk. Esther had never wanted to be a trader, never even imagined that one day she might hold a position similar to

Jason's. But here she was, not just doing so but handling the new duties on air. Live. Nationwide.

She checked Jasmine's latest note, jotted a swift response, handed it back, then said to the cameras, "Think of an earthquake. Anybody who has been through one knows the first thing that hits is not panic, but questions. First comes the worry of what it is. Then you want to know, are you at the epicenter? Is this the worst or is it stronger somewhere else? And then there are the aftershocks. Will there be a string of quakes, each worse than the last? All the unknowns triggered by the shaking of your world."

"Cascade," Suzie repeated for the fifth time.

"Right now, everyone is focused on Brazil. The pundits will talk about how the Dow has dropped another twenty-six hundred points, and the press conference is still ongoing. European aftermarkets trading is further off than the Dow, because their banks are far more deeply invested in instruments of South American national debt. And all the while we are missing the *real* event. Because what we *don't* see is that this is not the epicenter."

"How can you be certain?"

"Because this is my job. As an analyst I'm paid to see what's coming next."

Suzie gave that a beat, then almost whispered the word for the sixth and final time. "Cascade."

Esther turned and faced the camera directly. "A collective of international banks has gathered

346

together a war chest of eleven billion dollars. They have been lying in wait, secretly preparing for just such a moment. They are not intent upon profiting from events. They are not satisfied to benefit from the resulting downturn. They intend to use this moment while the global markets are teetering on the brink. They are going to blast away the cliff and send our economies tumbling into the abyss."

58

Sir Trevor's voice sounded as splintered as Reynolds felt. "Are you *listening* to this woman?"

"I have been all day." In fact, Reynolds had been so rattled by Esther's first announcement that he had called in sick. Reynolds had not missed a day of work since being named CEO. His wife was so alarmed, she wanted to drive him to the emergency room. Reynolds had finally locked himself into his home office and refused to answer when she knocked.

Reynolds asked, "Where did she get that lead on Brazil?"

"We're past that," Trevor snapped. "The question is, what *else* does this Larsen woman know? What *more* does she suspect?"

As though in response, Reynolds heard Esther Larsen say, "A twentieth century banker once told his employees, the best time to make money is when there is blood in the streets. Until now, bankers have used global events to turn a profit. But like we've been saying all week—"

"The rules have changed," the newscaster, Suzie somebody, supplied.

"Exactly." Larsen looked straight at the camera. To Reynolds, it felt as if she were reaching through the distance to take a firm grip of his heart. "Bankers are no longer content with the standard model of observation-analysis-response. They want to *control* the markets. They have forgotten that the money we entrust to them is not in fact theirs at all. All they can see is the power this money represents. They have lost their moral compass. To them, there is nothing more important than raising their quarterly profits."

Reynolds had forgotten he still held the phone until he heard Trevor groan, "She knows."

Esther went on, "Through most of the twentieth century, our nation's banks remained focused on servicing their clients. They knew the companies and the individuals who relied on their services. They were *partners* in the advancement of our economy. Nowadays, bankers scorn this construct as being out-of-date. The clients are seen as servicing the traders. The focus now is on two things, and two things alone. How to maximize the bank's short-term gains, and how to increase the size of their bonuses."

The newscaster broke into his response by asking, "So what are they going to do?"

"They have been waiting for this precise moment," Esther repeated. "When the global economy is weakest, they intend to push it over the ledge."

Suzie McManning protested, "But eleven billion dollars, if this truly is the amount they hold—"

"It is."

Sir Trevor said, "She knows *everything*."

"That isn't enough to push an entire nation's economy over the brink," Suzie said, "much less the world's collective markets."

To Reynolds's horror, Esther was ready with the answer. "Which is why they will most likely focus all their funds, all their efforts, on the one market that grants them the greatest amount of leverage."

Suzie nodded. "And that market is . . . ?"

"Forex," Esther said. "The foreign exchange markets grant large investors the ability to leverage their bets at up to ninety-eight percent."

Suzie McManning's expression mirrored the shock and dismay Reynolds felt, but for different reasons. "So their eleven billion—"

"Means they will be laying out leveraged bets worth five hundred and fifty billion." Despite the makeup, Esther Larsen's face was taut and pale as parchment. "In a highly vulnerable market, it might just be enough to cause the dollar to crash."

Sir Trevor said, "We have to stop her—"

Reynolds threw his phone at the side wall. The idiot was two steps behind the ball. There was no way they could halt anything. The bets were laid, their allies bribed, the action set out in a sequence of carefully timed events. It was too late to do anything but run.

He unlocked his office door and opened it to find his wife in a near-panic state. Which was altogether a good thing as far as he was concerned. She cried, "Reynolds, what is *happening?*"

"Pack a bag. Bring your passport. We leave in five minutes."

"Pack? But where are we *going?*"

"Anywhere. Away." Suddenly he felt not just weary, but a thousand years old. "And we're never coming back."

59

"Welcome back. We are live nationwide. It is three forty-five, the Dow is down seven percent on the day in heavy volume, and the SEC has just stepped in and closed the markets for a ten-minute cooling-off session." Suzie McManning offered the camera a tight smile. "This after Esther Larsen urged the authorities to do just that during the previous half hour of our program. You heard it first here, on ABC."

Esther felt as though she had aged a decade in

the past nine hours. Suzie McManning, on the other hand, appeared fresher and more alert than the hour after dawn. "So, Esther, if the dollar forex market is going to be used as the lever to cause global collapse—"

"It is not an issue of if, but when," Esther said.

Suzie merely smiled once more. "*If* this is happening, what do you see as the sign?"

"Indicator," Esther corrected.

"Whatever," Suzie said.

"The banks acting as perpetrators will have set up in advance a series of carefully timed steps. This will begin with the short sale of half a trillion US dollars."

Suzie's smile vanished, but her voice remained both crisp and bright. "For our viewers, a short sale means the banks have bet that the dollar will fall. This means that *if* they are successful, *if* they indeed push our economy over the brink—"

"They will reap billions in overnight profits," Esther said.

"Where have they placed these short sales?"

"Such a massive bet against the dollar will be spread all over the globe, concentrated in forex markets that defy international regulations and keep a tight grip on personal data. My guess is, Singapore, Bahamas, Luxembourg, Hong Kong, Switzerland, and Liechtenstein."

"Back to my original question. If we are unable to obtain the trading data from these countries, what will be the first"—Suzie gave a somewhat canted smile—"*indicator* that this is happening?"

"An ally of these two banks, either a major overseas financial institution or a foreign country's central bank, will announce that they have lost confidence in the US economy," Esther replied. She felt like the minuscule lunch she had eaten hours ago had become a concrete slab in her gut.

"Because, as we're seeing, the markets are in free fall," Suzie said.

"Correct. The calmer heads within their organization will be stifled. Their ally will insist that the group or central bank must exit their dollar positions while their holdings have some value at all. Because . . ."

Esther caught sight of the ticker tape streaming across the bottom of the central wall monitor. The words in her throat became a solid and unyielding mass.

On national television, anchorwoman Suzie McManning's calm façade broke wide open. *"Tell me what is going on!"*

Esther pointed at the screens. "The governing committee of China's central bank has gone into emergency session. An announcement is due within the hour. China holds more dollar-based assets than any other foreign country. It is, I have to admit, a brilliant start to the banks' assault on our economy and currency."

The frenetic activity that had filled the space behind their desk froze. Even the scurrying technicians and their electricians straightened slowly. Every eye was on the large wall monitors and the news headlines sliding across the bottom.

Suzie demanded, "What will happen next?"

"As soon as China's central bank makes its formal announcement, the bank's forex agents will simultaneously dump their shorted dollar positions." Esther no longer recognized her own voice. "This will be timed for right after the close of Wall Street. That was why the Chinese announcement was set for this hour, so the banks can wreak their havoc over the weekend through the electronic trading system."

"The algo traders will go wild," Suzie said. "The dollar will drop like a stone."

"Allies within the financial community are bound to have been tipped off," Esther went on. "They will begin dumping dollars in large volumes. The computer-based algorithms will hit their panic level. They will instantly sell every dollar-based stock, bond, and derivative. Within seconds the markets will be flooded with sell orders. Every dollar-weighted asset will drop to near-zero valuations."

As she spoke, the US markets began tumbling. The ribbon of indices ran red as a tide of blood.

It was Jasmine who called out, "We have to stop this!"

"Absolutely correct. Five things must happen before China's central bank goes public." Esther turned to the cameras again. "Everyone with any clout or connection, either to the Fed or the SEC or Washington, I urge you to drop everything and call your contacts and tell them to *do this now*.

"Step one: All markets around the globe must be ordered to halt trading. All foreign exchange trades must be shut down for the entire weekend. All electronic trades must be halted. *Immediately*. There has *never* been a time when urgent action by our government has been more important than today."

Suzie turned slowly in her chair and stared gravely at the same camera as Esther. The monitor showed the newscaster as slightly off-center, a position despised by most anchors since it suggested they were no longer in control of the set or the discussion. But Suzie McManning's gaze was locked tight as she began to nod, in time to Esther's words. In Esther's mind, Suzie's features were a mirror image of her own.

"Step two: The US government must declare that it will serve as purchaser of any and all dollar-based assets, including our nation's currency."

Gradually everyone in the studio began shifting positions. Esther saw it happening on the monitor. She heard the approaching footsteps. She observed how more and more faces came on-screen. All of them sharing the same grave intent. All of them, in unison, silently imploring the nation to pay attention, to act. While there was still time.

"Step three: All US financial institutions that are not taking part in this debacle must *immediately* start buying dollar-based assets. Even if this means a temporary decline in profits, it is the only way we will have a market on Monday."

Craig moved in behind Esther, his arms around his two daughters. She had not even noticed their entering the studio. But it was highly fitting for them to be here now. Because it was for all generations that the nation had to act.

"Step four: The Federal Reserve must *immediately* raise both the short-term interest rate and the overnight interbank rate to twenty-five percent, spurring investors around the globe to buy dollars.

"And finally, the US government must make a personal plea to all its foreign allies, requesting they too buy all outstanding dollar-based assets. Because their own economies will not survive unless they act, and act *now*."

60

Within twenty minutes, the White House switch-board was so swamped that the operators stopped answering. The server systems handling both houses of Congress crashed. Ditto for the SEC and the Treasury.

The voicemails of every congressman and senator, and every member of the Federal Reserve Bank, filled up and stopped accepting messages. All within twenty minutes of Esther Larsen's message.

Eight minutes before China's central bank was scheduled to make their announcement, the president's press attaché went on C-SPAN and declared that five executive orders had been issued.

The Treasury Department would serve as purchaser of any and all dollar-related assets that had fallen in value to a level classed as distressed.

All US trading floors were closed. The attaché assured the nation that business would resume as normal on Monday.

All global electronic trading in every class of dollar-based financial instrument and US stock was halted. The executive order would remain in effect for sixty-three hours, from that moment until nine o'clock Monday morning, eastern US time. Any foreign trader who broke with this order would be barred from trading on all US markets. Permanently.

The Fed had already instituted lifting of short-term dollar interest rates to *thirty* percent, effective immediately. The weekend interbank rate —the rate at which banks loaned to one another in order to maintain their overnight cash balances at legal liquidity—was set at the same position.

Finally, the president officially called upon all banks that had accepted the government's bailout funds to use "any and all measures" to assist the Treasury in acquiring distressed assets and stabilizing the markets.

Three minutes later, the station director called a break. Esther was checking the markets, preparing another roundup, when a grinning Jasmine walked up and said, "Somebody on the station phone would like to have a word."

Esther responded as she'd been doing all day, which was to delegate everything possible. "Handle it."

Jasmine set the phone down fast as she would a live coal. "Un-unh, honey, this is one call you gotta take."

Esther saw the station director step up next to Jasmine, sharing the tall lady's grin. She lifted the receiver. "This is Esther Larsen."

A woman's voice said, "Hold, please, for the president."

61

The crisis was over fifty-five minutes later.

Esther recapped the global positions and described the amazing view of markets around the world, buoyed by both the Fed's response and six of America's allies—Great Britain, Germany, France, Italy, Australia, and Japan. She listened as Suzie followed with a summary of incoming news briefs. Esther was too numb to be tired. But she could see the day's strain now in Suzie's face. No amount of professionalism could mask the fact that they had been working the story for twelve hours and counting.

Suzie set down the sheet containing the final news brief, turned to Esther, and offered her that canted smile of hers. It was Esther's only warning of the unexpected question to come. "If you had the opportunity to address the American nation at this point, a last word at the close of a very dangerous period, what would you say?"

For once, Esther found the question very welcome. Especially since she had been thinking about it all day. She looked straight into the camera and said, "A great deal has been said about our nation being exceptional. This is mostly directed at international diplomacy and military involvement. But in my opinion, for this to truly happen, we must start with a revamp of our financial system.

"America is built on business. Our banks are the engine. They must be brought into order.

"America's industrial might can only thrive when our financial system is built on long-term principles of stability and trust. Both of these principles have been shoved aside, replaced by a quarterly balance sheet and outrageous bonuses. All this must end. Now. Today. To survive, we must change for the better.

"Being exceptional means leading by example. We have served countless times as freedom's defender. Nowadays the banks claim we cannot be the first to enact laws that reestablish financial order. It would mean losing our global competitiveness. This present crisis is the only response we need to give. To do nothing means our eventual destruction.

"We must return to the forefront of moral leadership and end the current insanity. Banks must be forced to resume the practices that made our nation the greatest industrial force in the history of mankind. They must resume their role as merchants of trust."

Esther simply stopped. She wished she could say more. She yearned to *do* more. But the words were enough. Either they worked or . . .

From the shadows beyond the cameras, the station director said, "And we're off the air."

62

Saturday

The story dominated the entire front page of the *Wall Street Journal*'s weekend edition. Front and center was Esther's photograph. Below was the headline, *Local Analyst Rescues US Markets.* This was followed by the subtitle, *Esther Larsen dictates US national policy and halts a global economic meltdown.*

The right-hand column contained an unconfirmed report that the president had personally phoned the Chinese leader, who had intercepted the central bank's announcement just seconds before they were to go public. The official press bureau of China would say nothing except that one member of the central bank's ruling committee had been arrested on charges of corruption.

To the left of Esther's photograph was the story of the markets' wild ride. Below this was the report of a frozen international bank merger involving the seventh largest bank in the US, Carolina First Mercantile.

The bottom of the front page was given over to the news that a federal warrant had been issued for CFM's chief executive, Reynolds Thane, who was missing. The story also included a terse announcement that the head of the British conglomerate, Sir Trevor Stanstead, was assisting Her Majesty's government with its inquiries.

The bottom of the page included a brief notice that the financial authorities of Luxembourg, Switzerland, Singapore, Hong Kong, and Liechtenstein had leveled charges against the First International Bank of Hamilton, Bermuda. The bank was reportedly liable for $97 billion in unresolved short positions against the dollar.

Esther's trading team worked intensely through most of Sunday. All of them were exhausted, and yet all found the means to keep going. Trading was frozen for the weekend, which meant that in order to protect their investors, they needed to have their orders in place when the markets reopened.

At the close of business on Monday, investors in Esther Larsen's hedge fund realized a seventy-nine percent gain.

The dollar and the US markets closed up.

63

Three Weeks Later

Esther scarcely recognized her own kitchen. It was not the number of people, though there had never been so many friends in her home.

It was the joy.

The sense of impending threat that had

accompanied her through the days of crisis and tumult remained with her still. It was not by any means a constant companion. Now and then, however, she would stop, draw back, and listen. There in the background she could hear the faint hiss of warning. She knew her moment in the spotlight had not ended. And yet even now there was an abiding sense that everything had changed.

Esther Larsen was no longer alone.

She walked over to the two girls spreading a cake with dark chocolate icing. "The idea is to put the icing on the cake, not in your mouth."

"Abigail's the piggy," Samantha said.

"Then why is *your* mouth ringed in chocolate?"

"She did it." Samantha's smiles came a bit more frequently now. "That's my excuse and I'm sticking to it."

"Abigail, don't poke your sister with that spoon."

"She asked for it."

"I'm sure she did. Many times. Samantha, tell your sister you're sorry."

"No."

"Now tell her you love her more than chocolate."

"Yuck."

"There. You see?" She hugged both girls. "All better. Has anyone seen your dad?"

Abigail waved the spoon at the den. "He's in watching basketball."

Esther entered just as the TV viewers let out a unified groan. All except Lacy, who was rooting for the Pistons because, as she put it, somebody had to. Donald and Craig shared her sofa with Hewitt, a rawboned giant who had once played forward for Davidson. Esther settled her hand on Craig's shoulder. "Your daughters are misbehaving."

"Sorry, I'm off duty this afternoon."

"They're eating way too much chocolate."

"Wait. Let me check my pulse." Craig shook his head. "Nope. Couldn't care less."

"They'll get sick all over your car."

"You can drive them home." Craig turned to Hewitt, whose first name Esther now knew was Julian. "Do you believe that throw?"

Hewitt was the only one who did not appear totally engrossed in the game. "I missed it."

"You should have my husband check you out," Patricia said. "He knows all about the brain, except how to remember to take out the garbage."

Donald replied without taking his eyes off the screen. "I skipped that lecture."

The day was springtime fresh. The sliding doors to Esther's patio were open, as was the front door. A breeze laden with the fragrance of magnolia blossoms traced its way among the gathering. Esther reveled in the ability to ignore the whisper of future tension and give herself over to the simple delight of hosting friends.

Then she heard a car door slam. She walked down the front hall, spotted the new arrival, and called back, "Turn off the television. Hewitt, honey, it's time. Here comes your fiancée."

AFTERWORD

"The Federal Reserve's newest bank president, a Republican who served as a top Treasury Department official during the financial crisis, called for policy makers to consider breaking up big banks to prevent future government bailouts."

Wall Street Journal
Wednesday, February 17, 2016

ABOUT THE AUTHOR

Davis Bunn is an award-winning novelist and Writer-in-Residence at Regent's Park College, University of Oxford. His books, published in twenty languages, have sold over seven million copies worldwide. After completing degrees in international economics and finance in the United States and England, Davis became a business executive working in Europe, Africa, and the Middle East. He draws on this international experience in crafting his stories. Davis has won four Christy Awards for excellence in historical and suspense fiction and was inducted into the Christy Hall of Fame. He and his wife, Isabella, divide their time between the English countryside and the coast of Florida. To learn more, visit DavisBunnBooks.com.

Center Point Large Print
600 Brooks Road / PO Box 1
Thorndike, ME 04986-0001 USA

(207) 568-3717

US & Canada:
1 800 929-9108
www.centerpointlargeprint.com